HUNTED

EDGARS FAMILY NOVELS, BOOK 2

SUZANNE FERRELL

Copyright © 2012 by Sue

All rights reserved.

No part of this book may be reproduced in any form or by any electronic or mechanical means, including information storage and retrieval systems, without written permission from the author, except for the use of brief quotations in a book review.

❦ Created with Vellum

To my kids, Alison, Lyndsey and Eric,
for all your love, support and enthusiasm about having a mother who is
a writer.
You are the blessings in my life.

ACKNOWLEDGMENTS

There are many people to thank for this book.

To my critique partners, Sandy Blair, Jo Davis and Julie Benson, thanks for always being there to support me and force me to be a better writer.

To the Writer Foxes, Addison, Alice, Jane, Jo, Julie, Kay, Lorraine, Sandy and Tracy, thanks for all the support, laughter and good times. May they continue for years to come!

To the Romance Bandits, 17 of the best supporters a lonely little Bandita could ever have. The craziness that is the Lair is such an inspiration for us all.

Thank you to Officer Frank McElligot formerly of the Plano Police Department with help on technical issues and understanding the minds of writers.

Thank you to Eric Welsh for straightening out some technical gun and procedure issues.

Thank you to Lyndsey Lewellen of Llewellen Designs for her wonderful cover design. You always capture my ideas and make them work.

Thank you to Tanya Saari for all her editing work.

AUTHOR'S NOTE

Dear Reader,

Thank you so much for trying my Indie published book. I understand that there are many options for you to spend your money on and am honored that you chose one of my books. For that reason my team and I strive to put out the best product we can from the awesome cover design through the entire editing and formatting process. For my part, I hope to deliver an entertaining story that keeps you wondering what's going to happen next.

If at the end of this book you find you simply loved the story and characters, please consider giving it a positive rating or review. In this brave new book world, the only way for a good story to find its way into the hands of other readers is if the people who loved it let others know about it. We authors appreciate any little bit of help you can give us.

If, when you reach the end of this story, you think, "Wow, I'd love to know what's next in Suzanne's world of characters," then consider joining my newsletter mailing list. I only send out newsletters a few times a year, plus extra ones in anticipation of any new releases, so it won't be flooding your inbox on a weekly basis, but will keep you abreast on any changes I may have coming.

Also, I love to hear from readers. If you have any questions or comments, or just want to say "hi", please feel free to visit my webpage for some extra tidbits or check out my Pinterest boards. You can connect with me via Facebook, Twitter or through my email: suzanne@suzanneferrell.com

Now the important part: Here's Matt and Katie's story. I hope you will love them as much as I did while I was writing **HUNTED.**

PROLOGUE

Seated behind the prosecutor's table and flanked by two large men dressed in
government-issue blue suits, dark sunglasses and wearing stern expressions, Sarah shivered as she watched the devil standing before the judge.

"Jacob Strict, having been found guilty of conspiracy against the United States government in the Philadelphia Federal Building bombing and the deaths resulting from therein, you are hereby sentenced to be put to death on the date and time to be set by this court."

The judge's gavel hammered against the wooden bench frame. Despite her resolve to remain calm, Sarah jumped, her breath catching in her throat.

The judge's words echoed for a moment in the silence of the crowded courtroom.

Then shouts of victory erupted from the victims' families. Strict's "family" moaned and wailed. She felt neither jubilation nor remorse. Seeing that Strict received judgment for his crimes had driven her for months. Nothing else mattered.

The prosecutors shook hands and slapped each other on the

back. Reporters scribbled frantically in their notebooks or spoke softly into tape recorders. The rail-thin, white-haired man standing at the defendant's table didn't move a muscle—not even an eyelash. He stared ahead with deadly calm as if waiting for the perfect moment to strike—a consummate performer to the last.

Grasping the coat sleeves of the oversized navy blue suit the Marshal's assistant had given her to wear for the hearings, she closed her eyes. The tumult in the courtroom pounded in her ears and she shrank into the chair, praying she'd be swallowed up by it. Plain by most people's standards and rarely noticed in a crowd, she prayed that for once she could blend into the furniture. Only this time she knew her wish wouldn't be granted. No matter how little he'd shown it to his audience, the defendant's entire attention was focused on her.

She'd done the unthinkable. She'd defied the Almighty Prophet—dared to expose the monster to the light. There would be hell to pay.

The judge's gavel banged and banged. Shouted commands to come to order or have the courtroom cleared slowly registered with the crowd. People regained their self-restraint. Women dried their eyes. Men took their seats.

A cold chill settled in her bones. Fine tremors caused her hands and knees to shake. She dug her fingers into the nylon serge of her borrowed suit.

Once again the judge focused his attention on the silent man before him. "Mr. Strict, do you have anything you wish to say before this court, Sir?"

Tense silence filled the assemblage. Women gripped their husbands' arms tight. Some spectators waited to hear their prophet speak his last free words. Reporters' pens paused.

For her, time slowed to an eon. She sucked in air, every muscle in her body tensed for flight. *Words can't hurt me, words can't hurt me.* She silently repeated the mantra she'd practiced for years in her head. She just wished her body believed them as much as her mind wanted it to.

The Marshals moved a fraction of an inch closer, reminding her they were there to protect her.

Slowly, she exhaled, sat straighter and lifted her head.

Jacob Strict, the Grand Prophet of the People's Militia Movement, inhaled deeply. Only five feet eight inches tall, he appeared to double his height with the breath he took—a trick she'd watched him practice in front of the mirror for years. Slowly, he scanned the faces on the jury, his throng of supporters, and then the faces of his victims' families.

Finally, his gaze locked on hers. His eyes narrowed. He'd lived by one simple code for as long as they'd known each other. An eye for an eye—total retribution, no matter how large or how small the infringement.

She returned his stare without flinching. She'd be damned if she'd let him see her fear. From the moment she'd walked into the police station, half-starved and nearly frozen to death, she'd known her testimony would seal her own death sentence.

After a moment that seemed like an eternity, he spoke. "The chains of this illegal government cannot hold me. Soon I will be free. Then nowhere on this earth will provide safe haven for the traitor among us."

1

Matt Edgars searched for stranded motorists in the snowdrifts lining the roadside as he drove into work. The cold spell the weathermen had predicted blew in last week, layering one snowfall after another onto the Midwestern landscape, until six inches had accumulated on the ground.

Other state troopers didn't understand his need to find stranded motorists when he was on duty let alone on his way to work. They said he had a knight complex. He always needed a fair damsel to rescue or a dragon to conquer. His fellow patrolmen didn't get emotionally involved with the drivers they stopped to help, but he made a habit of it.

He had no choice. When his friend slowly bled to death in his arms on the roadside with no help in sight, he'd vowed never to let that happen to another person. He'd promised on his friend's grave that he'd help others when he could, even if it meant doing so on his own free time.

Winter in the Midwest held dangers for those stranded or ill prepared for the sudden storms that ripped through the area. Each morning he pulled his truck out of its warm garage to check for those in need of aid before beginning his shift.

Today he drove along Plumb Road toward the junction of State Route 3. A green Jeep sat pulled off the roadside at the red light. He slowed, pulling in behind the other car, its engine still running.

The person in the driver's seat slumped to one side. Apprehension crept over Matt's spine. After finding that old man frozen to death last week, he dreaded finding this driver dead, too.

Damn, he hated starting his day like this.

He stepped out of his truck and approached the driver's side. Unable to see clearly from that window, he circled the car, and peered in from the passenger side.

A woman, a rather pretty woman—with dark hair surrounding an oval shaped face, dark lashes fringing her closed eyes, a narrow, slightly upturned nose and pink lips—leaned against the driver's door. He leaned closer and wiped at the fog his breath had made on the window and studied her. There it was—thank God—the subtle movement of her chest under the wool winter coat, air being inhaled. Her breath fogged against the glass from the inside as she exhaled. She'd fallen asleep at the light. At least he hoped she only slept. Hell, he'd settle for passed out even.

Before waking the woman, Matt retrieved both his Breathalyzer and the thermos of hot chocolate he'd packed for himself that morning. His fellow officers liked to rib him for preferring hot chocolate to coffee. But today, it might come in handy for this young woman.

He returned to the car and tapped lightly on the driver's window. The woman didn't move, so he tapped harder. Still no movement.

Damn, maybe she was seriously injured. With a gentle tug, he opened the car door.

The movement jarred her. The woman gasped, then sprang away from the door, surprise and confusion filling her face.

"W-what?" she stuttered. Her eyes blinked rapidly as if trying to clear her mind.

"Are you all right, Miss?" Matt asked, temporarily caught in the gaze of two deep-blue—no, make that violet—eyes. Then his training kicked in. He searched her face and head for any injuries. "Are you hurt?"

She shook her head. "No-no, officer. I'm fine. I-I just fell asleep, I think."

"You aren't hurt at all?"

She glanced at him, and he was pretty sure it wasn't just the cold putting that pink in her cheeks. "No, really, I'm fine. I was just a little tired after working all night. This is so embarrassing."

Matt nodded. "May I see your license and registration, Miss?'

"Um, oh, yes..." She blinked again, a bit of confusion still crossing her face.

Matt fought the urge to chuckle as she searched through the backpack beside her, all the time mumbling that she couldn't believe this was happening to her. Finally, she found her wallet. Then she leaned over to open her glove compartment and twisted to one side.

Nice butt.

He barely managed to wipe the grin off his face before she straightened and handed him both the registration and her driver's license.

"Thank you, Miss..." he read her name off the license, "...Myers." Matt flipped open his notepad and wrote down both her name and address, then returned her papers.

A light blush filled her cheeks and she lowered her eyes. "Thank you, officer."

"Well, I hate to do this, but I need you step out of the car Miss Myers, and take a Breathalyzer test."

Her head snapped up and she fixed him with an intense stare. "You're kidding."

"I don't make the rules ma'am, I just enforce them."

The woman shot him an exaggerated sigh, her face tensing. Then she climbed out of her car. Her head only came to his shoulders. "I can't believe this. I just finished working a twelve-hour shift and fell asleep at the wheel. Honestly."

Matt moved back as she stepped away from the car. He hated making her go through the test, but regulations were regulations. He handed her the Breathalyzer and instructed her to inhale, then exhale deeply into the mouthpiece. He watched her follow his instructions. Anger flashed through her narrowed eyes.

Good thing looks couldn't kill.

After she handed him back the Breathalyzer, she folded her arms across her chest and tucked her hands beneath her arms. Despite the cold her attitude dared him to say something about her belligerent stance. She had bravado, he'd give her that much.

With great effort, he focused on becoming the professional cop again as he read the results. "Zero, point zero-zero. Good." Then he flipped open his book and wrote down the findings.

"May I go now, officer?" Irritation filled her voice.

"In a moment, Miss Myers." Matt picked up his thermos and poured some hot chocolate into the lid, blowing over the hot liquid for a moment. He watched her face through the steam. Then he offered her the cup.

"No, thanks."

He could see the drink's smell and warmth tempted her.

"I insist, Miss. The caffeine will help keep you awake for the rest of your ride home." Again he offered her the cup, and this time she took it. "Go ahead. I really won't let you go until you have at least one cup."

An exasperated sound escaped her, but she drank some anyway. Matt leaned against the car and waited for her to finish it. Something about her reminded him of his sister, Sami. Maybe it was her annoyance over his insistence, or her rising indignation?

The young woman finished the chocolate and handed him back his cup. "Now may I go, officer?"

"Edgars."

"Excuse me?" She blinked once more and tilted her head slightly to one side.

"Edgars, Officer Matthew Edgars, at your service, Miss Myers." Matt screwed the top back onto the thermos. "And yes, you may go." He opened her door for her. Just as she stepped in, he stopped her from closing the door. "You said you were on your way home from work, Miss Myers?"

"Yes, officer." She shot daggers at him once more, then tried to close the door.

"Where do you work, if you don't mind me asking." Despite her growing irritation, he couldn't help himself. He wanted to know more about her and he wanted to be sure she was awake enough to drive the rest of her way home.

"I'm a nurse, Officer Edgars. Now, if you don't mind, may I please be on my way?" She ground the words out between clenched teeth. Her lips closed in a firm line.

He straightened to his full height then stepped away from the car. "By all means, Miss Myers."

She slammed the car door. Even in her anger, she remembered her seat belt before putting the car in gear and driving through the green light.

For a moment he stood there, watching as she drove down the road, then he walked back to his truck. He pulled out his own car mug and filled it with the hot chocolate. Leaning back in the seat, he flipped open his notebook and sipped his drink.

Katie Myers.

After finishing his chocolate, he started his engine. He shook off the urge to follow her, pulling out and turning right at the light. He needed to get his half-shift finished. His mother expected him early today. No excuse would pacify Mary Edgars on a Sunday. Not even her son meeting a beautiful woman. All her children and their families were expected at her house for dinner.

IN THE WOODS THREE HUNDRED YARDS AWAY, THE MAN FIXED HIS target through the scope lens of his Dakota 76-longbow rifle. His finger caressed the trigger. His whole body hummed with desire to pull it.

Such an easy kill. One bullet. Straight through the head. Too bad his assignment wasn't to take the target out.

Frighten her. Force her to get on the move. Push her in the right direction. That's all the Prophet wanted—for now.

For ten years he'd been on the prowl, hunting his prey, never getting quite this close. Now that he finally found her, time was running out.

He lowered the sight to the rear of her Jeep. As soon as she pulled out, he'd take a shot. With the silencer in place she wouldn't hear it coming. But she'd get the message. She'd been trained to know an accidental blow-out from a staged one. Unless she'd forgotten everything she learned with the Family, she'd get the message loud and clear.

A millisecond before he pressed the trigger, a movement to his left caught his attention. A forest-green pick-up pulled up behind the Jeep. He watched as a highway patrolman climbed out and approached the target.

Dammit. He pulled his finger off the trigger, continuing to watch the pair through the sight.

Just what they didn't need, a witness. He'd have to wait and leave his calling card later.

Since he couldn't complete his mission, he lit a cigarette, inhaled the smoke deep into his lungs, and studied his prey a while longer. She'd grown up in the past ten years. Her hair was dark again. The Prophet wouldn't be happy about that. He'd wanted all the Family women blonde, either by birth or by dyeing.

She'd grown careless, too.

Ten years ago, she never would've been caught sleeping on the roadside. Hell, from the minute her mother brought her to live with the Family, she'd always slept with one eye open. Her survival back then depended on it.

Well, it was his job to remind her that the devil was on her tail and he wanted what belonged to him.

Her Jeep pulled out. Then the patrolman climbed back into his truck.

The man put out his cigarette, then packed up his gear. Patience. He'd deliver the first of his messages another day. Soon.

2

Katie let herself into her apartment and closed the door. For a moment she stared at the main room's monkish austerity.

House and Garden material it wasn't.

She kicked off her tennis shoes, standard work shoes for nurses even in winter, and dropped her backpack on the threadbare chair. Flopping down wearily on her couch, she heaved an exhausted sigh.

Man, what a night.

First, premature twins were born, which she had to stabilize for transport to the children's hospital downtown in Columbus. Then, three other newborns added to her already burgeoning nursery. To top it all off, that patrolman found her asleep at the traffic light. Could anything be more embarrassing?

And why did he have to be so darn handsome? Tall, with dark hair and serious, but kind, hazel eyes. When he'd awakened her, she'd thought she was still in some sort of dream, because men that handsome didn't notice her in real life.

Katie sat forward with her face in her hands and groaned.

Having to take a Breathalyzer test. She prayed he hadn't

decided to run her license plate or issue her a ticket. She groaned again. From his uniform to his strictly-by-the-book manner, he screamed good guy. The last thing she needed in her life right now was a guy, good or otherwise.

Well, this holiday season couldn't get any worse, that was for sure.

A shudder ran through her body. Yes, it could get worse. The Family could find her.

She pushed herself off the couch and headed to the shower, stopping first to turn on the electric blanket. She hated getting into a cold bed after working all night.

Stripping in the bathroom, she shivered before stepping under the steaming water jets. The hot water pounded on her aching back muscles as she lathered on the gardenia-scented body wash. It was her favorite thing to indulge in. No matter that no one else would ever enjoy the scent of it on her body, some things a girl just did for herself.

When the shower grew cold, Katie stepped out, shivered and toweled off. She pulled on her flannel pajamas, and a pair of thick socks. She liked the room cold, but her bed and body warm. Since working nights the past five years she'd discovered it was the only way to get any real sleep during the day, that and turning the phone ringer off. Finally, she crawled into her bed, and let out a long breath. Tucking one pillow under her leg, she turned onto her side and stared at the bedroom's bare white walls.

She'd called this one-room apartment home for nearly six months. Other than her father's picture sitting by her bed, she'd left no personal mark on it. How could she when she knew she'd have to leave on a moment's notice?

She couldn't remember the last time she'd had a home of her own. For the past decade she'd moved from place to place, never putting down roots, never having a real home. She'd never been able to trust anyone to become her friend, either. Besides, anyone who dared get close would be in grave danger.

She exhaled long and slow, then wiped at the wetness stinging her eyes.

How much longer can I bear this loneliness?

People complained all the time about their dysfunctional family holidays. If they only knew.

Next week was Christmas, and if the Family found her, it would be murder.

Literally. Hers.

———

Matt called himself a fool as he drove the Plumb Road to Route 3 route again. Every day for the past week he'd made the same trip, hoping he'd find Katie Myers asleep in her car once more.

Although he knew the chances of finding her asleep again were probably nil after that Breathalyzer test he'd insisted she take, every morning he found himself driving this same route.

For the first time in a long time, he'd met a woman he couldn't get out of his mind. It was stupid to be hung up on a woman with whom he'd had a ten-minute conversation, during most of which she'd been pissed off at him.

He blew out an exasperated grumble.

If he was smart he'd turn his truck around and head home. He'd been lucky enough to draw Christmas Day off, as well as the day after. After his shift today he needed to finish his shopping for his parents then drive down to their house for the family gathering.

That's what he'd do, turn around and forget about hoping to find Katie Myers again.

Coming to the traffic light where he'd stopped to help Katie, he put on his signal to make a left turn. He waited for the light to turn green. He believed in obeying traffic laws. He couldn't give tickets to drivers for doing something he'd done—illegal U-turns among them.

A white van appeared from out of nowhere from his right side. It turned in front of him onto Route 3 toward Columbus, and sped away.

Matt nodded to himself. There was a prime example. If he'd been on duty, he'd bust the idiot.

Out of habit he glanced at the retreating vehicle's rear plates. Pennsylvania.

As the light turned from red to green, a flash of light on metal farther up the road caught his eye. Curious, Matt switched off his turn signal and drove past the light. The road sloped downhill, revealing a familiar green Jeep sitting on the shoulder. He ignored the pleasure that surged in him, seeing her vehicle. As he drove closer he noticed the car leaned at an odd angle. Then he saw the flat rear tire, and Katie kneeling to study it.

He pulled in behind her car. She stood, a mixture of relief and embarrassment on her face. "Are you okay, Miss Myers?" he asked as he walked between the two vehicles.

"Um, yes. Officer..." She looked a little confused as she searched her memory for his name.

So much for making a big impression last week.

"Matt Edgars. But please call me Matt." He glanced down at the tire, then back at her. "What happened?"

She pointed down the road, holding her hand out and waving it with some frustration. "It just happened a few minutes ago. The steering became wobbly and the car was hard to control."

"You're sure you're not hurt? You didn't hit your head or anything, did you?"

He searched her face for any signs of injury. For a moment, he stared into her eyes. Fear, loneliness and something darker swirled in their depths. He had the greatest urge to wrap his arms around her and hold her for a moment.

Then she blinked and lowered her gaze. "I'm alright, really."

Taking a deep breath, Matt stepped back. "Let's get your spare and jack. We should have this changed in just a few minutes."

"I could call a tow truck," she said as she opened the trunk. "I hate to put you out."

"You're not putting me out whatsoever." He lifted the tire from the truck then reached in for the jack. He put the jack together and slid it in front of the flat tire. "And a tow truck would take forever on a Sunday. Not to mention Christmas Eve."

"It is Christmas Eve, isn't it?" She sounded startled by the information.

He popped off the hubcap and handed it to Katie. Then he hunkered down and loosened the lug nuts slightly with the lug wrench. He glanced at her. "Don't tell me you forgot?"

She shrugged. "I guess I've been too distracted at work to think about the holidays much."

After he jacked the car's fender off the ground he removed the nuts, tossing each into the upturned hubcap Katie offered him. He grinned at her. "You've done this before."

"Once or twice. I was helping my stepfather once and I lost one." A shadow passed over her features. "Using this technique, I never lost one again."

She lifted the hubcap to collect the bolts, holding herself just beyond his reach as if she suspected he might attack her. Even though they were strangers, he didn't like the idea she didn't trust him. Matt shook off the uneasy feeling and concentrated on fixing her flat.

Once he had the old tire off and the new one in place, he lowered the car back to the ground. He lifted the flat tire back in the jeep when something caught his eye. Laying the tire back on the ground he studied it. The tread was barely worn.

"Are these new tires?" He ran his fingers along the deep tread.

"I had them replaced last spring." She leaned down to watch him. "Why?"

"Most flats occur with old tires that have little tread left on them. It makes the tire more vulnerable to road hazards." Matt's fingers touched over a hole. His index finger slipped inside. He leaned over to look closer. "What the heck?"

"What's the matter?" Katie peered around his arm.

Matt sat back on his heels. "Tell me again what happened just before the car became hard to steer."

She nibbled on her lower lip while she considered his question. The sight of her teeth pulling on the soft flesh held him mesmerized.

"I was heading home, listening to the radio. Loud. I didn't want to fall asleep again." She blushed when she glanced back at him.

"So you didn't hear anything?"

"I heard a pop. Then I had to concentrate just to keep the car on the road. For a minute I thought it would flip over."

"I'm not surprised," he muttered, sticking his finger back in the hole. Except for some jagged edges, the hole's circumference was an almost perfect circle around his finger. A nagging sense of unease inched its way along Matt's spine.

Katie leaned close, her lips pressed tightly into a thin line. "What aren't you telling me?"

Instead of answering her, Matt lifted the tire. On the other side he found a larger hole, one with the reinforced steel and rubber poking outwards like a small explosion.

"What?" Katie grasped the tire's other side, to help support it.

Matt looked into her eyes. "Someone shot out this tire."

"No." Katie took a step backward, lifting her arms to wrap around her torso. Her eyes blinked rapidly, and once again she bit her lip. "You're mistaken, Matt. Maybe it was just a nail or something?"

Her use of his first name should've thrilled him, but the near panic in her face ruined the act. He shook his head and pointed to the first hole. "This is where the bullet entered the tire."

Then he pointed at the second hole. "And this is where it exited."

"No one could be shooting at me." Shaking her head, she took another step backward. "Maybe it was just a hunter."

Matt scanned the surrounding area. It used to be nothing but farmland and trees. But with Columbus bursting at its seams, new housing developments had crept into the area. Somehow he doubted a stray bullet from a hunter had hit this tire. At least not from someone hunting with a license.

He watched Katie for a minute. Her eyes swept from one side of the road to another. He felt her anxiety despite the distance between them. Her choice of words rang in his ears. *No one could be shooting at me.*

"Katie, are you in some sort of trouble?"

She shook her head, but edged further away from him and around the back of her car. "No. If you'll just put the tire back in the trunk. I need to get out of...I need to get home."

"We need to report this."

"No. It's just an accident." As she spoke she stepped around the truck's rear to the driver's side. "I don't want to get some innocent farmer in trouble."

Matt followed her. Grabbing her by the elbow, he stopped her from climbing back in the vehicle. "You can't ignore this. At least let me file a statement."

"No!" She jerked her arm out of his grasp. "I'm not going to, and I don't want you to, either."

Matt fought the sudden urge to shake her. If Katie didn't want to file a complaint, there was little he could do for her. He swallowed his questions and replaced her tire and jack in the jeep. The woman was spooked. His instincts told him she wasn't just in trouble, but that she knew who had shot her tire out...and why.

Finished, he walked to the driver's side window and took out his wallet. He pulled out a business card and handed it to her. "I don't know what's going on here, Katie. I can't force you to tell me, either. Here's my card. My cell phone number is on it. If you decide you want my help, or you want to talk about whatever has you so scared, then give me a call."

She didn't look at him as her trembling hand accepted the card. "Thank you, Officer."

Didn't the woman get it? Someone wanted her to die. He ought to shake some sense into her.

"Katie."

She turned huge frightened eyes to him.

"Don't wait too long to call me."

She blinked, then nodded, pulling onto the highway.

For a moment, he stood watching her disappear once more. This "accident" had all the earmarks of an ambush. Who would want her dead? And why didn't she want to tell him what she knew?

He walked a path from where her car had stopped back to where the skid marks started. The chances of him actually finding the bullet were next to nil, but he needed to look anyway. He stood for a minute and studied the area. Nothing.

Walking back through the light, Matt scanned both sides of the road. To the right was a new housing development. Cars sat in the driveways, and new swingsets dotted the backyards. To his left stood a grove of old oak and evergreen trees. A perfect spot for picking off a moving target. He'd guess the distance to be about two hundred and fifty yards. Far enough for a marksman with a high-powered rifle to shoot out her tire.

Matt hurried to his truck then drove back to the crossroad. The vision of the white van with the Pennsylvania plates flashed in his mind. The hairs on his neck tingled. He didn't believe in coincidences. Not when it might involve attempted murder.

He turned left and headed up the road in the direction the van had come. Less than a hundred yards from the light, a dirt road led into the trees. That nagging sense of unease now gripped him by the nape of the neck. Approaching the trees with caution, he stopped just on the grove's edge.

For several minutes he sat there, watching. No movement came from the trees. No cars or trucks hid in the area. Without a doubt this was where Katie's assailant had hidden in wait for her. The knot in his gut told him so.

He withdrew his service weapon from the truck's glove compartment. Nothing stirred in the area, but he didn't want to take any chances. He stepped carefully into the trees. Broken branches and smeared muddy tracks headed in and out of the underbrush. He followed them about twenty feet.

This was the spot. Matt hunkered down on his heels. Someone stood here for quite a while. The area was trampled down almost in a circle. Several cigarette butts littered the area. He lifted a leaf.

A spent cartridge lay at his feet.

3

Katie rushed into her room, slammed the door and locked all four dead bolts. For a moment she pressed her back against the wood and tried to calm her racing heart.

"Oh God, oh God," she whispered.

What to do now? Think. Must think.

For years she'd believed the Marshals were paranoid when they moved her from safe house to safe house on a whim. Now she knew better. The Family had found her.

"I've got to get out of here. It isn't safe anymore."

Still trembling, she pushed herself away from the door and grabbed her second backpack. She threw her clothes in it. During the past ten years she'd learned to exist on less than ten articles of clothes, not including her scrub suits, of which she had all of three sets. She needed to be mobile and ready to move on a second's notice. If the highway patrolman, Matt, was right, and her tire had been shot out, this just became one more of those seconds in her life.

She forced herself to take a deep breath.

Panic won't solve anything.

Glancing at the door once more, she checked all the locks,

then hurried into the bathroom and grabbed her makeup kit, toothbrush, and shampoo. All of which she tossed in the backpack's side compartment. Finally she pushed her father's framed picture into the pack with as much care as her nervous hands could manage. Even though he'd died twenty years ago, his gentle eyes still offered her peace and protection throughout this long ordeal.

One last thing to pack.

She reached into the bedside table and pulled out her Glock 9mm pistol and its case. Checking the clip to be sure it was full, she shoved it into place.

God, I hate these things. The Family never understood her aversion to firearms. They considered them an extension of themselves.

With a quick glance around the dreary room she'd called home for six months, she assured herself she'd left little evidence of her presence here. No mail lay anywhere in the place since she always used a post office box. She scribbled a quick note to let her landlord know she was leaving.

Peeking out the door to make sure no one watched, she slipped out and hurried down the metal stairs that ran along the antique store's side beneath the apartment. At the bottom of the steps Katie stood between the two buildings and observed the street. The only car parked on it was hers. No one moved. The small town of Sunbury hadn't awakened to start its day, yet.

She wrapped the note around her door key and dropped it in the antique store's mailbox. By the time the owner opened the shop for business, Katie planned to be long gone.

As she sprinted around her car, the spare tire on her left rear wheel caught her attention. A shudder ran through her, but she shook it off and climbed in the driver's side. She didn't have time to waste on fear, panic and what-ifs. She needed to find a safe place to spend the day until nightfall. Then she could hide in the safety of the hospital's nursery.

Normally this would be the last place she'd want to hide, however last year the hospital decided to update their security after a disgruntled boyfriend entered the hospital brandishing a gun. With its bulletproof windows and locked doors only accessible by key-pass badges, it was the most secure place for her tonight.

She drove toward Columbus, thinking about her shot-out tire. She glanced at the card on the passenger seat. If Matthew Edgars was right, then the Family had found her again. The question was, how?

THE TENSE BEEP OF HIS PHONE SOUNDED IN FRANK CASTELLO'S office. He glanced at the clock.

Almost six. He nodded to his secretary who was taking dictation for him. "That will be all, Leslie. Arrange the necessary paperwork for the prisoner's transfer by the time our agents leave tomorrow then you're through for the day."

Trusting her to follow his instructions, he watched her leave as he picked up the phone before it finished the third ring. "U. S. Marshals, Castello."

"This is Katie Myers."

The name of one of his witnesses in the Witness Protection Program had Castello sitting ramrod straight in his chair. The hesitant catch in the voice put him on high alert. "What's wrong, Katie?"

"My identity's been discovered."

"How do you know that?" Castello asked, even as he opened the file containing his list of safe houses. Katie wasn't a witness prone to panic. If she felt her identity had been compromised, the likelihood existed it had.

"Someone shot out my tire this morning."

"What?" Castello stood, the phone clenched in his hand. He

closed his door then sat again, willing himself to think rationally. "Where are you?"

"Somewhere safe."

"You know the rules. I need to come get you. Let me know where."

"No. I don't want to come in yet." She took a deep breath. "It's Christmas Eve, Castello. I want to work my evening shift. It's only four hours and I'll be safe there, behind the security doors. People are counting on me."

The plea in her voice shook him. "Your life isn't worth a job, Katie."

"I know, but...I promised. You can pick me up at midnight. At the hospital."

"Katie, let me come get you now. Katie?"

The phone line disconnected.

"Dammit!" Even if he'd had a tap on his phone, the conversation hadn't lasted long enough to trace. Besides, Katie always used a pre-paid cell phone when she contacted him.

Man, she had him over a barrel. If her cover identity was compromised, he didn't want to alert anyone she was on the run by issuing a search for her. If he wanted to get her to a safe house, he'd have to wait to get her at the hospital.

Fighting a surge of anger, he ground his teeth. Just out of sheer prudence, he ought to grab her on her way *into* the hospital.

He unlocked the bottom desk drawer, and pulled out the Katie Myers file. For a few minutes he stared at the girl's picture. He remembered how frightened the young woman had been the day he and his partner picked her up at the airport.

She'd put her life in jeopardy and her future in limbo when she'd provided evidence against the right-wing extremist group's leader behind the bombing. Fifty people, including ten FBI agents died in that blast.

Her only stipulation for testifying had been that the Marshals provide some way for her to finish her nursing studies. They'd locked her in a series of safe houses for several years while she pursued her dream of becoming a nurse. When the trial date arrived they'd dragged her back to Pennsylvania to testify then returned her to her isolated hiding place once more. Over a period of three years her only outside contact had been with her protectors.

He glanced at the picture again. Katie never panicked, even when cult members issued a public death sentence for her. Every time she'd been moved from safe house to safe house, she hadn't whined or complained as some of Castello's other protected witnesses did. Katie never asked for more than the right to live her life with anonymity.

If Katie wanted one more shift with her babies, then he'd give it to her. Besides, it would give him time to set up the safe house's security.

Castello started to lock the file in the drawer again, then stopped. Most witnesses' identities became known through some slip-up on their part, not the Marshals. Katie was the exception, she always followed the rules. They'd moved her at random intervals to new locations just as a precaution. Never once had her identity been blown.

Until today.

Could someone in the system have betrayed her? A little caution now might save both Katie's life and his career.

He pulled on his overcoat and slid the file inside under his arm, then grabbed his cell phone and left his office. He needed to arrange a special safe house and extraction team for tonight. He felt the file under his arm. Until he discovered how Katie's cover had been compromised, he needed to keep her file safe as well.

———

MATT STOOD OUTSIDE THE CHURCH WITH HIS BROTHERS AND brother-in-law before the Christmas Eve church services started.

He handed a plastic bag to Dave, his oldest brother. It contained the spent cartridge he'd retrieved from the woods earlier.

"And she refused to report it?" Dave examined the bullet casing through the plastic, then handed it to their brother-in-law, Jake Carlisle.

Matt nodded. "She's spooked, Dave. There's no question about it. The lady denied knowing anything, but I'll bet she knows exactly who shot out her tire today."

"Whoever it is, they're very familiar with sniper rifles." Jake handed the bag to Luke. "And she must be one hell of a driver, not to have flipped from the impact with the tire."

Matt agreed. "Judging by the skid marks, she handled the car like a pro. Another few feet and the shooter might have gotten the results he wanted. I dusted the cartridge for latent prints and there wasn't one. The cartridge is clean." He took a second plastic bag out of his pocket and handed it to Jake. "Could you have the FBI lab run the DNA off this cigarette butt?"

"Sure. I can find a way to make it an unofficial test." He put the plastic bag into his pocket. "You know it'll take weeks to get results since this isn't even an official case, don't you?"

Matt nodded. "If someone in the system pops up, then maybe I can convince the lady to let me investigate."

"If the lady doesn't want to make a big deal out of it, why are you? Seems like there's no case to me." Luke stopped studying the piece of evidence to grin at Matt. "Or is it the *lady* you're interested in?"

"At least my face won't scare a woman away, unlike your ugly mug." Matt resisted the urge to punch his younger brother and held out his hand for the bag containing the shell. "Besides, the woman needs help whether she knows it or not. There's nothing more to it."

Dave laughed. "Luke, with any other cop, he might be interested in the woman and not the case. But you know our brother, strictly by the book."

"You filed a report on your own, didn't you?" Jake asked.

"I found the shooter's hunting blind and processed the area as best I could." Matt shrugged. "In case the lady changes her mind."

His brothers and Jake exchanged knowing looks. All three were in law enforcement of one kind or another. They knew the procedures as well as he did. Just like some of his co-workers they believed some rules could be bent just a little on occasion.

But Matt knew different.

Years ago he'd learned that dire consequences came from not following the rules. There wasn't a day he didn't regret ignoring rules meant for their safety. He'd sworn on that day to never knowingly put someone in danger by steering off course again. Laws and regulations provided security for people, and he'd chosen to spend his life enforcing them.

The church door opened. His sister Sami waddled out to stand by Jake. Matt never considered a pregnant woman beautiful before, but his sister literally glowed with her happiness. After all she'd endured in her life, if anyone deserved to be so happy, Sami did.

"So, why're you guys freezing your tails off out here?"

Her husband wrapped his arm around her. "Matt was just telling us about finding his lady again today."

Damn, just what I need, Sami's comments on my love life, or lack of one.

Matt tried not to groan when Sami lifted one eyebrow at him. His dear sister wouldn't let that comment slide.

"The same girl he couldn't take his mind off last week?"

"Shouldn't you be inside? Resting, or whatever pregnant women are supposed to do?" Matt slipped the shell casing into his coat pocket.

"He's touchy on the subject." Jake leaned in and nuzzled her ear. "But he's right. You shouldn't be outside."

"The kids are going to start the carols soon. Nicky wants you there." She pinned each of them with her pointed gaze. "All of you."

Luke held open the door. "I'd much rather hear the kids sing than Matt moon over some woman he'll never see again."

Sami looked at Matt again. "Matt moon over a woman? He doesn't have a romantic bone in his body."

The others all laughed with her and went inside, but Matt stood outside for a moment. Maybe they were right. He wasn't one of those guys in touch with his feelings. Protecting and helping people took way too much of his time for that. He didn't spend his days writing poetry or making romantic dinners. He'd always believed when the right woman came along, he'd know it.

His fingers touched the shell casing through the plastic bag in his pocket once more.

Had he found the one woman for him?

4

The nursery evening shift went without a glitch. Katie gave report to the nurse for whom she'd covered half the Christmas Eve shift.

She grabbed her backpacks from her locker. Since she wouldn't be collecting this paycheck, she didn't bother to clock out. It wasn't like she needed the money. With nothing more than her living expenses to pay, she'd squirreled away quite a little nest-egg. Earlier in the day she'd visited the bank and emptied her account.

She peeked out the locker room door into the hallway and searched for anyone out of place.

The fruity tang of the hospital's floor cleaner solution drifted toward her. Kenny from housekeeping stood at the opposite end of the hall from the elevator. Mop in hand, he swirled it back and forth in a lazy figure eight across the tiled floor. Katie smiled. As always Kenny had on his headphones and whistled as he mopped, oblivious to everything around him.

She'd miss that. Who was she kidding? She'd miss almost everything about this job, the babies she took care of each night, the other nurses she'd called casual friends, even some of the doctors.

A spurt of anger shot through her.

Why can't they leave me alone? Why do they destroy everything?

Katie inhaled a deep calming breath. She didn't have time to wallow in self-pity or anger. She needed to get to the Emergency Room exit and find Marshal Castello. Until he had her in another safe house, her life could end at any moment.

Taking another deep breath, she stepped into the hall and hurried to the elevator. For once it arrived immediately. She took that as a good omen. She rode it to the main floor, then stepped out opposite the Emergency Room.

Adrenaline rushed through her body, sending her heart racing and her nerves into over-drive.

To get to safety she had to cross the sea of strangers sitting, standing or milling about in the Emergency Room's waiting area. Any one of those strangers could be the person trying to kill her. Even though she'd denied it to the highway patrolman this morning, she wouldn't lie to herself. Every second she remained outside the Marshals' protection she was a marked target.

On shaky feet she started through the waiting room, willing herself to walk, not run, to the exit. As she neared the door, a huge explosion racked the parking lot. The waiting room shook, and the panes of glass rattled from the force of the blast. Screams rent the air. Pandemonium broke out.

Along with half the room, Katie rushed to the windows.

Flames, bright as the sun against the dark, starless night, shot up in the distance. More than anyone in the room, she knew exactly where they came from. Three rows back in the rear employee parking lot, two slots to the left, exactly where she'd left her car.

Realization settled over her like a shroud. She hadn't registered her car with the hospital. No hospital employee could identify it as hers. The Marshals had secured her plate number with the local police. No one, but no one knew this was her car. Except the U.S. Marshals.

She went cold inside.

Someone who was supposed to protect her had set her up to be killed. Coming here was supposed to keep her safe tonight.

Oh, God. Someone could've been killed!

She needed to get away from people. Hide. She'd promised herself years ago that no one else would die because of her or something she'd done.

While the hospital security personnel and several male orderlies ran out with fire extinguishers, Katie stepped slowly away from the crowd at the window. Her pulse pounded in her ears, and the acrid smell of burning fuel assailed her every time the exit door opened.

As she retreated, she searched the faces surrounding her for some sign of recognition.

Everyone appeared focused on the confusion. She forced herself to walk slowly away from the scene.

Desperation filled every cell in her body. She needed to think. The Marshals were no longer a viable plan. Somehow she had to get to safety, to hide.

Katie turned the corner behind the ER. No one lurked in the hall. She ran as fast as she could to the women's restroom at the end of the corridor. Inside, with her back pressed against the door, she gasped for breath and tried to stop her uncontrollable shaking.

What do I do now?

Think. There had to be a way out of this. Someone inside the Marshals had given her new identity to someone in the Family. She knew that, as certainly as she knew the sun rose in the east.

I need someone to help me.

The image of Matt, the tall, handsome, serious Highway Patrolman who'd come to her rescue twice appeared in her mind.

He'd given her his card and told her to call him if she needed help.

Well, she needed help now. She opened her smaller duffel bag and searched for his card.

Please let it be here. Oh, God, I hope I didn't leave it in the car.

At the bottom, stuck to the side of her cell phone was his card. She took a deep breath and dialed his number.

Matt walked down the steps from his parents' home with his brother Luke.

"What time are you going to be here tomorrow?" Luke asked as he rounded his car.

"Probably about noon. Most of the package-ripping frenzy by the kids should be finished by then. I'm house-sitting for my friends, Craig and Nancy, watching their dogs while they're gone for the holidays."

Luke laughed. "Remember how great Christmas morning was when we were kids? Tons of presents littered the floor."

"Remember the year we all got new bikes, except Sami?" Matt laughed. "She stayed pissed off for six months."

"She was too little for a two-wheeler, but that didn't stop her from trying all of ours until Mom and Dad had to buy her one with training wheels."

"Our sister is one tough cookie. She always was."

The sound of The Lone Ranger theme broke into the night. Matt's family and friends gave him grief about his cell phone song. But The Lone Ranger had been his hero as long as he could remember.

"A little late for calls, bro. Thought you weren't on call tonight." Luke paused with his car door open.

Matt fished his cell phone out of his pocket. "I'm not." He glanced at the caller ID. No name.

He flipped it open. "This better be important."

"Officer Edgars? Matt Edgars?"

The hesitant voice on the other end threw him for a moment. "Katie?"

"Yes. Um, you told me to call if I needed help."

"What happened? Are you okay?" Every predatory instinct Matt had jumped to alert.

"I'm okay. Just scared." Her voice broke over the last statement. "Could you come get me?" Real fear laced her voice.

"Where are you?"

"At work, at my hospital."

"Which hospital, Katie?"

Luke closed his car door and leaned against the top of his car. "She's in the hospital?"

Matt shook his head and motioned for his brother to shut up as she told him which hospital. "Where's your car? What happened?"

"It's...not working, and I need to get out of here. Please, I know I'm asking a lot on a holiday night, but could you just come and get me?"

"Okay, I'll meet you at the ER entrance in about fifteen minutes."

"No! Not the ER. I'll be around in back, at the service dock. Blink your headlights three times so I'll know it's you." She hesitated again. "Please hurry."

The phone went silent in Matt's ear.

The hairs on his neck stood at full attention. Someone was after her. "What's up?" Luke hadn't missed one bit of the conversation.

"Katie needs a ride. Probably nothing more than a dead battery." He climbed into his truck. "I'll see you tomorrow at brunch, little brother."

"Oh, ho. Big brother's going to the damsel's rescue." Luke laughed then climbed into his car.

Matt headed north toward the suburb of Westerville and Katie's hospital. He couldn't explain why he made light of the problem to his brother. He didn't want to involve Luke in something until he knew exactly what the problem was. By the sound of Katie's voice, he knew she was in trouble.

Katie had called. Katie needed him.

———

A LIGHT SNOW FELL OUTSIDE THE HOSPITAL LOADING DOCK, covering the dark asphalt in a thin layer of white. Sirens still wailed at the front of the hospital. The nauseating smell of burning fuel and oil filled Katie's nose with every breath. She hid in the corner just outside the loading dock doors.

Through the window she could see anyone approaching from inside.

Headlights flashed to the right as a truck approached.

Please let that be him.

The vehicle slowed and blinked its lights. Once. Twice. Three times.

Thank God. Matt.

She hefted her backpacks and ran down the steps to his truck. She scrambled in beside him. "What's going on? What's the fire out front all about?"

"Go. Get us out of here."

Matt leaned his back on the driver's side door. The firm set of his lips announced he'd just become the patient, stubborn patrolman again. "No. Not until you explain..."

"They blew up my car. You've got to get us away from here and someplace safe before they find us."

"Katie, we have to go talk to the cops working the scene. You've got to tell them what's going on and who's trying to kill you. That's how the police handle things." He put the car in park. "I'm not going anywhere until I get some answers."

Crazy people are trying to kill me, and now probably him for helping me, and he wants to play by the rules?

God forgive her, she hated doing this. She reached into her pocket and pulled out her pistol. Pointing the Glock at him, she used the voice her stepfather had drilled into her over and over. "Drive. Now!"

5

Matt sat stunned. The Glock's barrel was less than six inches from his chest. At this distance she couldn't miss.

White hot anger surged through him. He'd come to her rescue and now she pulled a gun on him? He forced his hands to remain fixed on the steering wheel and not give her a reason to fire.

Desperate people always do desperate things. I knew the woman had bad trouble following her.

His gaze wandered from the barrel tip to her hands. They didn't shake. She gripped the weapon easily. No rank amateur's white-knuckle-grip for Katie. He looked at her face. Her lips formed a thin line, and she clenched her jaw tight. Then his gaze centered on her wide eyes filled with fear and desperation.

Whoever meant to kill her had her spooked. She meant business. If he pushed her, she'd shoot.

He had no doubt.

"Okay." He eased the car into drive. "Where are we going?"

"I don't know. Just get me out of here, before someone sees me with you." She squeezed her small body beneath the dashboard and the front seat. The gun never wavered.

Matt drove around to the service road, then onto the parking lot's main exit, avoiding the police, fire crews and reporters swarming around the hospital's front. He hated not reporting it was Katie's car in flames.

His gut twisted like a telephone cord. Great gaping holes existed in his database about Katie, her past and the danger she was in. Besides, he didn't like having a gun pointed at him.

"Where'd you learn to use that thing?" He turned onto the I-270 outer-belt and headed across Columbus' North side. "I assume you can use it."

"The nine millimeter Glock-19, triple action safety, magazine capacity of 15, weighs less than two pounds, fires a 9x19 caliber bullet and at this range I can't miss."

That answered that question. Her monotone as she listed the statistics about her gun sounded like a kid reciting facts for a class, or a cadet in the military.

"Where did you learn about guns? Were you in the army?"

"You might say that."

Okay. That subject is a dead end.

"You can sit on the seat now. We're far enough away from the hospital no one will notice you sitting in my truck."

Careful not to take her aim off of him, she wiggled onto the seat. She glanced out the rear window, then the side window. "Where are we heading?"

"To Dublin."

"Is that where you live?"

"No, it's where I'm staying for a while. I'm house-sitting for some friends." That information seemed to relax her.

"Good."

"Why is it good, Katie?"

"He won't be able to trace us there." She nibbled on her lower lip, a habit she seemed to have when she worried.

"Katie, don't you think you should tell me who is trying to kill you?"

"The Devil."

Matt watched Katie out of the corner of his eye as he made the last turn onto Craig's street. For the last several minutes she'd fought sleep, the gun wavering back and forth a few times. At any point he could've swerved hard on a turn or forced the weapon out of her hands. Yet something in her face and voice when she'd ordered him to drive kept him from taking the advantage.

She didn't trust him. Yes, she'd called him to get her, but he knew without a doubt if she'd had another option, she never would've dialed his number. Her comment about the devil trying to kill her still puzzled him. If he hadn't seen her car in flames and found the shot out tire himself, he'd think she was paranoid.

Helping her would be easier if she'd tell him what was going on. Of course getting her to put the gun down was his first priority.

He glanced at her again. Convincing her to get some sleep wouldn't hurt. The dark circles beneath her eyes and the compressed line of her lips spoke volumes of her exhaustion. He wondered when she last slept.

"How much longer?" She yawned and regained her grip on the weapon.

"This is it." Matt pulled into the drive and opened the garage door.

Once the car stopped she wiggled out her side, grabbing both backpacks with one hand and leveling the gun at him once more with a steady hand.

"Why don't you put that thing away?" Irritation radiated through him. Resentment welled inside him. Despite knowing she needed the gun right now to feel safe, he didn't like it pointed at him. "I'm not going to hurt you."

"I think I'll hold onto it a little longer."

Muttering he headed into the house. The woman's stubbornness pushed his patience to the limit. "I don't like being forced to help people, Katie, and guns pointed at me make me nervous."

Inside the kitchen he stopped to pet the three Boxers that met him with wagging tails.

"Hello guys. Miss me?" He patted their heads and bent to grab their food bowls. "You know if you want my help you're going to need to trust me, Katie."

The only sound from behind him was six sets of excited paws padding on the tile floor.

"Katie?" He turned to see what had happened to her.

As still as a statue she stood frozen just inside the door, her back plastered to the wall. Her gaze remained fixed on the three dogs sniffing her feet and legs. All color had left her face. Her violet eyes were huge, and her chest movement so shallowly he wondered if she breathed at all. She clenched both her backpacks against her with one hand, the other still holding the gun.

"Katie? What's wrong?" He approached her with slow careful steps.

"Dogs," she whispered.

Understanding filtered through his concern. The lady was scared of dogs. No, correct that, she was petrified. For a moment he stared at the three Boxers. He had to admit, they gave a pretty mean first impression. Their looks were deceiving. They wouldn't hurt her, but *she* didn't know that.

"Stay where you are, Katie," he ordered as if the dogs might attack if she moved. Then he walked to her side and carefully took the gun from her. He popped the Glock's clip out, pocketed it and set the gun on the refrigerator, then he stepped to the kitchen's far side. "Rocky, Sugar Ray, Ali, come."

The dogs immediately sat at his feet. He patted them all on the head and rubbed their chests, his eyes never leaving the stark whiteness of Katie's face. "You can come away from the door now."

With a trembling hand, she pulled out a chair, and sat on it hard. With great gulps she took in several large breaths.

"You...didn't...tell me...there were...dogs here."

"You didn't ask."

The color slowly returned to her lips, then her cheeks. She blinked a few times, her eyes filling with tears.

Guilt washed over him. He shouldn't have let her think the dogs would attack. "The dogs belong to my friend. I'm taking care of them, and watching his house. By the way, they wouldn't have bothered you. Craig jokes that if a burglar broke in they'd probably just lick them to death."

She glanced at them.

Rocky, the smallest, wagged his tail and whined at her. "They're not trained to attack?"

"A few squirrels and birds might argue with me, but no, they're just family pets."

"Pets." The word seemed to sound foreign to her. She continued to study the three brown and white dogs.

Matt laughed at her confusion. "You know, people actually have dogs as pets."

"We didn't."

"You didn't have dogs when you were growing up?"

Katie shook her head. "No, we had dogs. They weren't pets, though."

"What were they then?" Matt asked, not liking the odd sound of her voice.

"Guard dogs. Pitbulls. My stepfather kept them for...protection." She closed her eyes for a moment as if she relived something out of her past. From clear across the table Matt watched a shudder run through her.

"Do you want to tell me why you didn't want to go to the police and fire officials at the hospital to report it was your car that caught fire?"

"Blew up."

"Pardon me?"

She opened her eyes to stare at him. Fear, pain, and the truth were all present in that clear gaze of hers. "My car didn't catch fire. They blew it up."

Frustration built inside him. He wanted to shake the information out of her. Instead he leaned back in his chair, idly scratching behind one of the boxers' ears. "Who are they, and why did they blow up your car?"

Tucking a thick strand of rich black hair behind her ear, she hesitated so long he wasn't sure she'd answer him. Then she blinked. "The Family. They did it to warn me."

"Warn you?"

"They want me to know they've found me and that there will be no place safe enough for me, anymore." She unzipped her coat, took it off, then stood. "May I use the bathroom?"

"Of course, you're not a prisoner here. It's down the hall to the left."

The cold impersonal voice in which she matter-of-factly announced her own family was trying to kill her so shocked Matt all he could do was nod, and point in the direction she needed to go.

What kind of a family set out to murder one of their own? And she still hadn't answered his question. If someone was trying to kill her, why wouldn't she want to report it to the authorities?

———

KATIE BENT OVER THE BATHROOM SINK AND SPLASHED COLD WATER on her face, then closed the toilet seat and sat. Her hands began to tremble, followed by her arms, and then her body.

Desperate to stop the shakes, she gulped in air as quietly as possible, wrapped her arms around herself and rocked back and forth. Tears generated by fear and delayed shock coursed down her face. Over the years she'd found ways to control her emotions in front of others. Love, fear, happiness could all be used against you. Tears were weapons for your enemies. She'd learned that the day her mother died. It was the last day she'd shed tears in front of another human being.

Her panic started to subside. What did she do now?

Without Matt's help, she'd still be at the hospital, or even worse, back in the Marshals' custody. What had once been a source of safety now meant an easy conduit to the Family. Who in the Marshals had betrayed her? And why?

Nowhere on this earth will provide safe haven for the traitor among us.

Those words had haunted her since the trial. Over time, and especially for the past year or so, they'd faded into her subconscious, visiting her only in the depths of her nightmares.

A vision of a white-haired man, eyes so dark you could see hell reflected in them, swam before her. He lifted his arm to strike. Flames flared before her eyes.

She clenched her eyes shut, pounding her fist on the sink.

"No, no, no, no..." she repeated her mantra with each blow to the porcelain.

"Katie?" A male voice filtered through the door, followed by a dog's whining. She froze, her fist suspended in the air.

Where was she? Had he finally found her?

"Katie, are you okay?"

Coming out of her nightmarish past, she blinked hard. She wasn't at the bunker fearing the next lesson from her stepfather. This was the house where Matt had brought her, the present, not the past.

Dashing her hands across her eyes to wipe away the evidence of her tears, she stood and straightened her scrub shirt and pants. "I'm fine."

"You sure?"

She tried to ignore the concern in the tall lawman's voice. It would be too easy to give in to the desire to hand herself into his custody and let him turn her over to the authorities.

No, she'd learned a long time ago she couldn't trust anyone.

"Yes. I'll be out in a minute." She listened for his retreating footsteps outside the door. Leaning her head against the wall, she inhaled, then forced the air out, then opened the door and froze. The smallest dog sat outside the door intently watching her with huge brown eyes.

She almost slammed the door shut. She didn't have the option of hiding in the bathroom forever and she wasn't about to call Matt for help, again. She needed to face these animals on her own.

"Shoo," she whispered.

The dog didn't move. Neither did it attack.

Okay, I'll take that as a good sign.

Ignoring the flutter in her chest as her pulse quickened, Katie plastered her back up against the wall, her eyes watching the dog. "Stay."

She inched to the left. The dog stood.

She froze. Her heartbeat pounding in her ear.

The dog did the opposite of what it was ordered, but it made no attempt to get closer. She wiped her sweaty palms on her thighs once more and took another slow step to the left. The dog moved in the same direction, the nub of its tail wagging slightly.

Katie concentrated on moving slowly as she continued to slide along the hallway wall toward the kitchen. The dog moved parallel with her, never closing the distance, never baring his teeth, not even a growl. If it made one move toward her, she was out of here, no matter what.

A shadow appeared in her peripheral vision. Katie froze again, her eyes never leaving the dog.

6

"You can keep coming," Matt encouraged her from where he stood watching the odd ballet between woman and animal.

"I don't want to move too fast," she whispered.

She spoke as if she expected the dog to jump on her if she made a wrong move. Despite his reassurance that the animal wouldn't harm her, she didn't trust the dog, or it would seem, him, either. Yet she wasn't backing away.

"Come into the family room when you two finish getting acquainted." He walked away, leaving her to work past her fear.

Picking up the remote for the television, he sat on the oversized sectional, sipped his mug of hot chocolate, and tried to find a late local newscast. If she wouldn't give him the details of the car fire, maybe he could get it from the news.

He clicked past the reruns of local choirs singing carols. Katie's whispered conversation with Rocky and her wishes he would go away, drifted closer and closer. Finally, she stood in the doorway.

"You could have called him." Irritation laced her words.

"Did he attack you?"

"No," she mumbled as she eased past the dog in question to sit on the couch's other end.

"Did he do anything more than follow you?"

"No. He very politely stayed on the hall's other side all the way here." A surprised squeak escaped her. She drew her feet on the couch as the Boxer curled up on the floor right beneath her.

Matt shook his head. If her fear weren't so palpable, it would be funny. "If I had called the dog, you still wouldn't believe he wouldn't hurt you. Right?"

"Yes, but..." she started to argue, but he held up one hand to still her words.

"You're stuck with the dogs and me. At some point you're going to have to learn to trust us." He stared intently at her, trying to convince her of his sincerity. "The sooner you do, the sooner I can help you."

Their gazes held. Heat sizzled between them. For a moment she seemed to want to tell all her secrets, then the wariness and fear returned. She broke the connection, turning onto her side and curling into a ball. Hugging a pillow to her, she focused on the television, blocking him out. For now.

The lady wants to continue her silence. Fine.

Matt muttered a few curses. He preferred things up front. Straight shooting. But he also loved a good puzzle, a mystery. He had a feeling solving the enigma of Katie Myers and her problems would be worth the effort.

Glancing at the silent woman on the couch as he flipped to the all-night news channel, he watched for some sign of recognition in her as the reporters told their stories.

News about a homicide flooded the screen. She continued to watch. The weather came on, and Matt flipped to the next station.

The picture of a white-haired man in an orange jump suit and shackles came on the screen. On the other end of the sofa, Katie tensed. Her eyes widened and she sucked in a deep breath.

"Nearly a decade ago, convicted of the Philadelphia Federal Building bombing, militant militia leader, Jacob Strict, known to his followers as The Prophet, was sentenced to die by lethal injection," the reporter stated. "After years of appeals, the date of his execution has finally been set for December thirty-first."

Another picture filled the screen. The reporter moved on to the next headline.

Matt turned off the television and focused all his attention on Katie. "How do you know Strict?"

She pulled her pillow tightly to her, holding it like a shield, her gaze still on the now-blank screen. Fear radiated from her, even as she shook her head.

Matt scooted the dog out of his way and knelt in front of her. Gripping her shoulders, he pulled her to a sitting position, holding her there until she focused on his face. "You have to talk to me, Katie. I can't keep you safe if I don't know what's going on."

Tears filled her eyes, then she closed them tight for a minute. When she opened them again, he read only bleak despair in them. "There's no place safe for me."

"You're safe with me." His hands massaging her shoulders.

"For now. But he'll find me."

"Strict?"

She nodded.

"Why?"

"Because I betrayed him." She broke the current between them, staring down at her arms wrapped tight around the pillow in front of her.

Exasperated by her lack of trust in him and her apparent defeat, Matt released her. He stood, then grasped her by one elbow to help her off the couch. He tipped her chin.

The desire to kiss her overwhelmed him. It would be so easy to sample those soft, luscious lips. The warmth of her body so close to his, the feminine scent of gardenias filled his senses. But he wanted more from her. He wanted her trust.

"Get some sleep, Katie. Maybe in the morning, you'll feel like letting me really help you." He pressed his lips to hers, a gentle kiss. A promise. A comfort. A simple exchange of human contact. Before it could get out of control, he eased away and released her. "Take the second room upstairs. I'll sleep in the one closest to the stairs."

A bemused expression crossed her face as she moved away. She nodded and carried her pillow-shield up the stairs. Matt watched her go. He grinned to himself.

She didn't even notice the dog following her.

Katie climbed into the cold bed and snuggled beneath the sheets and quilt. She touched her fingers to her lips.

Matt had kissed her.

No one ever kissed her like that before. Her lips still tingled. She ran her tongue across them, tasting the hint of chocolate he'd left there, remembering the feel of his warm lips on hers.

She'd received her share of slobbering advances growing up. For years boys and men tried to garner favor from her stepfather through her. Once they learned she meant less to the man than his pitbulls, she'd been left alone.

Matt's kiss hadn't filled her with fear or revulsion. Instead a pleasant sense of warmth, comfort, and something akin to excitement had suffused her. When he'd released her and stepped away, she'd wanted to beg him to kiss her again.

This man's tenderness was dangerous. The comfort he offered would make her soft. To fight the Devil she needed to stay tough. She couldn't let Matt get too close, for his own sake.

And oh, she so wanted to wrap herself up in his promises of safety. She wanted to tell him everything. Not just today's troubles, but all the long terrible nightmare she'd lived through since the day her father died. She couldn't do it, though. She couldn't let herself fall into that trap. Once, years ago, she'd gone to the Marshals with her story and they'd promised to keep her safe.

What Matt didn't know, couldn't understand, was she brought as much danger to him as he did to her. The Devil was coming for her. Her day of punishment had come, and every second Matt spent in her company put him at risk of receiving the same. Anyone helping her would die right along with her.

Closing her eyes, she thought about Marshal Castello. He'd promised to keep her safe. He and his partner had been her last line of protection. Yet they'd betrayed her.

Nowhere on this earth will provide safe haven for the traitor among us.

She stared at the door. It stood about six inches open. Wide enough for her to see trouble coming. Years ago she'd learned to sleep lightly. She never knew when the Devil would come and drag her from her bed to torment her.

Those nights, his eyes filled with wild rage. She'd obeyed without question, hoping she'd only be forced to stand in the cold rain or snow in nothing more than her night shirt, quoting gun specifications or his own personal manifesto against the country's government and its leaders. The slightest sign of hesitation or question from her triggered more violent punishment. She rubbed the scar on her hip and thigh.

A shiver ran through her.

Sleep. She needed to sleep, to regain some strength. In the morning she'd decide what best to do.

She touched her fingers to her lips once more. The gift of Matt's kiss warmed her from the inside out. She thought of his deep hazel-green eyes, the feel of his hands on her arms.

Her body relaxed into the warm covers.

Tomorrow she'd give him a gift too. She'd protect him from the Devil.

Matt listened to her find her way to the rear bedroom, then pulled out his laptop and connected to the Wi-Fi before sitting at the kitchen counter. Now he had a few clues to the puzzle of Katie Myers.

He brought up a news service archive and typed in Jacob Strict's name. The computer screen took a moment to change then a page listing numerous articles appeared.

Scrolling down the page, Matt searched for the site he wanted. When he spied it, he clicked and watched the same image of Strict that had been on the TV fill his screen. The photograph didn't diminish the crazed gleam in the man's eyes. Matt clicked on the next picture in the series.

The Federal Building in Philadelphia just minutes after the bomb blast leveled two-thirds of it popped up on the screen. Black smoke plumed from the building. Firemen sprayed water over the smoldering rubble as others helped victims climb through the debris to safer ground. Matt remembered this scene well. This picture had haunted the news reports for weeks after the bombing.

Next came the funeral procession of one of the ten FBI agents killed in the blast. The tear-streaked faces of her teenage daughters as they escorted the casket to the cemetery had broken the hearts of many an American.

Moving on to the next image, Matt saw again the milling crowds of protesters and supporters outside the courthouse where Jacob Strict's trial took place. Riot police had kept Strict's followers apart from the friends and families of those injured in the bombing.

Finally, he hit upon the picture he'd been searching for.

A young woman exited the courtroom, flanked by two large men in dark suits and even darker sunglasses. Her white-blonde hair pulled away from her face with a headband, she wore a dark-blue suit coat and skirt with a white blouse beneath.

Matt cropped the picture, trying to enhance the image and get a closer view of the chief witness against Strict. The same oval-shaped face, full lips and large eyes fringed with dark lashes.

Seventeen year-old Katie Myers, formerly known as Sarah Strict, the Prophet's stepdaughter, almost single-handedly brought down one of the most charismatic militia leaders in the century's last fifty years.

And she slept upstairs in the back bedroom tonight.

Matt studied her image. In the enlarged picture's graininess he read the fear etched on her face.

Yet he recognized the strong set of her jaw. He'd seen that determination when she'd held the Glock on him in his car earlier. He also saw the steeliness in her posture. She might be scared out of her mind, but she would do what was necessary, despite her fear.

"Katie, don't you think you should tell me who's trying to kill you?"
"The Devil."

All of Strict's followers called him The Prophet. Katie called him the Devil.

Why after nearly ten years had Strict suddenly come after his stepdaughter? How had Katie managed to hide from Strict's followers for so long? And how had they found her?

Knowing who she was and who was after her had given him as many questions as they'd answered.

Had Katie been in the witness protection program? That would explain how she'd been able to change her identity. The feds must've helped her stay off Strict's radar all these years.

The question was, why now that she was in trouble, hadn't she insisted he take her to the FBI or the United States Marshals for protection? Why was she running from the very authorities who'd helped her for so long?

A vision of her haunting violet eyes filled with tears just before she closed them filled his mind.

He wanted to erase all the fear, mistrust and despair he'd seen in them since they'd met. He wondered what they'd look like if she ever truly smiled at him.

Deciding he needed to let someone know Katie was safe, he searched until he found a web site to contact the Marshals by e-mail. He typed in a message asking who he should contact regarding information on Sarah Strict, letting them know he was a highway patrolman and left his e-mail for them to contact him.

Matt clicked on some articles to read more about Strict and his obsessed followers. He wanted to know more about the man he'd be fighting in order to protect Katie.

THE PROPHET SHUFFLED INTO THE INTERVIEW ROOM IN HIS ORANGE jumpsuit, shackles on both his hands and feet. Sitting on the wooden chair, he looked through the pane of safety glass that separated him from his lawyer. For a long moment he stared at the balding man's heavy jowls, then at the blue pinstriped Italian silk suit he wore.

Jacob Strict glanced at the guard standing just inside the room. This last week he'd been under twenty-four hour observation. The government was afraid he'd cheat them of their glorious execution by taking his own life.

Little did they know him. He wouldn't breathe his last breath until the little bitch paid for her treason.

With a subtle nod, he signaled the other man to pick up the phone, then he lifted his own handset.

"Is it done?"

"There was a complication."

He narrowed his eyes. "What kind?"

"The fireworks were planned for midnight, as she left the hospital."

"And?" His lips pressed into a thin line.

"A car thief set them off."

Strict held the phone away from his head. Slowly, he tilted his head to one side, then the other.

The joints' cracking reverberated off the room's cement walls. "So, she's gone to ground?"

The lawyer nodded.

"And my retribution?" He tapped a finger on the counter.

The other man pulled at the silk shirt collar. "He's searching for her as we speak. His contact at the Marshals has been most helpful so far. There's little doubt his prey will stay hidden long."

Strict nodded. "Remind him she must not be allowed to escape punishment for betraying the Family."

"He's never let you down before."

The Prophet stared at the other man until beads of sweat formed on the lawyer's shiny head. "He has less than a week to fulfill my final prophecy."

7

Sunlight filtered through the drawn Roman shades and filled the room with a delicate softness. For a moment Katie snuggled deeper into the covers. Then she felt the hard lump in the bed beside her. Her eyes popped open. Stretched out in front of her, a dog lay on its back with one leg pointed skyward.

Swallowing a gasp, she scooted backward, only to encounter another long lump. Peeking over her shoulder, she saw another of the blasted dogs. Then she stretched out one leg and bumped into what had to be the third one.

I'm trapped.

Her heart pounded in her chest. *Take a breath and calm down.* None of them had attacked while she slept. That had to be good. Slowly, careful not to disturb any of the three, she eased herself toward the headboard. The littlest one, Rocky, she believed his name was, rolled into the vacated spot.

Katie froze, her knuckles blanched white as she gripped the headboard with all her strength. The dog wagged his tail just a bit.

"Look," she spoke to the animal watching her with big brown

eyes. "I don't want to be best friends. Just let me scoot off the bed and that spot's yours."

The dog wagged its tail faster. This time he was joined by the other two. Her pulse jumped to a faster beat. *Now I'm outnumbered.*

"Okay. You guys stay right there, and I'll let you have the whole bed to yourselves." Swinging her feet over the side of the bed, she kept her eyes on them until she stood against the far wall.

Her eyes closed, she pressed herself into the wall, fighting to breathe normally. Would this nightmare ever end? Every time she thought she'd found an island of safety, something new from her past popped up to haunt her.

She opened her eyes and studied the dogs. Her heart slowed to a natural pace. *I got away from those animals.* Now how to get free of Matt and his questions?

A sharp whistle sounded from below stairs. All three dogs bounded off the bed, and out of the room. Katie hurried to close the door behind them.

Moments later, yipping and a male voice came from below her window. Slipping over to it, she stood just to the side so as not to be seen from the yard. Matt and the dogs frolicked outside. Warm breath from all four swirled around them in the cold air as he threw tennis balls for the animals to chase and retrieve on the thawed wet grass left from the previous week's snowfall.

Dressed in a forest-green sweater that stretched across his broad shoulders and a pair of faded jeans that accented his thighs and long legs, Matt moved with power and energy as he chased the dogs about the yard. Mesmerized by his movements, a warmth started in the depths of her stomach. Remembering his kiss from the night before, her fingers caressed her lips.

Never had she seen anyone play with dogs with such abandon. Her stepfather had drilled his animals with the same determination he did his followers. He wanted them on alert at all times, ready to attack and defend.

Matt threw another ball for the smallest dog to chase then turned to stare up at her window. A shiver of awareness ran through her. Katie sucked in her breath and stepped farther into the curtains.

When she peeked out again, he'd turned his attention back to the dogs. She shook off the odd feeling of pleasure and gathered clean clothes, then headed to the bathroom.

If she stayed with him any longer, his life would be as forfeit as hers. While the shower heated, she stared at herself in the mirror.

The day she'd walked into the police station and asked to speak to a United States Prosecutor, her days on this earth became numbered. It was the price she'd paid to betray the devil. The sacrifice had been worth it to prevent the death of anyone else because she'd failed to act.

She wouldn't ask it of Matt Edgars. Her problems belonged to her alone. Enough innocents had died.

Stepping beneath the warm water, a deep groan escaped her. She soaped up a washcloth and began scrubbing her skin. No matter how much she tried, she couldn't seem to wash off the stench of evil that settled like a shroud on her with just the thought of Jacob Strict.

Finally, the water grew cold. Shivering, Katie dried herself then dressed in her favorite jeans and black sweater. Their well-worn softness comforted her. She toweled off her dark hair and finger combed it off her face.

Time to face Matt and convince him to help her get on a bus out of town.

―――

DOWNSTAIRS SHE FOUND HIM STANDING AT THE SINK PEELING AN

orange. Watching him pull off a slice, she licked her own lips as he slowly sucked on the end, then bit into the tender, succulent flesh. Her pulse quickened at the sight.

Could he look any more delicious?

She forced herself to step into the room, past the dogs milling about the floor. She retrieved a glass from the cupboard near the sink and poured herself a drink of cold water. She needed something to quench the fire that watching him ignited deep inside her.

Emptying the glass, she set it in the sink. "I need you to take me to the bus station today."

"Nope. Can't do that."

"What do you mean, you can't do that?" She watched him slowly devour another piece of his orange, unconsciously licking her lips. "I need to get out of town, before something else happens."

"Can't take you to the bus station or the airport," he said as if speaking to a child. "There's something else we have to do today."

Katie fought the urge to hit him. "And what is it we have to do that's more important than me getting out of town?"

"Christmas brunch at my parents."

"You've got to be kidding." Was he nuts?

"No, I'm not kidding. If I don't show up, my mother will worry and insist my father call the Highway Patrol office to see if something happened. Then we'll be paid a visit by at least one or more on-duty officers." He finished the orange then leaned against the counter with his arms crossed over his chest. "And I'm pretty sure you don't want that, do you?"

The idea of the State Troopers finding her didn't sit well with her, and he knew it. "I'll just stay here, while you go. There's no need for me to accompany you," she countered.

"Can't do that either."

His patient patronizing tone grated on her nerves. "And why not? You have three guard dogs to keep me company and keep me from stealing anything." Said fierce protectors all lay in a lazy pile on the floor.

"Until we know who's actually making these attacks on you, I'm not leaving you alone."

"I told you who was trying to kill me. And believe me, they won't stop until I'm dead."

He tucked a damp strand of her hair behind her ear. A shiver coursed across her neck.

"I know your stepfather is Jacob Strict, Katie." She started to interrupt him, but he stopped her with a finger to her lips. "Don't deny it. I researched pictures on the internet and found yours in stories about Strict. I know you believe he's behind these attacks on you. But think about it. He's behind prison bars. There's someone out there that's doing his dirty work. Until we discover exactly who and where they are, you need protection."

She stared into eyes that begged her to trust him.

"Since I'm your chosen protection, you either go with me or we both stay here and talk to my fellow troopers when they arrive. And believe me, they will."

"You're serious."

"Deadly."

How had she gotten into this? Spend a holiday with people she didn't know and a man who did funny things to her heart, or go into custody in a system that had already betrayed her. He didn't leave her much choice. The expression on his face suggested he couldn't be persuaded to change his mind, either.

Great. She'd spent her life getting around unmovable males. At least this one seemed to have her welfare at heart.

"Keeping someone from leaving against their will is tantamount to kidnapping and it's against the law."

He shrugged. "Report me to the police."

Throwing up her hands in mock defeat, she stormed out of the kitchen.

"Damn him. He can't force me to stay or to go to his parents' home." Katie stood in the back bedroom, still seething at his audacity.

Staring out the window, she studied the backyard's terrain. It couldn't be more than sixteen feet from the window's ledge to the ground. Shorter than the easiest height on the scaling wall back at the bunker. From there to the back gate was a sprint of about twenty yards. If the distance to the ground were decreased with rope, she'd be gone before he knew it.

The problem was no rope.

Her gaze drifted around the room, landing on the bed where Rocky lay watching her. She could tie the bed sheets together. It was old and cliché, but it was the only answer she had. If she cut six feet off the distance, she'd drop the remaining ten feet without trouble.

Ignoring the animal sprawled out on the bed, she busied herself gathering her few belongings and stuffing them back in her backpacks. As she opened the window a big blast of frigid air blew in. Snow was on its way again.

Hanging halfway out the window, she swung the first backpack out in an arc, letting go so it landed out on a pile of leaves. She stopped to listen. No sound came from any of the exits below. Good. With another toss the second backpack landed beside the first.

Now to convince the dog to move.

Taking a deep breath, she grabbed the corner of the comforter and gave a tug. "Get up, you."

The dog didn't budge.

Desperate, she gave a stronger jerk on the comforter, pulling it halfway off the bed. The dog jumped down, coming to sniff her legs, its tail wagging happily.

"I'm not playing with you, now go away." She tossed the

comforter to the floor then grabbed the flat and fitted sheets off the bed.

The dog sat at her feet, whining softly.

"Shh. If you won't go away, then hush."

She tied the sheets at the corner in a tight hard knot then tested her make-shift rope for strength. It only had to hold long enough for her to escape. Then she tied another knot at one end, so she'd know when she was close to the final length of her rope.

Now somewhere to anchor the sheets.

Twisting the sheet rope to give it strength, she tied one end around the bed's corner post. She tossed the other end of the rope out the window, then climbed onto the window ledge and straddled it.

The dog patted around at her feet, whining a little louder.

"Shh! You'll give me away. Now, quiet."

Looking below, she swallowed. She'd always hated this training exercise. As least Matt wasn't on to her plan.

Easing herself out the window until she held onto the sheets and the frame, she dangled precariously. She froze for a moment. The image of evil black eyes and white hair whipping in the cold breeze below her as she tried to repel off the bunker's thirty-foot wall for that first time fifteen years ago, flashed through her mind.

Get moving girl. Don't just hang there like a target. Or do I need to come get you and teach you a lesson about hesitating?

Strict wasn't here. She could do this.

Determination flooded her. Katie shook off the memory and wrapped her legs around the roping. Then gripping the cotton material with her hands, she slowly descended toward the ground. She hadn't done this in years. Just as her arms started to ache from the unfamiliar activity, her foot touched the knot tied in the sheet's end. She eased further down until her hands gripped the knot and she hung in midair.

Inhaling deeply, she closed her eyes and released her hold.

Matt listened to Katie storm upstairs to the back bedroom. Her sudden capitulation didn't fool him for one minute. As soon as his back was turned, she'd be gone.

The woman's mistrust ran too deep for her to accept his help. Self-preservation seemed entwined with her very core. Would he need a sledgehammer to get through the protective wall she hid behind?

The memory of the kiss he'd given her the night before filled his mind. Heat surged straight to his groin. He'd only meant to comfort her. Nothing had prepared him for the intense desire for her it evoked in him, then or now. The need to protect her hit him hard every time he looked into her eyes.

For the first time since he was fifteen years old he'd put his devotion to following the rules aside for the need of someone else and she'd fought his aid every inch of the way.

A whining sound drew him to the stairs. Whispered conversation drifted down from the back room, but he couldn't make out what Katie said to the dog. Something flashed in his peripheral vision. He looked out in time to see Katie's backpack land in the backyard.

Damn. The woman was going out the window. She'd kill herself before her assassins ever had a chance.

Grabbing his coat, he let himself out the side door. Perhaps he'd just give her a little surprise welcome when she came out the window. He stood at the corner of the garage watching the bedroom window. Both backpacks now lay in the wet leaves.

A long thick rope of material with a knot in the end dropped out the window. Even given its length she still had quite a drop from the end. Fool woman.

She stuck her head out the window and glanced around. He ducked back around the corner. When he looked again, she sat in the window with one leg hanging out. He held his breath as she eased herself over the edge and hung there.

Why didn't she move? Damn, she wasn't afraid of heights too, was she?

He started forward then stopped. She'd wrapped her legs and arms around the rope and slowly inched her way down. Her movements were as sure as any boot-camp graduate's.

Shaking his head, he moved quietly across the wet carpet of grass and stood directly beneath her just as she reached the end of her rope. Seconds before she landed in his arms he braced his body for the impact.

A surprised squeak escaped her as she hit his body and he wrapped his arms around her.

"What? How did you know?" She wiggled around in his arms.

Matt held her still, turning and carrying her back into the house. Anger kept him silent. Once in the family room again, he tossed her onto the couch. "Stay."

His body shook so badly with his own rage he didn't trust himself if she started demanding he let her go. He marched back outside to retrieve her things. Inside, he tossed them all on the couch beside her.

Out of frustration he grabbed her Glock off the refrigerator where he'd put it the night before.

He paced in front of the couch, trying to gain control of his anger.

"Are you trying to kill yourself before Strict's people can do the job?"

"No."

The despair in her one word answer caught his attention. "What were you trying to do then?"

"Leave before you get killed along with me."

"Katie, no one knows you're with me. Until I know otherwise, I intend to try to keep you safe. But it's hard to fight both the bad guys and you." He growled in frustration.

She scooted back into the couch, trying to disappear into it. Her face paled and her eyes grew wide with fright.

She thinks I'm going to hit her.

Hunkering down in front of her, he laid one hand gently on her knee, and held the gun out to her. "Here. This belongs to you. I'm not accustomed to hurting women, Katie. That includes frustratingly stubborn ones like you."

She hesitated a moment before taking the gun from him. Then her body relaxed.

"Now, let's get something straight. Until we discover who's tracking you, you aren't going anywhere."

"You can't force me to stay." A spark of anger filled her voice.

Good. He'd rather have her angry with him than scared of him. "Actually, I can."

"How?"

He stared at her. "In this state it's against the law to hold a gun on a law enforcement officer."

"You wouldn't press charges on me for that."

"Oh, ask anyone. I've locked up people for less."

Her eyes narrowed with suspicion. "What do you want of me?"

Matt fought the sudden image of her naked beneath him right there on the couch. If he told her what he really wanted, she'd probably pistol-whip him, then shoot him, before running off to who-knows-where.

He swallowed, hard. "Stick with me for a few days. Let me help you catch the person Strict has hired to kill you." Then he smiled at her. "And have Christmas lunch with my family."

Katie rolled her eyes. "Fine. I'll stay a while."

"And?"

"And I'll go to lunch with you, but don't expect me to have a good time."

8

Matt watched Katie talking with his mother, sister and brother Luke near the fireplace of his parent's family room, while he ate dessert with his father, brother Dave and brother-in-law Jake. Despite her promise not to enjoy herself, his family had made her so welcome she'd done exactly that.

While all the other adults in the house opened presents from each other, his mother produced a present of White Diamonds perfume for Katie. He suspected his sister had one fewer present to open today than she'd had under the tree the night before. His generous sister wouldn't mind at all. When Sami and his sister-in-law Judy found out Katie was a nursery nurse they'd cornered her on the couch to discuss newborns and Sami's impending delivery. At first, Katie appeared a bit panicked. After a few minutes, she seemed at ease talking with the other women.

Even Luke got into the act by telling her jokes throughout the meal. As he watched his younger brother bring a rare smile so easily to Katie's face something knotted inside Matt.

She should look that relaxed and happy all the time. Why wouldn't she smile for him like that?

"So how much trouble is the little lady in, son?" His father's question was barely louder than a whisper.

"Up to her neck, Dad." Matt took a bite of his mother's prize-winning pecan pie.

"Any fault of her own?"

His father had a way of cutting to the chase. He always had. Whenever any of his four children were in trouble, he always wanted to know the facts. His father was a fixer. The sooner the problem was laid out to him, the quicker he could come up with a solution. Matt liked to think he took after him.

He shook his head. "The only thing she did was put a monster behind bars when no one else would stand up to him."

"This is the same lady who had her tire shot out yesterday?" Dave asked him.

"One and the same."

"I take it you convinced her to tell you who's after her?"

Matt sat back in his chair. "Not exactly." He filled them in on what had happened last night and Katie's history with her stepfather. "Somehow he's arranging these attacks on her. I can feel it."

"Is there anything we can do?" Jake asked.

"I was hoping you'd ask. Any way you could quietly get your hands on the visitors log at the Lewisberg Federal Pen where Strict is being held?"

"Quietly?" Jake leaned closer, and the other men at the table seemed to be waiting for an explanation.

"She's been in the Witness Protection Program. Instead of going to them for protection, she ran."

Dave whistled softly. "She thinks someone sold her out."

Matt nodded. "That's the way I figure it."

"How do you feel about that?" Dave asked.

Everyone in his family knew Matt believed in the police system and doing things by the book.

Katie's fear was real and probably well founded. He'd have to deal with his own beliefs later, when she was safe. "I'd like to stay under the radar for a while on this."

Jake sat back in his chair. "How soon do you need the info?"

"Tomorrow would be good. I know it's a holiday, but I don't know how long I can keep her from taking off."

His father squeezed Matt's shoulder. "She'll be much safer with you than trying to hide on her own, son."

Matt studied the quiet woman seated on the room's far side. As if she knew he watched her she lifted her face, her gaze meeting his. His heart beat harder. "I know, Dad. I plan to stick close to her."

A TINGLING OF AWARENESS FLOATED ACROSS KATIE. MATT WAS watching her again. He hadn't taken his eyes off of her for more than a moment since they arrived. Half listening to the banter between Matt's sister and youngest brother, she looked to where Matt sat quietly talking with the other men. Their gazes locked.

They were talking about her.

Instead of feeling offended that he would share her problems with others, a warm sense of security filled her.

Her body flushed under his intense gaze. Something in this strong, dutiful man called to a part of her she'd long ago thought buried—her hope. The hope of a young girl wishing for a white knight to come to her rescue. Hope of love for a frightened teen. Hope of peace for a young woman.

With great effort she broke the sensual contact with Matt and turned to watch the game of checkers his brother Luke played with their nephew. She'd learned Nicky was from Russia, but adopted by Sami and her husband Jake. All of Matt's family seemed open and welcoming to strangers, even one with such danger riding on her shadow as herself.

This whole day with his family felt surreal. Growing up she'd read about families such as this one. People who enjoyed spending time with each other. Holidays filled with laughter. Some vague part of her memory tugged at her. She'd experienced this feeling long, long ago.

"Won't your parents be missing you this holiday season, Katie?" Mary Edgars asked.

"No, ma'am. My father died when I was six and my mother when I was just thirteen."

Mary took her hand and squeezed it, a soft smile on her face. "Then we're lucky to have you all to ourselves for the evening, dear."

Heated embarrassment flushed Katie's face. No one had ever considered it lucky to have her around. She doubted this kind woman would continue to think that if she knew all the things she'd done in her life or the danger that clung so tightly to her.

"Actually, we can't stay any longer, Mom." Matt's deep voice sounded behind Katie. She gave him a questioning look over her shoulder.

"There's snow in the forecast and the sky is getting dark." He held out his hand and she placed hers in it without hesitation. In his other hand he held her coat. "We have a few things to take care of before it gets late."

Katie smiled at Matt's mother. "Thank you for a lovely lunch, and the perfume."

"You're welcome anytime."

If she knew me, she wouldn't say that.

Her thoughts dragging her into the dark place of her past, she busied herself putting on her coat. While Matt said farewells to his family, she stood at the door, holding tightly to the first gift she remembered ever receiving, and watched. Sadness and longing crept through her. She wouldn't see any of them again.

Finally, Matt took her elbow and opened the door.

"Where are we going?" she asked as they headed for his car.

"To get some extra protection."

"We aren't headed back to the house?" Katie asked Matt as he pulled his truck onto the I-71 interstate again. Soft snow flurries danced in the headlights in front of them.

"Nope, we're going to my apartment. I left my Glock there for the holidays. I'd feel better if I had it with me."

On this holiday he needed his gun because of her.

She studied him in the flashes of light that filled the truck's cab whenever they passed beneath a streetlamp lining the freeway. His jaw had set in that same stubborn way this afternoon. "You should take me to the bus station."

"No can do, sweetheart."

"Why not? You can't keep me prisoner forever. I need to get out of town. Everyone will be safer if I do." She ought to punch him. When she'd called him yesterday, she hadn't known he'd get so muleheaded about things.

He shook his head. "Think, Katie. Your first instinct is to run, right?"

"Yes. It's the smart thing to do."

"But your stepfather believes he knows you well, right?"

She nodded. "He thinks he's an expert on everything."

"Then if you go to the bus station, or the airport, he could have someone waiting for you." He glanced at her then focused on the road once again. "The smart thing is to do the opposite of what he expects from you. Stay and find some way to catch whomever he sent to kill you."

"I did that once. It's hard to stand up to someone so powerful, so evil, by yourself. Sometimes it's almost impossible." A shudder ran through her.

Matt's hand settled over hers. He squeezed it. "You're not alone this time."

As much as she wanted to take comfort in the warmth and strength in his touch, she couldn't get drawn into his tempting offer. "I can't stand having another innocent die because of me, Matt. For both of us, it would be best if I just left town."

"Well, good thing you aren't making the rules this time. Until we figure out who Strict has sent after you, you're staying with me." He gripped the steering wheel again, his knuckles white with tension. "Besides, where would you go? Do you have a plan? Is there someone somewhere who can protect you?"

Katie stared out the passenger-side window at the gently falling snow. He had no clue what he was getting himself into. When he discovered all the things she'd done in her life, he'd come to regret this decision. Long ago she'd come to the conclusion that her life would be a solitary one.

She'd put her dreams of love and marriage away the day she learned to load and fire an AK-47 assault rifle. She'd learned self-defense and hand-to-hand combat to survive at fourteen. By sixteen she knew how to pack C-4 explosive and wire her own bombs. Every lesson protected her from the wrath of the man who controlled her life.

Absently she rubbed her thigh. Every lesson came hard and with a price.

The biggest lesson was not to trust anyone.

"And if I decide to go?"

"I'll follow you then press charges for holding me at gunpoint."

"You'd really do that?"

"In a heartbeat, sweetheart."

They drove on in silence through the darkening evening, past houses decorated for Christmas. Red, green, blue and white lights twinkled on roofs, doors, trees and windows, creating a glittering visual symphony for those who celebrated the season. She remembered once driving through neighborhoods with her parents to see all the lights. It was one of the few happy memories she had of her childhood.

Matt pulled off the highway into a subdivision of townhouses. He drove through the area and parked near a group of homes on the last street. When Katie made a move to climb out of the truck, he stilled her with a hand on her arm.

"I heard you tell my mother that both your parents are dead. You don't have any other relatives to go to? No aunts or uncles?"

"My father died when I was so young, I hardly remember anything about him or his family. We lived on our own for a while, but Mother didn't have many skills to provide for us. She was an only child and wanted us to belong to a family. Then my mother met Strict."

A shudder racked her body. "At first she seemed happy being married again and believing all his lies. Eventually, instead of the hero she wanted, he turned into a monster. Her disappointment in her choice, his maniac obsessions, and the oppressive environment we'd begun to live in took their toll on her."

"What happened to her?"

The tender compassion in his question put another chink in her armor. To fight her threatening tears she stared out into the dark. "She gave up her quest for happiness when I was thirteen."

"She killed herself?"

"If you mean did she take a gun and blow out her brains, no. She came down with pneumonia one winter. I think she just never put up much of a fight."

He slid one hand beneath Katie's chin, turning her head so she looked at him. "And she just left you to fend for yourself among the scavengers in Strict's pack of wolves."

"You want me to say I hate my mother?" Katie laughed bitterly. "The psychologists the Marshals made me see tried that tack. I don't need to face that I lived in a hell. Believe me that fact is well ingrained in my brain. But I won't hate the woman who tried her best to raise me and provide for me. She just wasn't tough enough to take on the devil."

"And you are."

She pulled her chin out of Matt's hold. "Yes, I am."

"Why?"

"Because he made me that way."

She jerked open the car door and climbed out. Seething, she stood next to the truck trying to calm her anger. She didn't need Matt using psychobabble on her. Not now when she needed to focus all her attention on staying alive. Couldn't he see that?

Count to ten. Get yourself under control. Don't let him see your pain. If you hide it, he can't use it against you.

"Which one is yours?" She nodded at the row of townhouses.

Matt finally climbed out of the truck cab and waited for her to come around the front of it. "The one on the end."

She should've known. Easiest place to see trouble coming and fewer innocent people to worry about if it did. Lighting just above the door prevented anyone from making a sneak attack. Perfect place for a cop to live.

"Are your neighbors at home?" Katie asked looking at the darkened doorway next to Matt's just as he finished unlocking the door. The femininely decorated wreath suggested at least one female neighbor.

He paused with the door an inch open. "Margo and Rachel are flight attendants. They do overnight flights to Europe and Hawaii on a regular basis."

"I suppose they're tall and beautiful?"

"Does it bother you that I have two sexy neighbors?" he teased, leaning a little closer to her.

Katie stared into the twinkling humor of his eyes for a moment, then out of habit she glanced at the top of the door he was inching open.

Oh, God. No.

White nylon rope stretched over the doorframe's top. "Matt!"

With all her might she lunged her shoulder into his bigger body. The surprise of her attack gave her enough power to knock them both to the ground just as an explosion came from the door's other side.

Glass and wood shattered around them like flying shrapnel.

Instinctively, just as it had been drilled into her for years to do, Katie covered her head and neck with her arms. Then searing pain in her shoulder, hip and thigh blocked out everything else.

9

Marshal Castello sat in his office reading the crime scene investigation file. The report told him little about the incendiary device that blew up Katie Myers' car. Everyone else in the department was home with their families on Christmas day. But he had a major problem to solve, a missing witness to find, and a departmental leak to fix.

If the bomb maker left a signature, the quirk each bomb maker used that identified the bomb as his own handiwork, Frank hoped to use it to pinpoint the member of Strict's family that stalked Katie.

What about Katie? Had she blown up her car herself to draw off the hitman on her trail? She had the skills.

Last night he'd arrived a few minutes before midnight at the hospital to retrieve her. Just as he'd pulled into the emergency room's ambulance bay to watch for her, the explosion from her car erupted in the parking lot. He'd run with the hospital security to the fire, afraid he'd find her body in the wreckage. It took two hours for the fire department to contain the area and confirm that no one lay among the rubble.

So where was Katie?

He'd interviewed her coworkers and found out she'd left the nursing unit just before midnight as she'd planned. But from that moment on, no one had seen or heard from her. She'd completely disappeared.

Even though he knew the depth of her indoctrination by Strict's militia, Frank didn't believe she was behind the bombing last night. All she wanted was to live a quiet, peaceful life. She'd talked about nothing else during the meetings they'd had over the past decade.

Had someone followed him to one of those meetings? Is that how they'd discovered who she was now and where she lived? He wracked his brain for the last time he'd met with her. Nearly a year and a half had passed since he'd contacted Katie. He doubted Strict's people would sit on the information for that long without acting.

Why now? With Strict's execution in less than a week, why try to kill Katie now?

Until Katie contacted him again, trying to find her would be like looking for a grain of salt in a sand pile. His hands were tied until—or if—she called again. His only option now was to attack the other problem facing him.

Who in the department had leaked her new ID?

Her file was sealed from all but the highest security clearance. He and his partner Pete Halloran had buried her identity as deep as they could.

Pete. He was the only agent with first-hand knowledge of Katie's new life.

Three years ago Pete retired to live in a cabin in the Northeast portion of the state. He'd wanted to spend his time fishing in the summer and hunting in the winter.

Pete couldn't have done this.

He knew Pete like a father. From the first day of their partnership Pete had led him through the ropes and given him the benefits of his years of experience with the Marshals.

But did anyone really know every detail of another person's life? Was there something the man had kept hidden from him? Something someone could use to find Katie? Had someone gotten to Pete?

Castello locked the report in his desk's bottom drawer for safekeeping. Later he'd compare it to other reports of car bombings by the militia. He typed a note for his secretary Leslie, letting her know he'd be out of the office the next day. He knew she'd pick up his e-mail and forward any messages to him, especially anything from Katie.

He looked at the late afternoon light. Neither he nor Pete ever celebrated the holiday with family. On Christmas Day traffic wouldn't be a problem. If he left now, he'd get to the cabin before dark.

It was time for him to go visit an old friend.

WITH KATIE'S INERT BODY SPRAWLED ACROSS HIM, MATT LAY stunned on the concrete sidewalk outside his townhouse, staring through the giant hole in his door.

What the hell had happened?

A shotgun, tied to one of his kitchen chairs, smoke billowing from the barrel, pointed directly at the door. A nylon rope extended from the trigger to the ceiling through an eyebolt someone had screwed in place, and to the door's top.

Katie had pushed him out of the line of fire.

"Katie?"

She didn't move.

Visions of another inert female body lying over him flashed through his mind. Chris had lost control on the wet road and smashed into a tree. She'd landed on top of him on the passenger's side. At fifteen her life had ended, and Matt's nightmares had begun.

Fighting the panic, he gently shook Katie's shoulders. She didn't move. His hand slid up to her throat. The rapid pulse in her neck beat against his hand.

Relief surged through him.

He ran his hand over her shoulders and back, then across her hips. A sticky wetness met his touch on her thigh.

Easing himself from beneath her, he tried to see her injury in the glow from the streetlight. It was impossible in the near dark. Gently, he lifted her into his arms. A soft moan escaped her as he carried her into his apartment. Careful not to disturb the shotgun and its rigging, he carried her to his couch and stretched her out on her non-injured side. Then he flicked on the light.

Damn. A piece of wood two inches thick stuck up out of her thigh at a forty-five degree angle.

Nearly five inches long from the outside of her jeans to the end, how much was on the inside?

Matt considered how to get the piece of wood out of Katie's leg. The bleeding had to be stopped. He opened his Swiss army knife, holding it poised over her thigh as he considered his options.

"Don't...cut my...jeans."

Katie's soft whisper startled him.

He lowered the knife and brushed her dark hair off her face. "Katie, we've got to get that chunk of wood out of your leg. You're bleeding pretty good around it."

"Take them off. I only have one pair."

"Sweetheart, they're ruined already. If I try to pull them over that wood they're gonna rip even more."

"Just pull it out. Then I'll take them off." Her hand lay on top of his, her eyes watery with her pain. "Please?"

He stared into her eyes for a moment. "You're sure?"

Releasing his hand, she gripped the sides of his couch, her knuckles blanching white. "Just do it quick."

For the first time since he'd met her, her eyes held a complete look of trust in them. *Damn, I'm going to hurt her, and now she trusts me?*

Gripping the door fragment in one hand, he broke eye-contact with her and braced his other hand on her soft rounded hip. The metallic smell of blood deluged his senses, gagging him momentarily. He fought off the sickening smell then pulled hard on the wood. At first it didn't seem to budge, then a tearing sensation started and the wooden stake ripped loose.

Fighting his own dizziness, Matt looked at Katie's pale face. Not a sound came from her, although she breathed in fast, shallow pants.

He swore under his breath. Grasping her face between his hands, he kissed her forehead and eyes. "I'm so sorry, Katie."

"Towel." The one word sounded like a whispered croak. The spot of dark red on her jeans was spreading.

With a muttered curse, Matt hurried to his bathroom for a towel. Pulling his cell phone out of his coat pocket, he dialed 911. Katie wasn't going to be happy with him, but he needed help. The last time he hadn't followed the rules a young girl had died. He wouldn't let that happen again.

After reporting the attack to the local police and requesting an ambulance, he returned. Katie stood beside the couch, trying to step out of her jeans. She wobbled with the effort. Grasping her by the arms, he caught her before she fell.

"I've got you." Gently he eased her back on the couch, holding the towel to her blood-soaked thigh then knelt at her feet to remove her shoes and the jeans. "I think between the rip from the wood and the blood, these things are history, Katie."

She lay back against his couch, clutching the towel to her thigh, her eyes closed. "I don't understand how they knew I was with you."

"You think Strict's hitman rigged this?"

She shrugged, then winced. "It has the earmarks of the ambush techniques we were taught."

Matt studied the rigged shotgun once more, fighting a flash of rage. What kind of life had she lived to give her knowledge most women never dreamed existed? He looked at the towel she gripped on her thigh.

"Better let me have a look at that."

"No." She gripped the towel tighter and tried to scoot farther into the couch.

"Katie, one of has to look at your wound." Gently, he encircled her wrist with his hand. For a moment, her arm tensed beneath his grip then she relaxed. As he lifted the towel from her thigh, he sucked in air in a low whistle.

The wound itself was no longer than a few inches, and the blood seemed to be congealing. A purplish bruise had started to form and was peppered with smaller splinters from the explosion of wood and glass that hit her. It was the skin beneath that shocked Matt.

"Damn. What happened here?" Releasing her wrist, he gently ran his fingers over the outer ridges of puckered and grooved scar tissue that covered half her thigh.

Her muscle tensed beneath his tender exam. She opened her eyes to stare at him. The depth of pain in her violet eyes rocked him to his core.

Instantly he knew the answer.

"One of Strict's pitbulls attacked you."

No wonder she feared dogs. Realization of how strong she'd been to face not one, but three dogs the past twenty-four hours settled over him. Then guilt slammed into him. He'd forced her to deal with it all on her own.

Before she could answer him, the wail of sirens filled the room.

"You called the police?" The betrayal in her voice surprised him.

Frustration surged through him. Didn't she see they were in over their heads?

"Katie, someone's trying hard to kill you, and now me. A gunshot in the city has to be reported.

Besides, you're going to need some medical attention for this wound."

"I told you, if the Marshals or the police take me into custody, I'm as good as dead." She tried to stand.

He stopped her with a hand on her shoulder. "There's nowhere to run, sweetheart. They're already here. Trust me, it'll be okay."

"Are you going to hand me over to them?"

The fear had returned to her eyes, and something more—pain. The knowledge that he'd put those emotions there burned in his gut. He wanted to convince her that he only wanted to protect her, but two policemen stepped through the door just then. "Mr. Edgars?"

"Right here, officer." He cupped her face in his hands a moment, willing her to listen to him. "Stay here, and let me do the talking."

KATIE WATCHED HIM THROUGH TEAR-FILLED EYES AS THE paramedics maneuvered around her, poking and prodding her hip and thigh. At some point they'd draped two warm blankets over her body and legs, exposing just the injured area they needed to work on. Despite their ministrations all of her attention focused on Matt and the two officers taking his statement.

When she'd awakened on his couch to find him about to cut her jeans off her, relief had flooded her. He hadn't been harmed from the shotgun blast.

She'd tried to hide her scarred thigh and hip from him with the towel, but he hadn't let her. Instead he'd insisted on looking at it. She wanted to crawl in a hole when he saw the scars. The gentle way he'd touched them, then the anger that hardened his features had nearly undone what little control she had left on her emotions.

She bit the inside of her mouth hard until the metallic taste of blood flowed over her tongue.

I will not cry. I will not cry.

"Miss, did you hit your head at all?" One of the paramedics leaned in closer flashing a penlight in her eyes.

Katie blinked, then shook her head. "I don't think so."

"She was unconscious for about three or four minutes," Matt said from clear across the room.

A warm sensation settled in her chest. Even though he appeared to focus on the officers with him, he still watched over her. It had been a long time since someone had cared that much about her.

Shaking her head, Kate forced those thoughts and the odd feeling around her heart away. From experience she knew she needed to depend only on herself. People let you down or betrayed you, especially those you let get close.

"Miss?" The pesky paramedic's face loomed before hers once more. "We need to take you to the hospital. The bleeding has slowed, but you may have a concussion."

"No, I don't need to go to the hospital." Katie tried to sit up, but a wave of dizziness and nausea flowed over her. The room took on a fun-house-mirror effect. As the medic eased her down onto the pillows, she closed her eyes.

"Can you tell me your name?" the medic asked.

She tried to concentrate on his questions, but Matt's voice filtered across the room.

"...last year's operation against a Russian mafia extortion ring..."

The medic lifted her eyelid. "Your name, miss?"

"Sarah." Katie answered automatically, swatting at the man's hand on her face.

"I thought you said her name was Katie Myers, Officer Edgars," the man in the dark-blue jacket asked Matt.

Katie closed her eyes tighter, and concentrated on listening.

"It must be the concussion, Officer." Through the ringing in her ears she heard concern in Matt's voice. "Her full name is Sarah Katherine Myers, but her family and I call her Katie."

"We're going to move you now, Sarah." The paramedic and his partner lifted her from the couch onto the stretcher.

Maybe she did need to go to the hospital. Her brain felt a bit scrambled, and she swore Matt just told the police she was his innocent girlfriend, a Russian mafia wanted revenge on him and the shotgun blast was meant for him. Matt lying? To protect her? At the moment not much made sense, especially Matt.

Closing her eyes again, she took slow breaths in through her nose and blew them lightly out her mouth, trying to calm the nausea the medics caused, rolling her out to their ambulance. Suddenly a warm hand lay over hers, fingers caressing her palm. The tingle that sizzled up her arm confirmed Matt's touch.

"Sweetheart," he whispered near her ear.

She opened her eyes and focused on his worried face. "I'm going to follow the ambulance to the hospital."

"Come with me." Katie clutched at his hand. The idea of being so alone, so vulnerable without him sent panic washing over her. God she hated that feeling.

"Shh, sweetheart. They won't let me travel in the ambulance with you." He kissed her lightly on the lips then moved his mouth to her ear. "Besides, if I drive the truck we'll have some way to get away if we need to."

She squeezed his hand, nodding. "You'll be right behind me?" The weak need for reassurance in her voice was only half an act for the police and medical personnel surrounding them.

For a moment he stared into her eyes, the promise that he wouldn't abandon her in his gaze.

Then he kissed her once more. "You have my word, sweetheart."

But the last thing she saw as the medics closed the doors behind her was the policeman pulling Matt aside for questioning once more. He'd forgotten his promise and her already.

———

IN THE HAZY MORNING LIGHT, PAIN IN HER HIP AND THIGH PULLED her from sleep. Slowly, she turned onto her back. A groan escaped her.

"Katie?" Matt's deep voice came from the room's dark corner. "Do you need the nurse?"

"No. Some water, please."

"The nurses said you could have some once you were awake and no longer nauseated. Want me to call them?"

"No." Shaking her head, she looked out the window away from him. She hated the fact that her heart jumped a little faster knowing he was at her bedside. Her heart wanted to believe he'd stayed because he cared. Her mind knew better. He probably wanted to be sure she didn't try to escape again.

The musky scent of the aftershave he'd worn earlier to his parents' house filled the air around her. Her skin tingled. He'd moved from his spot in the corner to the bedside.

"Katie, you needed stitches in that wound, and they pulled out several pieces of wood and some glass from around it. The nurse said if you woke and wanted some pain medicine to give her a call." He brushed her hair from her face.

She tried to swallow. Her mouth was as dry as cotton. "Is anything broken?"

"Don't you remember the docs telling you how lucky you were that your injuries were so minor?"

"Yes." The fuzzy memory crept into her mind and she nodded.

"When can I leave?" She steeled her jaw, fighting with every ounce of her willpower to contain the tears that threatened.

"The doctors said I could take you home as soon as they were sure your concussion hadn't caused any permanent damage."

"You should let me get out of town. They know you're helping me. It isn't safe for you to be around me anymore." She looked into his deep hazel eyes. Why wouldn't he understand? "Surely you see that now."

For a moment their gazes held. He slowly leaned in and kissed her softly, sending her pulse into hyper-speed and spreading warmth throughout her body. Then he held her face in his strong, warm hands and eased his lips off hers. The stubborn look had returned to his face.

"Wrong, sweetheart. What I see is the need for us to work together. The only thing Strict's people did by hurting you and invading my privacy, is hack me off." He pressed his lips to her forehead once more. "Now you close your eyes for a little longer, and I'll go get you something to drink."

Katie closed her eyes until she heard the door close. A deep sigh escaped her. She'd never been comfortable dealing with men's stubborn egos. The wise thing to do was leave before he got back. The determined set of his jaw and willfulness of his gaze flashed in her mind. He'd just come after her. With her luck, he probably *would* press charges against her for holding him at gunpoint. Ignoring the throbbing in her thigh and hip, Katie eased to a sitting position on the edge of the bed. She tested her strength while standing. Not too bad. Then she took one faltering step toward the bathroom. Pain shot through her hip. She froze, panting and waiting for the pain to subside. As soon as the stars before her eyes disappeared, she forced herself to take another step, then another.

The pain grew less intense as she made her way across the room, focusing on the purple bag with her clothes hanging on the bathroom door. She grabbed it on her way inside.

For a moment Matt's heart leapt into his throat as he stood in the doorway staring at Katie's empty hospital bed. Then the toilet flushed.

She hadn't left.

Relief flooded him, which was just as quickly replaced with anger as she exited the bathroom dressed in her bloody jeans and ripped sweater.

What the hell was she doing out of bed? And where did she think she was going? The woman had no sense.

Leaning back against the doorjamb, he folded his arms over his chest. It took every ounce of willpower not to take one of her arms and help her back to bed. "Going somewhere?"

"We have to get out of here. It isn't safe." She sat on the edge of the bed and wiggled her feet into her shoes.

He watched in frustration as she tried to bend over to tie her shoes, only to stop and pant as flashes of pain passed over her face.

Hell would freeze over before she'd ask for help.

"Here, let me." Kneeling at her feet, he lifted her right foot and set it on his knee, tying her shoelaces. "Why do we have to leave right this minute?"

"I assume you gave the admissions department my health card and Social Security number?" She winced as he lifted the foot of her hurt leg.

He nodded. "Sort of hard to get you admitted without them these days."

"The Marshals gave those to me. As soon as I'm admitted to a hospital, they're automatically notified. Then they'll come to bring me in."

Frustration surged through him. He knew she was scared, but she sounded like a completely paranoid conspiracy theorist.

Setting her foot back on the ground, he remained kneeling in front of her, one hand resting on her knee.

"Katie, the Marshals' job is to protect you. The longer you run from them, the easier it's going to be for Strict's hitman to find you."

Tears filled her beautiful eyes, but she simply swiped them away with the back of her hand. "You don't understand."

Gently he laid his palm against her cheek. "Explain to me so that I will."

"I did call them."

"The Marshals?"

She swallowed hard and nodded. "The morning after you found my tire shot out. They were supposed to be picking me up at work that night. Only..."

"Only your car blew up instead."

"They promised me if I followed their rules, no one would ever know who I was. When I called for help, they sold me out. You have to believe me."

He rose and paced the room, thinking about the message he'd sent to the Marshal's the night before. If she was right, then someone had traced that message back to his apartment. His action had nearly killed them both.

Stopping in front of the window, he stared into the early morning's gray light. Outside, a dark sedan pulled up near the hospital's entrance. Two men climbed out and hurried into the building.

"Damn. I do believe you and you're right. We do have to get out of here. Now." He took her by the hand and led her to the door.

Suspicion filled her eyes, but she didn't fight his hold on her hand. "Why? Why do you all of a sudden believe me?"

"Because I think the Marshals just arrived."

Opening the door just two inches, he peeked down the hall. The nurses' station was located at one end where several employees stood talking, their backs to Katie's room. A stairwell was on the hall's opposite end.

Easing her back into the room, he grabbed both their coats off the chair by the door. "How fast do you think you can move on that leg?"

"Not as good as before, but I'll manage." She slipped on her coat and pulled the zipper up tight, determination etched in the fine lines of her face.

For how long in her young life had she managed just to survive? He'd like to get his hands on the people who'd forced her to do that.

He pushed the protective feelings into the back corner of his mind. He'd examine them later.

Now, he had to get her to someplace safe.

"When we get in the hall, wrap your arm around my waist, like we're lovers. We'll head to the left and the stairwell. If we can get in there without being seen, we might escape before anyone comes looking for us." Touching her under the chin, he lifted her face and stared into her eyes. "Got it?"

She nodded. Smiling at her, he released her then stepped to the bed. He plumped her pillows and laid them lengthwise in the bed. Then he drew the covers up high.

At the door, he turned off the lights and whispered in her ear. "It never works on TV, but maybe it'll buy us a few minutes before they realize you're gone."

For the first time since he'd met her, she gave a small laugh.

He kissed her lightly then wrapped his arm around her waist. "Ready?"

"Yep." She wrapped her arm around him, her injured hip next to his. Her weight leaned slightly into him, and he adjusted to support them both.

"Not too fast now."

Opening the door, he checked to be sure the staff was still distracted. "Looks like they're busy."

"It's seven in the morning. Report time," Katie whispered in his ear. "We've got fifteen to thirty minutes before the nurses make rounds, depending on how long-winded the night shift is this morning."

"Let's go then."

Without making a sound, they slipped into the hall. Katie showed him how to close the door without any noise. Turning their backs to the nurse's station, they made their way to the stairwell. He prayed there weren't any alarms on the door as he opened it. Nothing sounded and he helped her through.

Just as he eased the stairwell door closed, the single up bell rang on the elevator at the opposite end of the hall. Quietly he clicked the door shut.

"We've got to move fast," he said in lieu of an apology. Before she could protest, he bent, lowering his shoulder and hoisting her up over his back fireman style. Air surged out of her lungs in a whoosh as she landed doubled over his shoulder, but they couldn't waste time with her bum leg or arguing about it. She could chew him out later.

One arm wrapped around the backs of her thighs, and the other on the hand rail, he hurried down the stairs, trying to distance them from the Marshals or whoever came looking for them.

At the bottom step, he set her on her feet again. They slipped through the door into the emergency room lobby, just twenty feet from the exit.

"My truck's not too far from here," he said, drawing in breath as she wrapped her arms around his waist once more.

Again the staff seemed preoccupied with switching shifts. Even the security guards reported off to each other. No one noticed the couple making their way through the front lobby.

Suddenly, alarms sounded inside. The guards rushed past them toward the elevators.

Forcing himself to remain calm, Matt led Katie through the

automatic sliding doors and out into the parking lot. Then he hurried her into his truck.

She turned to watch behind them.

"See anything?" he asked as he pulled out of the parking lot and headed toward the street. The urge to speed was overwhelming. Instead, he drove carefully away from the hospital.

"Nothing yet." She continued to watch until he'd pulled out onto the road then she slowly turned around. "Do you think they're searching the hospital?"

"With any luck they'll search every floor." He pulled the armrest down between them. "Why don't you lay your head down and rest until we get back to my friend's house?"

"I can rest at the house."

"You'll be too busy then." He felt her studying him.

"Doing what?"

"Answering questions."

10

"Just send it to the house by courier, Jake." Matt talked with his brother-in-law on his cell phone as he stood at the stove, flipping buttermilk pancakes.

Katie listened to him for a moment then searched in the refrigerator for milk for her coffee, but came up with hazelnut creamer instead. God bless the woman who owned this house.

Stirring the coffee, she maneuvered past the three furry beasts milling about the kitchen, their noses actively sniffing the air. She eased herself onto a chair, and watched them. Today, they appeared almost harmless in their efforts to convince the man cooking to share some of his feast. The man, on the other hand, seemed anything but harmless.

"No, I don't want you to come over here. You stick close to Sami. Katie and I need to handle this ourselves." He divided a pancake into three pieces and flipped them to the dogs. "I don't want anyone else involved. It's too dangerous."

Ever since they drove away from the hospital, he'd radiated an awareness that crackled the air around him with tension. Gone was the Dudley-Do-Right Highway Patrolman she'd met that first morning a week ago. In his place was every action figure she'd ever seen on television with a little of an ancient barbarian thrown in for good measure. If swords had been legal, she could have easily imagined him strapping it on his hip as he prowled around the kitchen.

Once they'd arrived at the house, she'd expected him to grill her immediately for information. Instead he'd dialed his sister's number and begun making breakfast, mumbling something about working better on a full stomach. Something in his manner suggested he was trying to calm himself before starting his question and answer period.

Katie studied him as he moved around the kitchen. Never in her life had she met a man like him. Strict and the men at the bunker always asked questions with their fists. They believed a man acted immediately. Indecisiveness or any hesitation was a sign of weakness to be exploited.

Yet, despite his anger, Matt worked hard leashing it before speaking to her. Even though his anger was palpable, she knew instinctively that it wasn't directed at her in any way. He seemed determined to gather as much information as possible, but she had a feeling that if she didn't have the answers he wanted he wouldn't punish her for it, either.

"If you can find any files on Strict's people, especially pictures, send them to me via e-mail. I'll call you later." He set a plate with two large pancakes in front of her and one with twice as many across the table for himself then he winked at her. "Yes, tell Sami that except for some bumps, bruises, and a few stitches, Katie's all right."

Katie lifted her fork and began eating, trying to ignore her heated blush of embarrassment. She couldn't remember the last time anyone showed concern over her welfare. To have Matt's sister ask about her caused an odd sensation to settle in her chest, one she didn't want to ponder.

Hanging up the phone, Matt sat across from her and ate half

of his plate of pancakes before stopping to drink his hot chocolate.

The man had a real thing for hot chocolate in the mornings.

"Jake has a copy of the sign-in log for the past two years at the U.S. Penitentiary in Lewisberg, Pennsylvania. He's sending it over by special courier this morning."

"Why do we need that?" She set her fork aside, her hunger satisfied and her appetite suddenly gone.

"Strict contacted someone on the outside to set up the hit. I'm hoping the log will give us some clue as to who we're searching for." He finished off his pancakes and pushed his plate to the table's center. Sitting back in his chair, he sipped from his mug. "In the meantime, we should concentrate on finding out who at the Marshals sold you out. Tell me exactly what happened the day of your tire shooting, after you left me."

Katie sipped her coffee, thinking back over the past several days. It seemed like months ago now. "As soon as you said the tire had been shot out, I knew I had to get the Marshals to retrieve me. I'd been through the drill numerous times while waiting to give my testimony against Strict."

"How many times have they moved you?"

"At least ten. The pattern was always the same. A threat would come in, I had to be packed in less than ten minutes, and before anyone knew what was happening, they'd whisk me off to another safe house."

The lines around his eyes deepened, and his jaw tensed once more. "And you've continued to live out of two backpacks."

She sipped her coffee, ignoring the anger in his voice. "Once I had things packed, I abandoned my apartment and headed to a hotel room. That's where I called the Marshals."

"Who's the person you're supposed to contact in this situation?" He took out a notebook and started making notes.

"His name is Frank Castello."

"How long have you known him?"

"He and his partner, Pete Halloran, have been assigned to my case since the beginning." Setting her half-empty cup aside, she filled him in on the details of her arrangements for being extricated that night and how she'd spent her day huddled in the corner of her hotel room praying the hitman wouldn't find her. Matt didn't say much, just wrote down most of what she said, his body tensing when she described seeing her car explode.

"Then I called you to come get me." She sat back in her chair. Rocky sat beside her, nudging her uninjured thigh with his nose. Tentatively she patted his head, all the time watching Matt study his notes. The other dogs lay at her feet.

"You didn't speak with anyone but this Castello?"

"No one. I have a direct number to him." Relaxing, she let her fingers inch into the warm, soft fur on the dog's head. "What I can't understand is how they knew I was with you. Someone, either the hitman or the Marshals, must've seen your license plate when we left the hospital."

He rubbed his hand over his jaw. "I don't think that's how they found out."

Something in his tone set the hairs on her arms on end. Ignoring the pain in her hip, she eased forward and leaned her elbows on the table, studying the tension around his lips. "Why do you say that?"

"That first night, when you wouldn't answer any of my questions, I decided to find my own answers." He pushed himself away from the table, stood and strode to the opposite side of the kitchen and back. "Once I figured out who you were, I decided I should let someone in authority know you were all right."

"What did you do?" She dug her nails into the palms of her hands, anger surging through her.

He stopped pacing and set both hands on the table, leaning in and staring intently at her. "I sent the Marshals an e-mail letting them know you were with me."

"And Strict's hitman used that information to rig the shotgun ambush at your apartment." She shoved her chair away with her good leg. The dogs scattered. She, too, leaned her hands on the table, her nose inches from his. She glared at him. "I told you we couldn't trust anyone."

"When a witness is in trouble, the first thing a lawman has to do is let the Marshals know. It's the rules, Katie."

A muscle in his jaw ticked. Silence spread between them like a chasm. Anger and disappointment filled her heart.

"You and your rules are going to get us killed, Matt."

———

CASTELLO EASED HIS SUV INTO FOUR-WHEEL DRIVE AS HE TURNED from the highway onto the snow and ice-covered road leading to Pete Halloran's cabin. Several times on his way north he'd nearly swerved off the highway.

Stopping outside the cabin, he sat in the car and studied the area, his gaze moving over the main building, garage, and the boat. Nothing moved. Snow lay in a pristine layer over the ground. Not one track, human or vehicular. Nothing.

Something's wrong.

Man, don't let Pete be here.

Frank pulled his gun from the glove compartment and released the safety, then stepped out of his car. The thin layer of ice covering the snow crunched beneath his feet as he approached the front door. He stepped onto the porch. A board creaked beneath his feet, sounding like a gunshot in the woods' eerie silence.

His pulse rate shot up over a hundred. *Take a deep breath.*

The sinking feeling he got right before a stakeout or witness delivery went bad knotted his stomach.

He reached for the doorknob. It turned easily. Not good. Pete wouldn't leave his home this vulnerable.

Pushing the door open, Castello looked inside, letting his eyes adjust to the room's shadows in the dim evening light. The stale mustiness of a room that hadn't been aired out in some time assailed him as he stepped into the main room.

"Pete?" he called, moving farther into the cabin and leaving the door open behind him. He prayed Pete had gone to Florida or anywhere else for the holidays, but the nagging sense of unease continued to beat the back of his neck.

Carefully checking the closet and the kitchen area, Frank found nothing. He paused in front of the fireplace studying it. A pile of ashes lay in the center. Pete always cleaned out the fireplace after each use. He was obsessive about it, ever since his younger brother died when smoldering ashes in their family fireplace re-ignited one winter.

With his gun arm extended for his own protection, Frank checked out every corner for any evidence as to where his old partner might be. At the bedroom door, he moved to the side and took a deep breath before pushing it open.

Empty.

No one in the bed or under it. The closet held only clothes.

Frank started to close the closet door when he noticed the box on the top shelf. He had one just like it at home—for his service weapon. Reaching for it, he prayed he'd find it empty. The box's weight confirmed his fears. Wherever Pete was, he'd gone there unarmed.

Only one room left in the small cabin to check.

Pushing open the door to the bathroom, Frank used the same methodical caution he'd used upon entering the other rooms. Again, empty.

Slipping his weapon into the back of his belt, Frank returned to the cabin's main room. Maybe he was overreacting. Pete retired three years ago. He didn't have to report his comings and goings to his old partner or anyone else at the Marshals, for that matter.

Castello stepped out on the porch, deeply inhaling the cool

crisp country air and relaxing for a moment. He hadn't found Pete dead in the cabin like he'd been so sure he would. His old partner would've told him, don't overthink a situation.

Read your surroundings, Rookie. Listen to your gut and act accordingly. If it feels wrong, it is *wrong.*

His gaze wandered over the landscape, moving from the entrance in the woods to his car. Then he scanned toward the rear of Pete's property, past the tree line to the garage—and the boat sitting outside it.

Frank stared at the boat, his pulse quickening again. That was what bothered him.

Pete always stored the boat inside during the winter.

Slipping his gun out of his belt, Frank started toward the garage. His pace quickened with each step until he was moving at a dead run.

The garage had turn-of-the-century doors which opened out, like a barn, instead of lifting up like modern garages. He paused for a moment, catching a steadying breath.

Then he reached for the door latch. The stench through the wood doors assailed him immediately.

Decaying flesh mixed with blood wasn't a scent a person ever forgot. He pulled off one glove and covered his mouth and nose.

God, he didn't want to go in here.

Dragging the door as far open as he could, he closed his eyes for a moment. Then he forced himself to look.

Pain hit him square in the chest like a sledgehammer. "Oh God, Pete."

Frank sank to his knees.

Pete hung from the old garage's rafters, his hands cuffed, a chain lashed over the beams, stretching his arms above his head. Naked, he'd been systematically sliced, his blood caked over his torso in the many paths it had taken to drain from him body.

Frank gulped in air.

His mentor, his friend, his partner had suffered greatly at the hands of his torturer.

Frank staggered to his feet. The bastard had made a grave error. He'd just called down the government's powers on his head.

If it takes me the next twenty years, I'll put whoever did this six feet under.

He fought the urge to lower Pete's body. The crime scene needed to stay intact. He flipped his cell phone open and dialed the local sheriff's department. His boss would get the second call, then the FBI.

Now it was imperative he find Sarah Strict, alias Katie Myers.

MATT OPENED THE PACKAGE FROM THE OVERNIGHT COURIER service. He dumped the contents onto the kitchen table. Jake not only sent the log, which consisted of a series of photocopied sheets from the actual log, but a bundle of pictures also. There was something else stuck in the package's bottom. He turned it upside down and shook it hard. Into his hand fell a box of gauze and a tube of antibiotic ointment.

"Sami to the rescue." Then he laughed.

But he knew his sister was right. Since they'd literally fled the hospital, the responsibility for Katie's care rested squarely with him. Guilt washed over him. Hell, it was his fault she'd gotten hurt in the first place. Earlier in the morning she'd made that fact obvious.

When she strode from the room her back ramrod straight and a new limp to her stride, he'd never felt so angry or so low. He had wanted to go after her to make her see reason. She was in danger and if he'd known all the information he knew now, he never would've sent that message. Hell, he'd been so frustrated he didn't know whether to shake her or kiss her.

He blew out a deep breath.

"She's had plenty of time to cool off," he said to Ali, the largest Boxer, sitting at his feet. "Time to get down to business."

After picking up the visitor's log, pictures and first-aid supplies, he went in search of Katie. The sunroom was where he finally found her. He stood in the doorway, watching. Sitting on the floor, she had spread newspaper out in front of her. On it lay all the pieces to her Glock. She sat cross-legged, cleaning and oiling each piece, with methodical precision.

The woman and her ability to adapt amazed him. On either side of her lay a dog. A woman with as much reason to fear them as Katie did should be screaming at him for letting them anywhere near her. Yet there she sat nestled between them, accepting them for what they were—harmless, gentle companions. They'd proven they could be trusted.

A spark of frustration burst to life inside him. When would she realize she could trust him?

When you start showing her she can.

Where had that thought come from? From the truth. If he wanted her to trust him, he'd have to give her reasons to.

Matt fetched his coat from the hall closet and returned to the sunroom. Laying the papers and medical supplies on the sofa, he fished his own Glock out of his coat pocket.

"When you finish cleaning yours, how about doing mine, too?" He held the gun toward her, barrel end first.

She stared at the weapon. "When did you get this?"

"After the paramedics left with you for the hospital. It's what I stopped by my apartment to get in the first place. I figure I need to stay armed until your hitman is captured."

For a moment she hesitated, then nodded and took the gun, and laid it beside the pieces of her own.

Matt relaxed.

Chalk one up for the good guys.

"Is that the log you asked your brother-in-law for?" she asked, going back to her oiling and cleaning.

"Jake sent along what pictures he could find of the known members of Strict's family and Sami sent this to you." He held the gauze and ointment out to Katie.

"For me?"

The surprised look on her face both pleased and irritated him. He was glad his sister's thoughtfulness would be appreciated. Yet he read in Katie's eyes the idea that she didn't deserve this simple act of human kindness.

If Strict weren't dying in four days, he'd kill him himself. "Yes. For your wounds."

"Please tell her thank you." A light blush filled her cheeks. She blinked hard against the tears that filled her eyes, and set the boxes by her side.

Matt coughed hard to clear the lump in his throat. "Why don't I read off the names of Strict's visitors while you work. If any of them sound familiar, you let me know. Okay?"

She nodded.

"Want to start first to last, or last to first?"

"Last to first." She glanced at him, the corners of her lips turned up in a semi-smile. "Maybe we'll find the person in the first name, and I won't have to think about my stepfather too much."

He winked at her. "Attagirl." Flipping to the last page, he read off the latest entry. "December twelfth, Thomas Pike."

"Strict's lawyer. Pike was never a real believer of Strict's plans, but my stepfather said a man should always have the best lawyer and the best doctor he can afford." Concentrating on what she was doing, Katie pushed the barrel of her gun down into the frame from the rear, then replaced the captive recoil spring.

"Strict could've used him as a conduit to the hitman." Matt wrote down Pike's name and how Katie said he functioned for Strict. "December first, Hank Wooten."

"Hank was the accountant. Most Family members believed my stepfather was simply a religious leader, but I knew better. He was out to make himself rich and famous. Hank was in charge of the rich part."

"He could've arranged for a hitman's payoff. An out-of-towner, perhaps?"

Katie shook her head, sitting straighter and pulling both her shoulders back for a moment. "He could've, but the Devil never paid for anything he could get for free. He would have used one of his own people."

"I'll put the accountant on the list, just in case Strict was desperate enough to hire outside help."

"Why're you asking me questions, if you're not going to accept my answers?" Deftly she moved the slide backward onto the frame, squeezing the trigger and letting the striker find its proper position on the frame, locking it in position with the slide lock.

Matt watched her hands work with lightning speed as she reassembled the Glock. She had nimble fingers and great dexterity. How much had she inherited, and how much had she learned in order to survive?

Shaking his head, he studied the log once more. Focus. He needed to focus on the task at hand. "The lawyer was the only visitor Strict had for the previous two months."

Finished assembling the Glock, Katie pushed the magazine into place. She laid down her weapon then reached her right arm over her head, scratching at her back. "He had followers, not friends. Once he was sent to Lewisberg penitentiary, the Family scattered."

"September twenty-third, Christian G. Anders visited."

Her face went blank as if she was trying to recall the name, then she shook her head. "I don't have a clue who that could be." She switched arms, again scratching at her back.

"Could it be an alias?"

"Who knows." Shrugging, she lifted his weapon and quickly disassembled it. "Many Family members used them. A number of men spent time in prison."

And this young woman grew up in that environment? He studied her face. Concentrating on her task, she looked as young and innocent as a student performing an assignment for a grade.

Living among hardened criminals and men who placed their own needs and desires above the law, had she really managed to stay innocent? He knew some paramilitary groups used their women like toys.

The idea of Strict using Katie as a prize for his men made Matt's blood go cold. She wouldn't have been able to prevent the abuse. Considering everything else she'd been through, Strict wouldn't have been above using rape as a way to control her. Self-preservation ran strong and deep in Katie. She'd learn to adapt, even to that.

A wave of nausea rolled over him. The room filled with stars. Intense heat pressed in all around him.

He needed to leave, quick.

He shoved himself out of the chair then stumbled toward the door.

"Matt?" Katie's concerned voice followed him.

He stopped at the door, signaling her to stay where she was. "I'm all right, I just need a little air."

Without looking back, he bolted for the kitchen. After grabbing a bottle of whiskey from Craig's liquor cupboard, he stepped onto the back porch. Inhaling deep, he let the winter air fill his lungs. The shocking cold returned his world back to its axis. He unscrewed the top to the whiskey bottle and took one large drink. The liquor burnt his throat then sent a fire all the way to his stomach.

Pain blurred his eyes and he choked. Coughing for a moment, he bent at the waist, his head hanging below his knees.

Damn, he hated even the possibility that Katie had been raped and used by Strict's men.

That was Sarah, not Katie.

His mind cleared. Those things, all of them, had happened to Sarah, not Katie, not the Katie who stood up to Strict and his clan.

He could deal with that. He'd just keep her two identities separate in his mind. He slowly took another steadying drink of whiskey, then screwed the cap back on the bottle. What was past was past. Now she needed him to help her catch the person sent to kill her.

———

"FEELING BETTER?" KATIE ASKED WHEN HE RETURNED TO THE sunroom. She had his gun dismantled on the newspaper before her.

Matt nodded. "A little. Let's see who else we can add to our list." Picking up the log he flipped through the next few months, finding Strict had no contact with anyone other than his lawyer. "April sixth, Maura Allen."

A soft smile spread across Katie's lips. "Maura. She was one of the few people in the Family I liked. She functioned as the clan's midwife and secretary. I think she fancied herself in love with Strict."

"She was kind to you?" Matt liked the idea of someone caring about her.

"As much as anyone was allowed to be, yes." Finished cleaning the parts, she quickly reassembled his Glock.

Fascinated, Matt watched her quick and precise hands. "You're an expert at that."

"I was drilled on it every day for six years. Some things you never forget." She laid the gun on the floor next to the other weapon. She sat straighter, wiggling her shoulders, then reaching back to try and scratch between her shoulder blades once more.

"Got an itch?"

"It's more like something is poking me there that I can't quite reach." She twisted to one side, reaching from the bottom.

Matt set aside the log. "There's no other new names in the log. Why don't you let me see if I can find out what's bothering you."

He scooted the dogs away and sat next to her on the floor. Gently he turned her so she sat between his extended legs. She sat ramrod straight, her body tense again. He wanted to grip her by the hips and pull her snug against him, but he fought the urge. Winning her trust was important to him.

"Where's the spot?"

"Here." She pointed to the area between her shoulder blades.

Matt looked at her top. The light-blue cotton sweater was dotted with small brown spots. "Have you been scratching at this long?"

"Just since we got back from the hospital. Why?"

"I think you've made it bleed. There's some dried blood on your sweater." He grasped the bottom of her sweater and gently pulled upward. "Let me take a look—"

"No." She grabbed the shirt and held it down.

What the hell?

He held onto the back to keep her from moving away. "Katie, I think you're bleeding and I need to see what caused it."

Shaking her head, she held the shirt down tight.

"Let me look. I promise not to do anything else." He leaned forward, his lips a hair's breadth away from her ear. "Please?"

A shiver ran through her.

"You can trust me."

They sat that way for a moment in their silent tug-of-war then her head drooped.

She released her hold on the sweater. Her body tensed tighter.

He wondered if he blew across her skin if she would shatter into a thousand pieces.

Gently, he lifted the material from her back, exposing the creamy skin beneath. As he lifted higher, he leaned closer not believing what he saw.

Long razor-thin scars striped her mid-back in crisscross fashion.

He paused, holding her shirt halfway up her back. He couldn't be seeing what he was seeing. "The son of a bitch. He whipped you?"

"With an antique horse whip." Her voice trembled. Gripping the sweater again, she tried to pull it back down.

With great restraint over his rage, Matt managed to still her efforts. "It's okay, sweetheart."

When she released her hold on the shirt, he took a deep breath to steady himself for whatever else he might discover. Pulling upwards, he saw the beginning of puckered scars, the same kind she had on her hip and thighs. He wanted to swear. But he'd seen how his anger affected her and forced himself to hold all the words inside. He eased her top up to her shoulders.

The scars from dogs' teeth left long ridges over the upper half of her torso. Beneath them lay more lash marks from the whip. There was no question she'd been tortured—more than once.

God, how had she survived it all?

Suddenly, she shivered beneath his fingers. Was it from the cool air on her skin or embarrassment? Trying to reassure her, he rested his hands on her shoulders, gently rubbing them through the material.

"Is my back bleeding?" Her voice trembled again.

Gently he pushed her forward so her back arched a bit. Light from the windows caught something clear on her back and numerous pinpoints flashed at him.

"Dammit. Your whole back is peppered with glass slivers. How did they miss that at the hospital?"

"I didn't feel any of it until we arrived here. Between my concussion and my thigh injury, I'm sure no one knew to look for an injury on my back." Once again she tried to pull her top down.

"Stop that." He held the material at her shoulders. "These need to come out of there, and you can't do it yourself. You're going to have to let me get them out for you."

Her shoulders slumped beneath his hands. "I guess you're right."

Her capitulation wasn't enough. He wanted something more from her.

"Katie, you're going to have to take off this sweater and your bra. Can you trust me long enough to sit here exposed while I work these slivers out?"

She hesitated. For a moment he thought she'd fight him again. Then very slowly she nodded.

Easing away, he stood for a moment gazing at her. She was almost huddled on the floor at his feet. For the first time since he met her, she looked frail and helpless. Even unconscious she'd seemed to have more fight in her than she did at this moment.

She needed him, not just to pull shards of glass from her flesh, but to restore part of the innocence Strict stole from her. By accepting all of her, her past and her scars, he could return some of her dignity.

Matt strode from the room, praying he could do what had to be done without inflicting any more pain or damage on Katie. Searching through the bathroom cabinet, he found a pair of tweezers and a bottle of peroxide. When he returned, Katie still sat huddled in the same spot. Her top and bra were off, and she held them to her front. Adding the gauze and ointment to his supplies, he slipped in behind her once more.

"I'm going to try not to hurt you too much, sweetheart, but I don't think I can help it."

"Scar tissue has fewer nerve endings than regular tissue."

She sounded like a robot. Just how much control did she have over her emotions right now?

And if he did the wrong thing, how would she deal with it?

Forcing all his questions away, he began the long process of pulling each glass sliver from her flesh. Every so often he stopped and rubbed her arm or shoulder.

"How're you doing?"

"Okay. It feels good to have them gone. But I'm dying to scratch."

"Let me get them out, and I'll be happy to scratch your itch for you."

Returning to his chore, he was glad the fragility he'd seen earlier was disappearing. She'd almost relaxed under his ministrations.

Finally, the last piece of glass slid out. He handed her the bottle of peroxide. "Pour some of that on the gauze."

"Be gentle," she said, handing the soaked gauze to him. Wincing in sympathy he laid the astringent cloth on her back.

She hissed out a sharp breath, shaking her head back and forth as he dabbed at her skin. "Geez."

"That's done. Now, you want some ointment on it?"

"Yes. If you don't mind?" Her voice sounding almost normal, she handed him the tube. "There's painkiller in it."

After squirting the gel onto another piece of gauze, he gently dabbed it over the numerous spots on her upper back. With his left hand, he continued to rub her upper shoulder, accustoming her to his touch.

Her skin grew warm beneath his hand. His eyes wandered over her scarred back. Without thinking, he leaned down and let his lips touch one of the old scars in a gentle kiss. He lowered his hands to the small of her back, his fingers caressing over the faint scars there.

She shivered, but didn't pull away.

He took her stillness as permission to continue. Working his fingers upwards, he slowly caressed each and every one, bypassing the recently injured spots. Occasionally, he dropped a soft kiss on a particularly ugly scar.

Her shaking started when he'd worked his way two-thirds up her back.

"Am I hurting you?" If she said yes, he'd die. He didn't want to hurt her. She'd been hurt more than anyone ever deserved.

She simply shook her head. "Want me to stop?"

Without words, she shook her head.

Taking as much care as he could and fighting his own desire to do more, he continued his gentle caressing touch. Her shaking grew harder.

She sniffled.

His hands stopped on her shoulders.

"Katie?" He leaned closer, his chest gentle against her back. He touched her chin with his finger and turned her head to look at him.

Tears rolled down her cheeks.

11

Katie stared at Matt through her blurry veil of tears. Every inch of her body shook. She needed to find a hole to crawl into and hide.

If he kissed her she'd lose what little control on her emotions she still had.

Please God, don't let him kiss me.

Slowly he inched closer. She held her breath. His hand touched her cheek, gently stroking her skin with his fingers.

Then she felt a tug on the sweater she clutched to her chest. She gripped the material tighter.

The condition of her back embarrassed her. It made her less than whole.

Yet he'd touched, caressed and kissed all her scars. Could she bare the rest of her body for him? She was twenty-seven years old, and no one had ever seen her naked. Until this very moment, she'd planned to never allow anyone this much intimacy. He was slowly changing her beliefs about many things. Could she trust him with all her body and all her secrets?

He leaned in closer. "Sweetheart, let me have the sweater."

His eyes said trust me. His warm breath sent tingles

throughout her body. Slowly she relinquished her hold on the blue cloth.

His gaze never left hers.

Cool air caressed her skin as the material slipped from her fingers. She shivered, from cold or the sudden awareness of him, she wasn't sure which.

Bunching the material in his hands, he made the opening in the top a wide circle then gently pulled the material over her head.

Realizing he didn't mean to press his advantage she numbly stared at him. "You're sure?"

"I'm sure. Now isn't the time. When you're ready, you'll know it."

"What if I'm never ready?"

"Then the choice will still be yours." He helped her get her hands through the sleeves then gently pulled the sweater down over her. His fingers lightly touched the outer swells of her breasts as they passed by.

She gasped. He smiled at her and finished lowering her top into place.

Then he did the one thing she'd feared. Cupping her face in his hands, his thumbs brushed away the wetness of her tears. He leaned toward her, pressing his lips to hers in the softest of kisses.

It was the one thing she couldn't handle now—not on top of his tenderness. The dam burst. She tore her lips away from his.

Her body shaking, she couldn't stop the soft wail that escaped her or the torrent of tears that flowed unchecked across her cheeks. She curled herself into the warm shelter of Matt's body, keening from all the pain and suffering she'd endured.

The reality of everything that had happened to her in the past three days hit her like a tidal wave.

"Someone…is trying…to kill…me." She clung to Matt's shirt,

needing to get closer to his warmth. The shaking grew worse. "Three...three...times."

He wrapped his arms around her and slowly rocked her. "I know sweetheart, I know."

"Nightmare's...coming...true." She hiccupped. A second wave of tears hit her.

"So...so...long...alone. No one...then you came...to my...rescue."

She found herself lifted in Matt's strong arms and carried to the sofa. Still clutching his shirt, her tears soaked the cotton as he settled her on his lap. She turned her face so her ear pressed against the steady beating of his heart. His warm hands continued to rub up and down her arms and the uninjured part of her back. Their heat and strength soothed her.

"You're not alone anymore."

He murmured the words over and over against the top of her head. His voice rumbled in his chest against her cheek, sending an odd feeling of comfort through her. Slowly the monsoon of tears ebbed, until she closed her eyes, reveling in the calm sea she'd found in Matt's arms.

Emotional exhaustion took its toll. Her eyes drooping, she didn't try to fight it.

LONG AFTER HE FELT HER CALM DOWN AND HER BODY SLUMP against his, Matt continued to rock her. He whispered words of reassurance and acceptance, as much for his own need as hers. Steel gray clouds, filled with the snow the weathermen had predicted, darkened the afternoon sky before Matt had the courage to release his hold on her.

Careful not to wake her, he eased her onto the overstuffed floral sofa in the sunroom. He smoothed her hair off her face, pressed a kiss to her temple then pulled a green and yellow afghan over her.

How long had she held those tears inside? Any other woman would've given in to the past two days' stress the minute her car exploded. Yet she handled danger like an everyday occurrence. It had taken kisses on her scars to break through that hard shell she showed the world.

One hand resting gently on her back, he felt the ancient scars' telltale ridges beneath the cotton shirt.

How had she endured such torture?

He wanted to kill Strict. Hell, he wanted to find every member of that damn cult and treat them to the same torture they allowed to happen to her.

Signaling the dogs to lay near the sofa to guard Katie, he strode from the room. He needed to hit something.

———

"Exactly when were you going to inform me you had a witness missing, Castello?"

Frank watched the vein on his boss' forehead bulge and throb, a sure sign his ass was on the line. Jeff Davis was known for his calm, methodical approach to problems. When it came to solving a messy situation though, Jeff could play the hard-ass with the best of them.

"It started out as a simple retrieval, Captain. Nothing more than picking her up at her work. Then it all went to hell." Castello ran his hand across the stubble on his face. He hadn't slept, shaved, or showered in over forty-eight hours. "To be honest, I think the department has a bigger problem than just a missing witness."

"Besides a dead retired Marshal?"

Frank winced. Still raw with pain over his partner's death, he'd spent the entire night and most of the morning with the state FBI forensic team and the local sheriff working the crime scene at Pete's cabin. But the captain was right. He'd kept him in the dark and now Pete's death escalated the situation. The media would go on a feeding frenzy.

"Captain, I think we have a leak in the department. The only two agents who knew the new identity and whereabouts of Sarah Strict were Pete and myself."

"Maybe your little witness decided to garner some attention by leaking the information herself."

"After ten years of living a quiet anonymous life? That's what she'd always wanted, Captain. I don't think she'd trade that in for a little media attention."

Davis pulled out a cigar and clamped it between his teeth. He'd promised his wife to quit smoking them years before, but he still liked to chew on the ends while thinking through a problem. "You're sure she didn't have any contact with anyone in the Family?"

Frank handed him the file photos of Katie taken the day she walked into the police station to give information regarding the bombing. "She has no love for anyone there. The Family and Strict are responsible for all those scars."

"Shit." Captain Davis closed the file, shaking his head, and handed the folder to Castello. "Who knew you were extracting her from the hospital?"

"Katie and myself."

"And you haven't heard from her since?"

"Not a word."

"Dammit, that ties our hands. We'll have to approach this on a need-to-know basis. You pick the people you need to help you. They'll be told we're doing our own investigation into Pete's death. You'll head the task force. I know I should put you on desk duty since he was your old partner, except in this case you'll be the only one knowing we're also looking for your missing witness."

Castello nodded. Relief surged through him. He'd been afraid he'd be sidelined for the remainder of the investigation. "What about the FBI? They're not going to like us stepping on their toes."

"Screw the Feds. This was our man. We're not going to be their water boys while they play first string quarterback." Davis took the cigar out of his mouth and laid it on the glass ashtray. "You look like shit. After you set the task force in motion, grab a few z's."

"I'm okay, Captain—"

Davis held up a hand. "Save it. Nothing we do in the next hour is going to lose us Pete's killer, and your witness has been gone thirty-six hours. If she's hiding, she won't mind you getting a nap. If she's dead, well, she still won't mind."

Castello nodded and gathered his files. He knew Katie was still alive. But maybe the captain was right. He'd function better if he wasn't exhausted.

Damn. He was going to have to break the news about Pete to Leslie.

As a rookie agent, he'd partnered with Pete. Pete's secretary, who had been with him for nearly fifteen years at the time, took him under her wing as much as Pete had. Three years ago, she'd been killed in a car accident. Leslie Bell had come up from the secretarial pool to be the interim secretary for the pair. Despite her efficiency and calm demeanor, Pete couldn't adjust to the loss of his first assistant in such a tragic way. Saying, *"You never know when your time will be called,"* he'd retired to enjoy the rest of his life, never knowing how prophetic his words were.

At his office door Castello stopped and took a deep breath before opening it. Inside, Leslie sat, smiling and talking on the phone.

"Leslie, I need to speak to you in my office," he said as he passed by her desk. A few minutes later, she took her seat across from him, her notepad in hand.

"Did I interrupt something important on the phone?" He ought to just tell her and get it over with. But he just couldn't.

She smiled. "No, sir. Just talking with an old friend on my break."

Good. A friend might be able to ease the shock of what he was about to tell her. "Leslie," he started, then swallowed.

"Yes, sir?" She had an expectant look on her face.

Shit. This was going to be harder than he'd thought.

He swallowed again. "Leslie, I have some bad news." He gripped his pen tight between his two hands. "Pete Halloran is dead."

"Oh, no!" Her hand flew to her throat. Tears welled in her eyes. "How?"

Castello walked around the desk, leaning one hip on the edge. He took her hand in his. "I found him at his cabin last night."

"Was it his heart?"

He shook his head. "Pete was murdered."

She gasped and the color drained from her face. "Why? Why would someone want to kill Mr. Halloran? He's been retired for nearly three years."

Castello poured her a glass of water from the carafe she kept on his desk and handed it to her. He knew the news would hit the young woman hard, even though she'd only worked with Pete for a few months. She was tender-hearted that way.

In the twelve years he'd been with the Marshals he'd never been very good at breaking bad news to family members. That had always been Pete's area.

"We think it may be related to an old case of ours." He patted her hand once more. He didn't want to tell her the rest, but it would go down better coming from him than the rumor mill. "Leslie, there's something you need to know. Pete wasn't just murdered."

"He wasn't?" If possible, she went even paler.

"Someone wanted information from him. They tortured Pete to get it."

"Oh dear God." She gulped the water then set the glass on the desk with shaky fingers.

Castello took her hand in his once more. "I'm going to need your help finding out who did this to him, but if it's going to be too hard, I'll request a different secretary for this case."

She shook her head. "No, I'll be fine. Really."

"You're sure?"

Some color returned to her face. "Yes. I want to help catch who did this."

Castello smiled. "I knew I could count on you.. I'm forming a task force to spearhead our investigation." Assured his secretary wouldn't fall apart on him, he returned to his seat. He wrote a list of names and handed it to her. "Have these people meet with me at one this afternoon. Tell Bob Crestview to contact the FBI and get what he can from them. He'll be our contact with the bureau."

"Where will you be?"

"In my office. The captain ordered me to sleep. I'm counting on you and Dave to organize the information for everyone before the meeting."

She started to leave.

"Oh, Leslie?"

"Yes, sir?"

"Were there any messages for me?"

"A few, sir. I'll have them on your desk before the meeting."

"Any from a woman?" He doubted Katie had contacted him, but right now he could use a break in this case.

Leslie shook her head. "No, sir. Not by phone or e-mail."

He nodded, then reached in his top drawer for his antacids. At thirty-four he'd developed an ulcer that spoke to him when things were going bad. Right now it was sending him SOS signals even the East Coast Naval stations could receive.

For a minute he stared out his office window at the gray sky.

Soft fat flakes of early winter snow fell past. Then gruesome images of Pete hanging in his garage filled his mind. Willing them gone, he pinched the bridge of his nose tight, and closed his eyes.

Damn, he hoped Katie had found a safe place to hide. He didn't want to find her in the same shape as Pete.

12

The gnawing pain in her stomach woke Katie. Slowly she sat up on the couch in the darkened sun room. Dogs scooted out from under her feet. They sat watching her expectantly, their stub tails twitching side to side.

"You guys hungry, too?" The dogs pranced around in circles when she stood. "Or is it Mother Nature calling you?"

With a smile at their bouncing desire, she let them outside then watched them run and frolic in the new-fallen snow.

How long had she slept? The sun was low in the sky, and the ground outside the French doors lay covered with an inch of snow. A chill ran through her.

A week ago, she would've been content to sit in the dark alone, contemplating the snow. She'd grown accustomed to isolation during the past decade. After living with the Family, she'd craved nothing more than peaceful solitude.

And now? Now her peaceful existence had literally been blown away by her past. She had no home, no family, no one to trust.

Except Matt.

The memory of his fingers and lips on her scars sent a

shudder through her body. He'd seen her flawed body and hadn't been repulsed. How could any man look at her and not think she was a monster?

She leaned her face against the cold windowpane. Memories flashed in her mind. Standing in the freezing cold rain for hours, dressed in only a tee-shirt and shorts. Strict's face in front of hers, expressionless as she repeatedly recited gun specifications. Her mind skipped forward, to sitting bent over the bomb making table for hours, happily building her latest creation. Smiling to herself as she worked because she'd found a way to please Strict. No one had the ability to make his latest toys like she did. Then that fateful day when Billy was killed.

It's your fault little girl. He died because of your mistakes.

With Strict's voice echoing in her mind, she squeezed her eyes tight to dispel the images. Matt might not see her as a monster, but she knew the truth. She'd earned every one of those scars. The monster inside her needed the punishment.

The house's quiet crept in around her. Rubbing her arms against the cold that filled her from the inside out, she wandered in search of Matt. The kitchen was empty, as well as the living room and office.

As she climbed the stairs her pulse quickened. She hurried through all the bedrooms. His bag lay in the middle of the floor, clothes hanging out of it.

Where was he?

Panic rose inside her as she ran down the stairs and jerked open the garage door. His truck was still parked there. He hadn't left.

She stood, willing her heartbeat to slow. If he hadn't left, where was he? Another surge of adrenaline hit her heart. Had someone found out where they were? Had something happened to him?

Then she heard a sound from below. A slap against leather. A grunt.

She retrieved her gun from the table in the sunroom and followed the sound to the basement door. Opening it as quietly as possible, she eased her way down the stairs. The slaps continued. The grunts came in rhythm with them.

Had someone gotten in the house? Was he being tortured? God, she couldn't stand another innocent person being hurt because of something she'd done.

Staying against the wall, she silently made her way toward the sound. At the stairs' bottom she took a deep breath, lifted her gun then slowly looked around the wall into the other side.

Relief flooded her then her breath stopped in her throat.

Matt, dressed only in a pair of boxer shorts, his hands and feet wrapped with tape, had his back to her as he rhythmically boxed and kicked at a large leather bag suspended in the center of the home gym.

His dark hair lay wet against his neck and face. His broad back glistened with sweat. Each muscle tightened and stretched with his exertion. The powerful muscles of his long legs flexed and relaxed with the effort he put into his kicks.

There wasn't a mark on his body. He was perfection.

Men had always been a source of pain and suffering for her. But this man—with his rules, his compassion, and his flawless body—made her want things.

She ached to touch him. In all her life she'd never wanted to touch someone as much as she wanted to stroke her hand over his skin at this minute.

MATT'S HANDS AND FEET STUNG WITH EACH THRUST AGAINST THE leather bag. After holding Katie while she wept, he'd needed to work off the anger surging through him.

How could anyone torture another human being like she'd been tortured?

He slammed his taped knuckles into the bag once, twice, three times. The sting felt good. He only wished it was Strict's face he was smashing.

What kind of sick man would take out such hatred on a young girl? With a swell of raw power his left foot slapped the bag's side.

Forget lethal injection. He wanted just ten minutes alone with the bastard.

Bouncing on the balls of his feet, he slammed his fists back into the bag. His chest heaved.

With slower movements he rolled his shoulders forward and back. How long had he been down in Craig's gym?

Long enough to work out some of my rage.

Women and children were meant to be cherished and protected. Katie never had that. He wanted to avenge the young girl who'd suffered so greatly at the hands of a monster.

Was there a way to erase all the pain and betrayal Katie had dealt to her in the past? Matt wanted to protect the woman she was now. How did he keep her safe? And how did he convince her to let him?

He ran his hands through his hair.

It wasn't just his rage he'd needed to work off either. Since the first day he'd seen Katie she'd intrigued him. At first it was just her beautiful face with those entrancing eyes.

Hell, don't lie to yourself. You wanted to make love to her at first sight.

With a wave of frustration he attacked the bag again. The voice in his head was right. Since the day he'd met her, he'd fought this underlying urge to sink himself inside her. The primal need was a constant electrical current humming inside him.

Despite the strength she showed the world around her, Katie possessed a very vulnerable core.

It was what kept his own needs in check.

That and having sex with a witness is a major rule-breaker.

Technically, she wasn't a witness for any case his department was investigating, yet.

Yeah, but she's under my protection and wrong is just wrong.

Hell, she'd been taken advantage of enough in her life. He'd just have to find some way to curb his own desires. Focusing on Katie's physical protection instead of her physical pleasure was his priority.

A soft sound came from behind him. His body hardened with her nearness. Slowly, he turned.

The fragile woman he'd held in his arms hid behind her tough exterior shell once again. Only this time something was different.

Her breasts rose and fell with each breath. Her eyes wide with desire, her lips parted and she slid her pink tongue out to wet them.

Desire, hot and needy slammed deep into his gut. His body responded to the wanton passion emanating from her as she stood in the door staring at him.

Without thinking, he crossed the small distance separating them, and stopped inches from her.

Cupping his hands around her face, he slowly forced her to look into his eyes.

Her lips parted again.

Her unconscious invitation pushed him over the edge.

Holding her still, he took her mouth in a devouring kiss. He stroked her lips then pressed his tongue deep inside. With all the passion humming through his body he probed inside her. He needed to taste her like a man in the desert needed water.

The sound of the gun falling from her hand to the concrete floor clattered in his brain.

A little moan escaped her. She gripped his elbows then slid around to spread her hands across his back as she pressed herself closer to him.

Suddenly it wasn't just his need he fed, but hers. As her

fingers dug into his back muscles, he slid his hands down her shoulders and back, finally gripping her buttocks. With a groan he pressed her closer, grinding his erection into the junction of her thighs.

Not breaking the deep kiss between them, he maneuvered her the short distance to the wall.

Holding her beneath her soft bottom, he pressed her against the cold concrete.

The need inside him boiled uncontrolled. He wanted to possess her, all of her.

Don't break this rule, man. Not like this, not now. If you make love to her before she's sure of what she wants, you'll be no better than all the people in her life who've used her.

The unbidden thought acted like a bucket of cold water splashed on his senses.

He wouldn't take her, even if she appeared so willing. Until he had her trust, this would be nothing more than pure sex for either one of them.

With great effort, he released his hold on her bottom, gently easing her away from his raging hard-on. Reaching behind him, he pried her fingers loose from his damp skin where she clung to his muscles.

He wrapped his fingers in hers, pushing her gently against the wall. Lastly, he eased their torrid kiss into something gentle, soft, almost caressing. Their lips slowly separated.

Bringing their entwined hands up between them, he softly kissed each finger as her violet eyes blinked then opened, confusion and passion swirling in her gaze.

"Why?"

"Because you're not ready." He released her hands, once again cupping her face.

"Oh, yes I am."

Standing so close, he felt her tense from head to toe.

"Katie, you're a federal witness. I'm a cop. My job is to protect you, not take advantage of your weakness."

"I'm not weak." She shoved at his chest.

He held his ground. Damn the woman. Didn't she know he was trying to protect her from more hurt?

"Okay, call it vulnerabilities, then. Right now, we're in a highly dangerous situation. You've been injured. Your life and mine have been threatened. You're feeling things intensely. You don't know what you want. If we do this now, it will be just sex."

"So, you're saving me from myself?"

Something in the way she said that set off his internal warning system. He chose his next words carefully. "No, I'm saving us both from making a mistake we'll regret later."

"Let go of me." She pushed him again.

This time he moved back a pace, giving her room. "You understand, don't you?"

"Oh, I understand all right."

The muscles around her mouth tightened. Anger resonated from every inch of her.

"You're a liar. If you find me revolting, not as perfect as you, all you had to do was say so." With lightning speed, she slapped him. "You won't be the first person to reject me. I just wish you'd been honest about it."

Stunned as much by her accusation as the stinging slap he didn't try to stop her as she ran from the room.

13

Katie stood beneath the stream of hot water pouring from the shower, her hands covering her face, tears of humiliation coursing down her cheeks.

How could I be so stupid?

She'd trusted him with her body and all its imperfections. She'd been ready to give him all of her, and he rejected her. All her life she'd been unlovable. She'd hoped maybe somehow Matt had found something about her to love.

The taste of his kiss still lingered on her lips. She could still feel his body pressed against hers. Her hands ached to hold his firm muscles and smooth skin once more. For the first time in her life she'd wanted to make love to someone, and he called it just sex.

When would she learn? Her father died when she needed him, then her mother put her in the hands of the Devil and she died, too. She'd tried to fit into the Family, but even there she was such a failure. After Billy Hagen died because of her, she knew she was cursed.

You're useless, girl. If I didn't need your skills, I'd bury you with your piece-of-trash mother.

With a groan, Katie covered her head with her arms and huddled into the shower's corner.

There will be no place safe for the traitor.

She didn't want to remember how Strict made her feel, his berating comments about her and her mother, the way he tore her ego down.

"No, no, no." Slowly, she rocked herself. Visions of that first night her torture began flashed in her mind.

The Devil grabbed her by the hair as she stared at the badly burned body of fifteen-year old Billy.

"Girl, you screwed up. Look what you did! We needed that bomb for tomorrow's attack." He dragged her back to the bomb-making shack, more concerned about the setback in his plans than the young life that had just ended. "You will get back in there and make me another one, or I'll beat you until you can't stand!"

"I won't."

The words actually came out of her mouth.

Except for the wails of Billy's poor mother, silence descended on the Family. No one in the Family had ever defied Strict, their Prophet—certainly not his stepdaughter.

"You think you can refuse me, girl?" He released her hair with one hand, as the other delivered a stinging open-handed slap to her face.

Her head jerked to the side, blood oozing from her lip. She wiped at the blood and stared defiantly at him. At that moment she'd made her decision. No matter what he did, she would never build another bomb.

"I won't build another one." Strength surged through her body once the words were out.

"No one defies me, girl." He grabbed her again, this time, hauling her to the wooden flagpole centered on the main meeting room's front lawn. "Gideon, get the whip and rope."

Women in the group gasped, the men cheered their leader on. She didn't care. Her soul already ached. Dying was preferable than causing another death.

His second-in-command returned with the rope. She didn't struggle as they lashed her arms above her head to the pole. Billy was dead because of her. She deserved this punishment. "You have one chance to change your mind, girl."

"I won't ever change my mind."

"Yes you will, bitch."

He grabbed her shirt by the collar and yanked, ripping the worn out material off her body and exposing her flesh to everyone watching.

The horsewhip's first blow stung so badly, she thought she'd die. Then the second one came and she prayed for death. The men in the crowd began to count.

She listened to the numbers, forcing her mind to focus on something other than the pain, the first time Billy watched her working in the explosives shack. She'd protested, but Strict had insisted he learn from her. The boy had seemed happy to be around her.

Eight...Nine...

God, her back was on fire.

Think of something else. Billy had gone to the explosives shack to load their creation into the bag. She'd wanted to do it, but Strict had insisted the boy do it, not a girl.

Thirteen...Fourteen... Please let me die.

The pain cut deeper with each lash.

Think about Billy. He'd stopped in the drive and reached into the bag. Knowing how delicate the device was, she'd watched him, horrified. Then the explosion ripped through the night.

Nineteen...Twenty.

"Enough, Jacob. If she dies, no one will know how to make the bombs. Right now she's the only one who can." Gideon's words stopped his master before another lash fell on her back.

"Cut her down. If she refuses again, then she'll get thirty."

Gideon had been the one who cut her down, cleaned her back and slathered salve all over the cuts. He'd whispered to her as he worked. "He'll kill you, Sarah. Don't doubt it."

"I don't care. I won't kill another person."

"So be it."

She'd heard his voice predict her future, even as she collapsed to unconsciousness on the bed.

That was the day her nightmares began.

The water in the shower grew cold, bringing her back to the present.

Why couldn't she get Strict and the memories out of her head? For years she'd ignored him, shoved him into her mind's darkest recesses. In the last few days his presence resurfaced in her life. He wanted to control her, to defeat her.

Well, he wouldn't win this time. She wouldn't let him.

With every ounce of determination she forced herself to stand.

Come hell or high water, she'd beat the Devil. She'd survived this long. No matter the cost, she planned to outlive Jacob Strict.

Turning off the shower, she considered her next step. It was time to attack. If she learned anything from Strict, it was that power lay in the offense's hands.

But who, when, where and how?

The prison log hadn't helped. Maybe she could glean some information from the pictures Matt's brother-in-law had sent. She needed to figure out who the Devil had sent after her. Then she'd know how to find them.

———

ROBERT HAGEN STEPPED INTO THE SOUTH-SIDE BAR AND immediately felt transported back a decade. Seventies classic rock music blared from the jukebox. The neon Budweiser mirror flashed in the dark, smoke-filled room.

To his left a man dressed in khaki camouflage pants and a black tee-shirt leaned over the pool table, making his shot. Three other men, similarly dressed and sporting various stages of facial hair hovered nearby.

At the bar sat two bleached blondes, wearing low-cut tops and high-cut skirts. Each *lady* leaned over to whisper in the ear of, or touch the arm of the older man sitting beside her. Probably giving the gentlemen sneak peeks of what they were buying.

As his gaze adjusted to the dim, hazy light, Robert searched the room for the man who'd summoned him here. Then he saw him. Sitting in the last booth, facing the room, he'd placed himself close to the rear exit, should the need for a getaway arise. The man never forgot his training.

A shudder ran through Robert.

The man known as the Prophet's Angel of Retribution hadn't aged much in the past ten years. As a boy, Robert had feared him on sight, making himself as invisible as possible whenever the Angel passed by. Now as a grown man, every time the Angel contacted him, the reaction to run and hide still gnawed at him.

Only this time the Angel hadn't phoned, he'd summoned him to a face-to-face meeting. This time, there was nowhere for him to hide. As he'd always feared, his past had caught up with him.

He made his way to the bar's rear then settled himself on the worn leather seat opposite the quiet man. Neither said a word as the bartender came and took their orders for beer. Once they each had a frosty bottle in front of them, the other man raised cold gray eyes to Robert.

"The Prophet needs your help, boy."

Robert took a deep breath and let it out slowly. He'd known this day would come.

The morning after the bombing, Strict's stepdaughter Sarah disappeared, along with files of pictures and documents linking the Family to the explosion. Within days, State and Federal agents surrounded their bunker. The adults that hadn't fled went to jail, Strict among them. The kids and teenagers were sent to live with relatives or put into foster homes.

Robert, then fourteen, went to live with his maternal grandmother. He'd excelled through high school, amazing a legion of psychiatrists and social workers the government had insisted he see until he turned twenty-one.

None of them understood he'd been trained well by the Family at Strict's Bunker. It was his duty to succeed and find a place where he might be helpful to the cause.

"What does he want me to do?"

Robert dreaded the answer. He'd come to Columbus at the Angel's instructions a year ago and joined the local government in the Department of Motor Vehicles. Strict supplemented his income through the Angel in exchange for keeping track of the Family's current and former members.

Now he had to pay. He just hoped he didn't have to kill someone. "The traitor has surfaced."

He hadn't expected that. The news felt like a knife in his stomach. "Sarah?"

The other man nodded. "At the moment she's escaped me, so now it's time for you to help make her pay for killing your brother."

The knife twisted deep in his gut. Sarah. The one person in the Family who'd been kind to him and his twin brother. He needed to fulfill his obligation to the Family, but he didn't want to hurt Sarah.

"Where is she?"

"Somewhere in Columbus. But she's gone to ground for the moment. That's where you come in."

Robert nodded. "What do you need?"

The Angel slid a piece of paper across the table. "This man is hiding her. I need the make and model of his vehicle and license plate number."

Robert read the paper. A name and phone number were all that was on it.

"When you get the information, call me at that number."

"That's all?"

"Give me what I need to find her and your obligation to the

Family will end." The Angel stood then disappeared out the rear entrance without another word.

Robert heaved a sigh. He was almost free from the nightmare of his youth. One simple task. That was all that he needed to do. So why did he feel as if he were signing Sarah's death warrant?

14

When Katie entered the kitchen, Matt stood at the indoor grill, cooking three hamburgers. "Hungry?"

She felt him watching her. The jerk.

If her stomach hadn't growled, she would've ignored him completely. However she knew in order to fight Strict, she needed to maintain her strength…and damn those burgers smelled good.

She slapped the file of pictures she carried down on the table. The resounding smack ricocheted off the walls.

"What I am is ready to find out who's trying to kill me." Her voice sounded strained even to her own ears. What did he expect? For her to act as if everything was normal? Well, too bad. It wasn't.

"Katie, we need to talk about what happened downstairs earlier."

Taking a deep breath, she tried to still the anger inside her. Never give anyone power over you. Stay calm and in control at all times. "You don't have to worry about me throwing myself at you again."

"You didn't throw yourself at me. I wanted to kiss you."

His deep voice sent goose bumps shivering along her body.

"That's over now. It meant nothing, just two people letting off some frustration. What we need to focus on are these pictures. Maybe one of them will trigger an idea of who Strict sent after me."

For a moment, she thought he was going to argue with her. He opened his mouth, then shut it, gave her a nod, and resumed fixing the burgers.

Her fingers trembled slightly as she reached for the first picture. *Dammit.* She clenched her fingers into a fist then relaxed them.

No matter how much she pretended otherwise, the kiss and his rejection affected her greatly. She couldn't afford to become an emotional blob now. Her life, and his, depended on her ability to think one step ahead of Strict.

MATT FLIPPED THE MEAT ONTO THE BUN, AND FOUGHT THE URGE to slam the grill pan into the wall. The woman was driving him insane.

There she sat, as cool as a cucumber, acting like nothing had happened to her, when less than an hour before his whole world had tilted on its side with one sizzling hot kiss. How did she shut her emotions down like that? And how could he say this electric tension between them meant nothing?

With a shake of his head he inhaled and exhaled deeply, trying to fight his own frustration.

Maybe she was right. Maybe what they needed was to focus completely on which Family member might be the hitman.

He set one sandwich in front of her then settled across the table with his plate. The trouble was he'd much rather look at her lips than those damn pictures.

"Tell me about each person." If she could play it cool, so could he.

She glanced through the pictures, pulling out one of a middle-aged woman with dark curly hair and kind eyes. "This is Maura."

"The secretary/mid-wife?" He studied the picture a moment, committing the woman's face to memory.

"Yes, she's the nearest thing to a human in the Family." Katie took a bite of her burger. A bit of bread dangled from the corner of her lips. Her tongue darted out to catch it.

Matt fought a groan. "Who else do you see?"

She handed him the picture of a bald man with a scar across his cheek. "That's Stryker. The name fits. He liked to hurt things, especially those smaller than him." She tossed out a picture of a young teenager. "That's his wife. She was his anger's usual target."

From the looks of him, the man had probably served time in prison, which put him first on Matt's list for the hitman. The girl looked like she'd been used hard and put away wet. Her life hadn't been an easy one.

Had Stryker touched Katie?

Once again white-hot anger shot through Matt. He set the picture aside, the man's face permanently fixed in his mental file.

He took a few bites of his burger to prevent him from crumbling the pictures in wads. Katie continued to search through them. Every so often a flash of sadness or a wince of pain crossed her beautiful face.

"This is Cody. He supplied guns for Strict." She set a picture of a man with a long beard, dark glasses and stringy black hair onto the table. A second picture of a thirty-ish woman with matching stringy dark hair landed beside it. "That's Kat, his woman. She liked to pretend she was an equal to the men. But we all knew Cody beat her when she crossed the line."

Matt added the wife beater to his mental list of possibilities.

Two pictures landed on the table simultaneously. In both, the men wore military-style short haircuts and olive-khaki tee-shirts.

"Who are they?"

"Michael and Gabriel Whitaker. You can eliminate them from the list of suspects."

"Why?"

"They were two of the three Family members who died at the Federal Building explosion."

"Who was the other one?"

A sad, faraway look crossed her face for a moment, but then it quickly fled. "Gideon."

"Where's his picture?"

"He never had one, and no one ever took one of him."

"Who was he?"

"Strict's right-hand man. He treated me kindly once in a while, especially after the times Strict had meted out my punishment."

Matt fought the jealousy that roared through him. She'd cared about this Gideon. "Was he a young man?"

"If he'd lived I guess he'd be over fifty. I think my stepfather and he were in the Army together." She picked up another picture. "He's dead now, so it doesn't matter."

As she went through the file's remaining pictures the litany of abusive people continued and so did Matt's list of possible suspects. Each man resembled the others, cruel and dangerous. The women, their faces full of pain, were held in submission by the men's violent natures. The pictures littering the table resembled a collage of despair and hopelessness. Not even the children's photos changed the bleak collection.

Cold chills slithered down his spine. "How did you survive this?"

She slipped the last piece of her burger past her lips, chewed, then swallowed. "I survived because the alternative was to give up and then my stepfather would've been right."

"How?" Her apathetic summation irritated him. Why wasn't she angry at the life she'd been forced to live?

"He told me repeatedly I was nothing more than a useless woman. That I'd die long before he did. Proving him wrong was what kept me going."

"Because you helped get him convicted for the bombing?"

"Yes. I put an end to his plans." She lifted a picture and stared at it a long time. "But not soon enough."

The way she studied the picture piqued his curiosity. The boy in the image meant something to her, more than the others she'd discarded on the table.

"Who's that?" He nodded at the picture.

"Billy Hagen. He was in the sixth grade when his parents joined the family. This picture is from the last time he attended public school."

Matt glanced at the children's pictures scattered on the table. Many were simple wallet-sized school snapshots. His mother had pages in her scrapbook plastered with the same size pictures of him and his siblings, one grade after another.

"What happened to him?"

She shook her head and laid the picture gently on top. "He died before they blasted the Federal Building."

"How?"

The corners of her mouth turned down as she stared out the window into the dark night. "I killed him."

His cell phone rang before he could ask her another question. He mumbled a curse, then flipped open the phone.

"Where the hell have you been all day, Edgars?"

Hell. Just what he needed, his boss looking for him. "I'm still on holiday leave, Captain."

Katie gathered their plates and carried them to the sink. The curve of her bottom and the gentle sway of her hips distracted Matt from the phone conversation. As she moved about the kitchen, the new soft limp in her gait tore at his gut.

She'd gotten that limp trying to protect him. Men were supposed to protect women from injury, not the other way around.

"You want to explain to me why your front door was rigged to blow you away?" His boss ground the question out into his ear.

Matt's attention snapped away from Katie's body. "How did you know about that, sir?"

"The city's Chief of Police was only too happy to forward the report to me in person. While we're on the subject, who wants you dead enough to set up an ambush? Is this related to a case you're working on?"

Damn, Captain Brown was in the mood for blood—his. What he had to say next wasn't going to make him any happier. "It's not something I'm at liberty to discuss over the phone, Captain."

Katie stopped rinsing the dishes and turned to watch him. Her whole being stilled, as if every cell of her body was poised for flight.

Matt winked to reassure her that the phone call wasn't anything important. To her well-being, at least. His career, on the other hand, was another matter.

"I don't give a shit what you think you can explain or not, Edgars. I've spent the entire day bending over for the Chief of Police to kick me in the ass. Who, by the way, also wants to know where you are."

"The local police, sir? Not the feds?"

"Don't tell me the feds are looking for you, too."

Matt held his tongue. As likely as not, the Marshals would visit the captain next.

A derisive snort sounded on the line's other end, followed by a string of expletives insulting Matt's ancestors. "I want you in my office first thing tomorrow morning, before the feds come knocking on it, Edgars. Bring some answers with you. Understand me?"

Matt's balls felt the vice-grip squeeze his boss had on them. "Yes, sir. I understand." The conversation ended abruptly.

Matt closed the cell phone.

KATIE WATCHED HIM RUN ONE HAND THROUGH HIS DARK HAIR. His lips pressed into a firm line. The phone call upset him.

She focused her attention on cleaning the grill pan. The last thing she wanted to hear was how much trouble she'd gotten him into. This wasn't about him. She couldn't afford to worry about anyone other than herself, no matter how much her heart and body wanted otherwise.

"I have to go into the department in the morning."

"I'm not going with you."

"I didn't think you were. Besides he just wants me to explain about the ambush at my apartment. I'll feed him the same line I did the police, that the Russian mafia I helped put away last year are behind it."

She stilled her hands and stared at him. "I didn't dream that?"

He tilted his head to study her. "You thought you dreamed what?"

"When the medics put me on the stretcher, I heard you tell the policeman something about the Russian mafia having set up the ambush." Heat filled her cheeks. "I believed I had imagined you saying that. As much as you want to go by the book, I knew you couldn't be lying to protect me. I blamed it on the concussion."

"As far as I knew it was the truth, Katie. At the time I didn't have any way of knowing Strict's man knew you were with me. I assumed it had to be retaliation from last year's case."

Great. Now she'd made a complete fool of herself, again. She concentrated on scrubbing the grill pan. "So, you didn't lie to protect me."

"Technically, I did, twice." He voice sounded from right

behind her. Somehow he'd moved from the table without her hearing a sound.

"How?"

"You asked me to protect you, so I gave them a false name, sweetheart."

"And the other time?" she asked, looking over her shoulder at him.

"When I told them you were my girlfriend." He took her face in his warm hands and forced her to look at him. "I do believe in following the rules, Katie. If my boss doesn't mention you or Strict, I'll leave the subject closed."

"And if he does?"

His lips pressed into a thin line, the muscle in his jaw jerking slightly. "Then I'll be duty-bound to tell him the truth."

"He'll turn me over to the Marshals." Why did he stubbornly stick to the rules?

"Katie, you have to trust me. I'll do everything in my power to protect you from Strict's man, but I won't lie to my boss about the situation."

She stepped away from him, wiping her hands on a towel. "And I keep telling you, the only way to survive is to stay hidden."

"At some point, you have to quit hiding."

They stood just an arm's length apart. It might as well have been a mile. "I've been hiding too long to change now."

"If you don't come out of the dark soon and face your fears, you may never."

Suddenly, she knew they were talking about more than just hiding from the hitman—and it scared the hell out of her.

―――――

CASTELLO LOOKED AROUND THE ROOM AT THE FEW MEN AND ONE woman who formed his task force on Pete's murder. Dave

Crestview served with Pete before they were partnered. Kevin, Al, and Greg all had equally long careers with the Marshals.

He'd chosen them because he knew each man's work ethic and he couldn't trust any of the younger agents. Someone in the department had leaked information to Strict. So anyone with less than ten years' experience was questionable.

"As you all know, Pete Halloran was murdered. According to the Medical Examiner, he'd been dead about a week. The FBI is already on the case, but because Pete was one of ours, the Captain wants us doing our own investigation."

Frank took his seat at the conference table then nodded to the man seated at his left. "Dave, tell us what you've gotten from the feds."

Dave passed folders to the task force's other members. "The ME gives the official cause of death as heart failure secondary to exsanguination—basically, Pete's heart gave out from the massive amount of blood he lost during the torture."

"What kind of weapon?" Al glanced up from his copy.

"The ME thinks it was either an Army field knife or large blade hunting knife."

"See if you can get a better ID on the weapon, Al." Frank nodded at the man at the table's other end. "Then see if we can find out who might have purchased one lately. Check with local sporting-goods shops, and online sales, too."

"Any prints?" Kevin was a details man. He'd be asking about fiber analysis next.

Castello listened while Dave gave a report on all the evidence, or lack thereof, disclosed by the FBI report. The somber mood of those gathered illustrated just how much his team wanted to find who butchered their old comrade.

Now, all he had to do was steer them in the Federal Building bombing and Strict's direction. Then the hunt for who was stalking Sarah/Katie would begin.

He waited until their discussion ran its course, then he

nodded to Leslie to pass around the copies of five files to each investigator.

"These are the major cases Pete and I worked the last few years before he retired. Study them and see what you can come up with in the way of leads connected to his death."

The men opened their files, flipping through the witnesses' names in the protection program.

Suddenly Greg froze with a file half open in front of him. "Frank, this might be important."

Castello's pulse kicked into high gear. "What've you got?"

"This Sarah Strict? Her name popped up on our warning service last night."

"How?"

Everyone's attention riveted on the task force's oldest member.

"The social security number came in from a local hospital. Two team members went over this morning to interview her and get details as to her injury, but she'd skipped out without being discharged."

"Did they find out anything about her injuries?" Frank prayed it wasn't too serious. Greg shook his head. "Not much other than it was some sort of shotgun blast."

"That may be the connection we're looking for." Frank already knew it was. He focused his attention on each member of his task force. "I think we should concentrate on this witness' case as our main probable link to Pete's murder."

So much for discretion. His chief witness was on the run and possibly injured. The stakes had just doubled. Katie's life depended on how fast the task force moved in finding Pete's killer.

15

The black sedan drove through the parking lot outside the State Highway Patrol Headquarters on the near north side of town. The driver searched for a black Ford pick-up. Carefully the Angel studied each license plate, looking for the number Hagen provided. Too bad the young man had become another loose end he couldn't afford to leave behind. Another time, he might have proved useful.

Focusing on finding the girl, the Angel continued his search for the vehicle he needed. The only connection he had to her was the highway patrolman she'd run to for help. To find her he'd have to track the patrolman back to their lair.

But he always enjoyed the hunt. Even against formidable prey such as the girl.

For a female, she'd always been amazingly resourceful. That trait drove the Prophet crazy. No matter the amount of torture he put her through she survived. Her stubborn streak had propelled her down the scaling wall's side and more than one cliff during her training.

And her need to protect others added to the punishment her stepfather doled out. Once, a child failed to field strip a weapon properly. When he was sent to bed without food, Sarah had taken it upon herself to sneak the child some dinner. Strict had gone crazy. He'd forced the girl to stand in the freezing sleet, dressed only in her pajamas and recite the entire weapons manual the family used. Her ensuing pneumonia would have killed a weaker person.

Strict had never understood that about her. He'd always underestimated her abilities. Even now, when the Prophet ordered his plans carried out before midnight on the thirty-first, Strict expected the deed to take little effort.

He, on the other hand, knew she'd be a difficult kill.

Right now, his first priority was to find the patrolman's truck then he'd find the girl.

Finally, he drove through the lot's front lane. There was the truck, parked close to the door. A slow smile split the Angel's lips. The patrolman planned a hasty exit.

No matter. Now he had their scent.

———

CASTELLO LIFTED THE PILE OF E-MAIL AND PHONE MESSAGES LESLIE had laid on his desk after the task force meeting.

Two calls from his sisters in California, wishing him a Merry Christmas.

He shook his head. Every year they invited him out, and every year he chose to work. You'd think they'd get the message. He didn't want happy family time. Never had.

When Katie was safe, he'd have to make time to call the girls and apologize, again.

An e-mail notification regarding Strict's execution date and time. He set that to one side.

In all his years of protecting witnesses from scum like Strict, he'd never actually attended any of their executions. This time he might make an exception. He'd like nothing more than to watch the Prophet meet his maker.

As he read the next message, he sat straight in his chair. He reached for the file on his desk. The guy's name, he'd seen it before. He flipped through the file until he found it.

Matt Edgars.

He'd been the man listed on the hospital report as contact for Katie. The same man the nurses told the investigators had slept by her bed all that night. The same man they believe she left with. He compared the date on the message to the one on the file. The message came in on Christmas Eve. The hospital admission was just before midnight on Christmas night.

Dammit. What the hell had happened to Katie? And who was this—he glanced at the note again—highway patrolman to whom she'd gone for help? Had someone from his office given the patrolman's name to Strict's man?

He was tired of being ten steps behind his own witness.

It was time to find this Matt Edgars and hopefully, Katie. Castello slipped the note into his pocket.

Frustration pushed him out of his chair. He grabbed his coat and headed out of his office. "Leslie, I'm on my cell if anything important comes up," he called as he stalked out the door.

"Where are you going, sir?" She followed him from the office, catching him as he stopped at the elevator.

He waited for the door to open, then stepped inside and pushed the lobby button. "I'm going hunting."

MATT FORCED HIMSELF TO STROLL OUT OF THE HIGHWAY Patrol's general headquarters and quite possibly his career. He'd spent more than an hour enduring the third-degree grilling by his captain about the ambush at his apartment. Each time Brown asked him about a possible tie-in with a case, Matt had suggested it was due to his involvement with the Russian Mafia case he'd worked on with Jake the year before.

But Brown hadn't gotten to the rank of Captain by being stupid. When Matt hedged on information regarding the woman with him, Brown had stopped his questioning and sat back in his chair to study him.

Matt met his intense gaze without flinching. He'd already decided his first duty as both a law officer and a friend was to protect Katie.

"You're not telling me everything, Edgars."

Matt started to give him a vague answer, but the captain held up one hand to stop him.

"Before you say anything, answer some questions. Is this incident in any way related to a case in our department?"

"No, sir."

"I can't believe I'm gonna ask you this, but are you mixed up in anything illegal?"

Matt blinked at that. "No, sir. You know me better than that."

Brown lifted one eyebrow. "I also know you usually don't hedge on telling me the details of a case."

Matt's gut clenched. Never in his career had anyone had a reason to doubt him. Withholding information from a superior officer went against every code of conduct he'd ever had, not to mention amounting to gross insubordination.

His career virtually circled the drain.

Brown looked through the papers on his desk. "This woman. Anyone I should be concerned about knowing?"

"Captain, she's not in trouble with the law. But I promised to keep her identity quiet for the time being."

His boss studied him for a moment. "Is she worth your career?"

Matt didn't hesitate. "Yes, sir, I believe so."

"Then take your vacation time now. You have one week to get

this mess cleaned up, or I'll have to ask for the details of the case. And Matt?"

"Yes sir?" The guillotine blade rose above his head.

"Because of your past record and excellent job performance, I'm cutting you some slack this time. But get this straight. If you refuse to give me answers next time you're here, I'll be forced to ask for your badge. Got it?"

Matt had nodded and exited the office before the captain could change his mind or grill him further.

Now he needed to get back to Katie. Their search for the assassin just received a time limit. If he had any luck at all, they'd be able to catch the killer before his career went down the toilet. More importantly, before the man found Katie.

He'd meant what he said to the captain. She was more important than his career.

Outside the building, he sprinted to his truck. The need to see Katie burned inside him. Turning the Ford onto Seventeenth Street, he drove past the Ohio State Fairgrounds to the interstate entrance.

The light caught him before he passed under the freeway. He sat there thinking about everything that had happened since he'd seen Katie's tire shot out four days before.

Like a Midwestern tornado, she'd turned his well-ordered life upside down. He should've explained the whole affair to his boss and brought in more help. But when he tried to do what was expected of him as a law officer, they'd both ended up in more danger.

Since he'd met Katie, not only had his world changed, but so had he. He seemed to hover in a strange space between constant sexual arousal, tender desire to comfort her, and anger.

His anger focused first and foremost on anyone who'd ever hurt Katie. Underneath that solitary shell she presented to the world lay the young woman who wanted acceptance. He included the Marshals on that list. When he got his hands on the person that leaked her name, their life expectancy was nil.

Then there was Katie, herself. Her mistrust, no matter how well-founded, tied his hands. "Dammit." He hit the steering wheel. "I should be able to call on all the power of law enforcement to find this guy and protect her."

But she'd never forgive me.

Light flashed on metal in his rearview mirror. As he watched, a black sedan slowly pulled out of the parking lot he'd just exited.

The hairs on his neck tingled a little as it approached his tail.

The light turned green. Slowly, he drove his car under the interstate and onto the entrance ramp and headed north. As he settled into traffic, he glanced into the rearview mirror again. No sign of the sedan.

Great. Now he was imagining someone following him. Next, he'd be inspecting his phone lines to see if they were tapped, and seeing conspiracies in everything.

Switching into the middle lane he continued north. After passing several exits, he glanced in his rearview mirror, then his driver's mirror. Nothing but regular traffic. Then he glanced into the passenger-side mirror. A beer truck moved right to the exit ramp, and there it was. The same black sedan.

The hairs on his neck tingled again and his pulse rate jumped two notches. Coincidence?

"Well, let's just see."

He stepped on the gas, and maneuvered his truck into the left-hand passing lane. Frequently, he checked the traffic behind him in the rearview mirror.

Yep, the sedan changed lanes. It moved just enough to keep him in its sights.

Okay, I'm not imagining it, I'm being tailed.

He eased his foot off the accelerator, letting the truck settle into pace with the cars around him.

The guy kept just enough distance to track him, not attack him.

The question was who was on his ass? The Marshals? Strict's hitman? Had the police decided to put their own tail on him?

Whoever it was, they were looking for Katie. He felt it clear down to his bones.

Think, Edgars. How can I turn this to my advantage?

With one hand on the steering wheel, he slipped his cell phone's earpiece into his ear, then dialed Luke's work number.

"This is Edgars."

"Luke, it's Matt."

"Oh, ho. Got away from the lady long enough to contact your brother and let me know you're still among the living, huh?"

Matt clenched his jaw and ignored his brother's off-handed reprimand for not contacting him since the ambush. "Can you leave the office now?"

"Sure, why?"

"I need your help."

There was a pause on the other end. "What's up?"

"I need to shake a tail."

"Whatever you need, man."

Matt explained his plan to Luke, then disconnected.

Now to keep his tracker occupied until Luke could follow his directions. He shifted lanes through the midday traffic, back to his right, and headed northeast, away from Katie.

As he drove through the apartment complex's lot, Castello checked the address he'd gotten for Matt Edgars. He doubted the patrolman or Katie would actually come back to the apartment, but it was the only place he had left to look for them.

His trip to the hospital, while providing details of why Katie was admitted the other night, did little to aid him in actually finding her.

A low whistle burst out of him as he pulled up to the last apartment in the complex's rear. Coercing Edgars' address from the hospital administration had been another waste of time. He hadn't needed to.

Yellow police tape marked off the apartment's entire front. A crew of three worked to mount a new front door. The old one, with a hole big enough to drive a Hummer through, stood propped against the outside wall. It was a wonder that Katie and Edgars survived at all.

Parking his car, Castello pushed his black sunglasses on his nose. Time for the big bad federal agent to step on some local law-enforcement toes.

The work crew's oldest member looked up as he approached them. "Hey, mister, can't you see the police tape? You can't be here."

Castello took out his ID case, flipped it open and let them all see his shiny Marshal's badge. "Which of you is in charge here?"

"That'd be me," the older man replied and offered his hand. "Ralph Bender. I'm the maintenance foreman for the complex."

Castello shook hands. "How long has Mr. Edgars lived here?"

"About three years," Ralph answered then instructed the other two workers to finish repairing the front door.

"Has he had any trouble like this before?"

Ralph shook his head. "Not like this. He only complained about the regular leaks and electrical problems all the other tenants 'round here have."

"Okay, thanks." Castello watched until they had the new door in place then went inside.

Yellow police paint circled the tiled entranceway where the chair and shotgun rig had sat. The chair, weapon and rigging he assumed now sat in the police evidence room.

Without touching anything Castello walked through the

townhouse's front living room and into the kitchen. He wanted to get a feel for the man who was aiding Katie. The apartment was neat, but not fussy. Apparently, Edgars liked a little order to his life, but wasn't obsessed with it.

Using a pen from his pocket, Castello pushed the play button on the answering machine. "There are no new messages," said the mechanical voice. Not that he'd expected any.

"The tape was clean when we got here."

Castello turned to see two men in dark blue suits standing just inside the sliding glass doors to the patio. Their neutral expressions hinted they were the lead detectives on the case.

Well, he was just going to make their day.

"Gentlemen, I'm Marshal Castello." He gave them his ID and badge. "And I have a problem."

"Actually, you have several. The biggest one being you're standing in the middle of our crime scene," the shorter detective said.

Great. A cop with attitude. Well, right now his attitude was bigger.

"Gentlemen, since one of the people involved is a federally protected witness, this just became my case, and you are the ones standing in *my* crime scene."

A slow smile spread over Castello's face as the detectives' expressions darkened. Oh yeah, it felt good to pull rank.

KATIE SAT CURLED ON THE COUCH IN THE SUNROOM, FLIPPING through the Family's pictures once more. She'd hoped never to look upon any of these faces again. Every one of them brought back some bleak memory.

The day she'd escaped she'd managed to pilfer these photos from Strict's office. The last time she'd seen them, she and the pictures had both been in FBI custody. Somewhere in this file had to be the person Strict sent to kill her.

But who?

Several of the men were currently serving life terms for their participation in the bombing's planning. She could eliminate them easily. The Marshals would've contacted her if any of them had been paroled.

You believed they'd protect you, too.

The thought startled her. If someone with the Marshals had sold her out to Strict, then perhaps she'd been kept in the dark regarding any convicted conspirators' releases.

Maybe she needed to ask Matt to look into the possibility one of the five men having been paroled. If so, she'd have to eliminate possible suspects based on the skills she knew they did or didn't possess.

Whoa. When had she started relying on Matt?

When she'd called him to get her away from the hospital he'd simply been a conduit to safety.

She should've bolted that first night before she'd gotten to know him, before he ever kissed her.

Visions of him standing in his boxers, sweat glistening on his skin, passion etching his face washed over her. Heat ignited deep in her stomach and traveled downwards.

"Stop it."

Her command to herself was so loud it shattered the house's silence and startled the dogs. They came to attention at her feet.

"Not you guys."

They all tilted their head in different directions as if asking who else she would be talking to. "What, haven't you ever seen anyone go crazy before?"

They wagged their stubby tails at her.

"Great, now I'm talking to the dogs." She shoved herself off the sofa and headed to the kitchen. "Come on, let's see if we can find something for lunch."

She laid the folder of pictures on the table then searched the drawers for some paper and a pen.

One drawer's clutter amazed her.

"Look at this," she addressed her companions. "Spools of thread, coupons, rubber bands, a deck of cards." She rifled through, finding small bits of everyday life.

"I've never seen a drawer like this."

Then it hit her. In all her life she'd never been in a place of such permanence and security that she could collect such odds and ends of normalcy.

Rage surged through her.

She slammed the drawer shut.

Strict stole her past and had put chains on her present. Somehow she needed to claim back her future from him and his poisonous beliefs.

The dogs whined at her. "What?"

They sat next to their bowls wagging their tails, expectant looks on their faces.

"I guess you guys just want food, huh? Must be nice. The only worry you guys have is wondering when the next meal is going to be."

Shaking her head, she found their food, and scooped out a bowl full for each. "You know I don't know how much you're supposed to eat."

They didn't answer as they stayed seated, rooted to the spot, waiting for something.

"Oh, go ahead, eat." She waved her hand at the bowls.

They scampered to their food in a mass of wiggling tails, paws and muzzles. She watched them for a minute.

Visions of another time, another place filled her mind.

"Mama, I'm hungry."

"Hush, child. Don't let him hear you complain."

"But why do we have to wait for him before we can eat? Daddy never made us wait."

Her mother finished setting the food on the table. It looked so tasty and she was so hungry.

Without thinking of consequences she reached for one hot, tender biscuit.

The Devil grabbed her from behind. She screamed.

"What do you think you're doing, girl?" He shook her hard then set her away from the table. "You know the rules. The man of this house will tell you when you can eat. Even my dogs are better trained than you."

She knew better than to say she was sorry. He'd call her a sniveling brat and punish her for speaking without permission.

"You'll stand there while your mother and I eat."

When her mother started to protest, the Devil turned on her. "Quiet, woman, or you'll join the brat in her punishment."

She watched the pain and anguish fill her mother's face.

Oh, please choose me, mother, she'd wanted to scream. But in the end, her mother meekly sat at the table with him.

She stood near the wall, her little hands clenched in fists, while he and her mother ate the delicious smelling food. Her stomach grumbled at first, then hurt with the pain of emptiness, but it couldn't compare to the pain of her empty heart.

When they finished, her mother set leftovers on a plate for her. But the Devil wasn't happy with the look on her face and so he fed every last scrap to his precious dogs.

And so her training began.

A shiver ran over Katie's body, bringing her out of her nightmarish memories. She'd worked hard to bury her past. Looking at the Family's pictures had opened the door for the memories to surface easily.

She pulled ham for a sandwich from the refrigerator. She'd learned her lesson well that day. Never let someone know how starved you were, and never go without food when it was available.

As she ate her sandwich at the table, she glanced at the clock on the wall. It was after noon. Where was Matt? He should've been back by now. What if something had happened to him?

What if the Marshals found him? Or worse, the hitman?

Stop it. He's a big boy, he can take care of himself.

Oh, yes, he was big all right. She felt so tiny in his presence. But oddly enough, she didn't feel small or threatened.

In fact, she'd never experienced this kind of acceptance and freedom in her whole life. Sure, she wasn't allowed to leave, but she could speak her mind without fear of reprisal.

That freedom wasn't something she was used to. She looked at the clock again.

So, where was Matt?

The dogs stopped eating, their heads tilting to the side as they each listened to something outside. A low growl came from the largest.

Katie grabbed her gun, and locked a round into the chamber. She eased her way to the front window and peeked out. An electric blue firebird sat in the drive. She ducked away from the window.

Oh God, oh God. Her stomach dropped, and her heart ached. Matt had betrayed her, too.

She moved behind the front door. As it opened, she lifted her Glock.

16

"Don't move."

Cold metal pressed against Matt's neck.

He froze. "I won't, sweetheart. But please don't blow off anything important I might want to use later."

"You're late."

"I had a problem with the truck." He heard her ease the trigger back and cool air caressed his neck as she lowered the weapon. Only then did he relax.

"What's wrong with the truck?" She moved away, allowing him into the house.

"It was being tailed."

She froze halfway to the table. Slowly she turned, that quiet, wary stillness on her features again. "You're sure?"

"I've driven the entire north side freeway system making sure." He grabbed her hand and headed to the stairs. "Get your stuff together, we need to get out of here."

She dug her heels in and tried to pull her hand away. "Why?"

"Because I don't know who was following me. Could have been the hitman, could have been the Marshals, could have been the police. It might even have been my own people." He let go of her hand to grip her by the shoulders. She needed to understand. "If anyone at my work remembers I'm house-sitting for Craig, we could have visitors at any moment. Right now, the only people I trust knowing where we are is my family."

"Matt," her eyes filled with the glisten of unshed tears. "I don't want anything to happen to you or anyone in your family because of me."

He released her shoulders to cup her face in his hands. "Sweetheart, nothing is going to happen to anyone in my family. Mom and Dad are spending the next week with Sami and Jake. Besides, Mom wants to be near Sami in case the baby comes. Dave and his family are down in Cincinnati. No one's going to bother them."

"What about Luke?"

He rolled his eyes. His little brother didn't need her worrying about him. "The boy genius is going to meet us where we're going."

"Where are we going?"

"A cabin in the woods, totally unconnected with you." He kissed her once, deeply, then moved away before it could become more. "Now get your stuff together, woman."

She started up the stairs. Halfway, she stopped and looked back at him, concern on her face. "What about the dogs?"

"We can't stay here just to care for the dogs. Craig and his wife will be home tomorrow. They'll be fine for a day, and Luke will see to letting them out before he joins us."

"We can't just leave them here, alone."

"I thought you hated dogs."

"I don't hate dogs. I just…they scare me. But these guys…" She hesitated a moment. "They're not too bad."

"Katie, they can't go with us."

"Wouldn't they be able to stay at the cabin with us?"

He shook his head. "I don't know how long we'll be there."

"Where else are we going?"

God, he hated telling her this, but she needed to hear it.

"When I played football I always hated being on the defense. I prefer to attack."

"Who are we attacking?"

"Everyone. First the Marshals, then your hitman. Even Strict if we have to. It's time to get some answers."

Katie relaxed as they drove along through the winter woods. They'd traveled south from the city for nearly an hour, finally turning off the highway onto a single lane road. Then they pulled onto a gravel road that led further into the Hocking Hills Matt drove through a metal gate and up to a modern day log cabin, complete with covered porch for sitting outside. "Whose cabin is this?"

"It belongs to my sister and her husband. Last year Jake put in some security features."

"Why?"

"It's a complicated story having to do with the Russian Mafia and my nephew, Nicky. Right now it's the safest place for us to stay."

His explanation left her more curious than before. Since she had darker secrets than most people, she decided not to push him. If he wanted to tell her more later it would be his decision. If not, well, that was his decision, too.

He parked the car then reached for a remote control lying on the console between the seats. With one press of the button, the gate closed behind them. Then he pressed a second one and the interior lights came on in the house.

"Neat trick."

He winked. "I can get radar sweeps and set motion sensors if we want them."

"Don't you think that's overkill?" she asked.

The humor left his eyes, and his lips pressed into a thin line. "They've tried three times to kill you. I think anything we use to protect you is justified."

She blinked at the passion in his words. Unable to voice the raw emotions coursing through her, she opened her door and stepped out into the cold December air. "Just don't set the motion detectors until your brother gets here."

He chuckled, the intensity gone. "It might be fun to watch him set them off."

Inside the cabin, she marveled at the rustic charm combined with the high-tech kitchen and electronics. The river-stone fireplace ran from floor to ceiling in the main room. Off to one side was a small niche completely filled with a twin bed, and in the room beyond was a large wrought iron bed.

"You take the back bedroom," he said from right behind her, making her catch her breath. "Luke and I'll camp down out here."

"How long will we be here?" She set her bags on the big bed.

He stood in the door, completely filling it, and watched her. "That depends on what Luke finds out and you."

"Me?"

"Yes, you. If you can think of who Strict might have sent after you, then we'll make plans to trap him."

"I can't figure out who it is, Matt. I tried all morning while you were gone." She turned to stare out the window at the snow covered pine trees, frustration humming through her. "When I look at those pictures, the only things I see are bad memories."

His arms came around her, and he pulled her back against his warm chest. "I know, sweetheart. It's got to be hard for you to remember what you went through back then. But you're the only one who knows Strict's people well enough to pinpoint the hitman. Somewhere locked in your past is the name."

"I don't want to do it anymore."

"Katie, if you give up now, Strict wins."

"I know."

He held her for a long time, the cabin's stillness only interrupted by the steady strong beat of his heart against her ear. She could stay like this forever. But there would be no forever for her, here or anywhere else, if she didn't stop Strict's plans.

Shoulders slumping she groaned. "I guess I can go through the pictures one more time."

His lips pressed against the top of her head. "Just try to relax. Don't fight the memories. Remember they can't hurt you anymore."

"They do hurt." She moved out of his arms and into the cabin's main room. Picking up the packet of pictures, she sat at the table then turned her head to study him. "Only this time, I know I have the right to get angry about what happened and no one is going to punish me for it."

"Did you remember anything this morning?" He pulled out a chair opposite her and sat.

"Nothing helpful." She flipped through a few of the pictures. "The problem is, none of the people have the skills to bomb my car, rig that shotgun explosion, and shoot out my tire with such accuracy."

He rubbed his chin. "Who would have those skills?"

"That's what I was trying to figure out this morning. Five men were arrested and sent to prison as co-conspirators. Were any of them released recently?"

He shrugged and seemed to consider her question. "I don't know, but we can have Jake see if he can find out for us. There's a great advantage to having an FBI agent in the family."

He turned over a piece of paper from the file and started writing names. "Were they the only ones who possessed that combination of skills?"

"No. There were three more."

"Who were they?" he asked, his pen poised to write.

She shook her head. "It doesn't matter. All three were killed in the Federal Building blast."

"You mentioned them before. What were their names, again?"

Damn, he was bullheaded.

"Gideon, Strict's second in command. Michael, his most devoted follower, and Gabriel, a young member." She rolled her eyes. "He gave them all biblical aliases. I think it made him feel more powerful."

"A judge and two angels. His ego needed the reinforcement." Matt winked at her and added the names. "Just so we don't forget anyone. We'll list everyone you can remember from that time, okay?"

She nodded. It felt good to be doing something. But she also knew it was pointless. The only people capable of all the attempts on her life had died a decade ago. Strict was going to win, and there was nothing she could do to stop him.

17

The Angel waited in the mall's parking lot an hour.

Time to face facts. The patrolman had given him the slip.

Somewhere along the line his tail had been made. They'd traveled north, stopping several places along the way. Each time the patrolman had entered a store and come out within thirty minutes. Finally, he'd stopped at this mall, and hadn't come out again.

Maybe the girl had found someone smart enough to help her this time.

Slowly he unfolded his six-foot frame from the sedan. He grabbed his duffel bag and slung it over his shoulder. The weight inside barely changed his posture. He was used to lugging his weapons with him.

He'd make one pass through the mall, just in case the officer truly was making one last errand stop. Although he doubted it. Somehow the guy made him, dumped the truck and hightailed it back to the girl.

He knew it as sure as he knew the clock was ticking.

The crush inside the mall was worse than the one in the

parking lot. Two days after Christmas, and everyone was trying to return presents they hated or didn't fit. The ones not doing that were redeeming gift certificates before any good merchandise disappeared.

Strolling casually from the entrance to his right, he scanned the crowds as he moved. His mind recalled every detail of the tall, dark haired officer he'd watched exit the patrol headquarters.

At a pretzel stand the Angel stopped and watched the crowd behind him. No one seemed to be pacing him. He bought a cinnamon pretzel and indulged in just a bit of everyday suburban life.

People milled about like ants, running in and out of stores as quickly as they could, not a care in the world.

With one sweep of my Uzi, I could drop at least a hundred in a split second.

Now wouldn't that make lovely news for this holiday season?

But that wasn't on his agenda, so the little clueless people were safe for another day. Time to find the girl and carry out the Prophet's plans.

He finished the pretzel, licking the cinnamon from his fingers. Then he headed for the exit opposite the one he'd entered.

Early this morning he'd gotten the Patrolman's license plate number from Robert Hagen then tied up that loose end. Now he needed to dump Hagen's sedan just in case the patrolman had noted the license plate. Then he had to find alternate transportation. Luckily for him there were thousands of possibilities to choose from in the mall's lot.

Since following the patrolman was no longer an option, he'd have to fall back to his usual source of information. He smiled slowly and slipped his sunglasses in place.

He stood just outside the mall door in the cold December air and flipped open his cell phone. Punching a button to autodial the US Marshals' number, he waited for the usual two rings before it was answered.

"Hello, love."

Matt poured Katie another cup of coffee. She'd finished three since they'd arrived. She ought to be wired. Yet she sat and studied those damn pictures as if her life depended on it.

He ground his teeth. Her life did depend on what she remembered and how much they could use the information to protect her.

Earlier, they'd talked to Jake and he'd informed them that the co-conspirators were all still firmly behind bars. That ruled them out as Strict's hitman.

He hated this feeling of complete helplessness. There had to be something he could do.

"Think, Katie. One of those people is the one Strict has trying to kill you." He set the mug down in front of her.

"I'm trying. I've done nothing but stare at these pictures for the past three hours."

"And nothing has triggered a memory that could help us?"

She pushed the file across the table, spewing its contents onto his lap. "Oh, I remember things, Matt."

"Tell me. Maybe I can figure it out," he ground out between clenched teeth as he caught pictures threatening to fall on the floor.

"You want to know what I see when I look at those pictures? I see the time I stood by and watched Strict and my mother eat a meal, then feed the leftovers to the dogs without sparing one small bite for me. I remember how hungry I was that night, and how my mother betrayed me."

She stood, her hands braced on the table, her eyes blazing with fiery anger.

"I see the first time Strict dragged me out into the freezing rain in my pajamas and forced me to recite the family's weapons manual. I remember being stranded on the top of a cliff, scared to death of falling, Strict standing below calling me filthy names and threatening to leave me there for the wolves to get. I was all of thirteen."

Matt stood, dropped the slapped-together pile of pictures on the table and leaned over it. "You have to be missing something, Katie."

"Don't you see, Matt? I remember everything—every time I was beaten, the pain, the fear, the humiliation. Not one bit of it points a finger at who's trying to kill me."

They stood that way, barely a foot apart, the heated air in the kitchen rising by degrees, electricity sparking between them.

A cough at the front door broke the tension in the room.

"Did I interrupt something?" Luke stood there, a shit-eating grin from ear to ear.

A low flush crept across Katie's face. Matt fought the urge to throw something at his brother. "No, and where the hell have you been?"

Luke closed the door and dropped his bag on the floor. "Well, after you left me at the car rental and took off with my car, I circled back around to the black sedan."

"Dammit, Luke, I told you not to get too close. This isn't a game. We're talking about someone not afraid to kill."

Luke slapped him on the shoulder. "Not a problem big brother. It took me an hour to get back. By the time I did, the car was empty."

Matt leaned back in his chair, the urge to throttle his brother decreasing slightly.

"So you found nothing," Katie asked as she righted the pile of pictures on the table.

Matt watched her movements. The same awareness that had flashed between them still hummed through his body.

Luke grinned at her. "I didn't say that."

"Quit flirting with Katie and spill the news," Matt said, the option of strangling his brother still a distinct possibility. He felt Katie watching him as she went to pour her coffee out in the sink.

Ignoring the sensation of her gaze on him he sat, his attention totally focused on his brother.

A serious expression spread over Luke's face. "I got the car owner's name. It belongs to a file clerk in the Department of Motor Vehicles named Robert Hagen."

Chinaware crashed in the sink.

Katie's face went pale and Matt grabbed her before she could sink to her knees.

"Hey, what's wrong?" Luke pulled out a chair for her and Matt helped her onto it.

"Hagen…I…know that name."

"Get her a glass of water, Luke." Matt knelt in front of her, rubbing her hand between his.

"Didn't you tell me he died?"

"Billy Hagen. He died from a bomb I built."

"You built a bomb?" The information punched Matt in the gut. His Katie built bombs? Hell, why should *that* surprise him? And hell, when had he started thinking of her as *his*?

She nodded then gulped at her water.

"So this Robert Hagen, is he related to the one that died?" Luke asked, sitting across from her.

She nodded. "Bobby was his twin brother."

"Would he be about twenty-five now? Dark hair?"

"How do you know?" Matt, still kneeling in front of Katie, sat back on his heels to study his brother, who'd gone quite serious.

"Because I figured the good government employee hadn't abandoned his car. I also figured he hadn't given it to our hitman of his own free will, so after I got his name and address from the DMV, I drove over there."

Matt didn't like how this was sounding. "What'd you find?"

"Just what you'd expect. Hagen had been shot once in the back of the head. Point-blank, execution style. He lay sprawled on his kitchen floor like he was leading his assailant to the door."

Katie inhaled, her fingers gripping the glass tight. Matt pried them loose then set the glass on the table. He lifted her, sat in the chair and cradled her in his lap.

He and his brother stared at each other over her head. This was getting deeper by the minute.

The hitman was leaving no loose ends or live witnesses.

"Did you notify the police?"

"I hightailed it out of there."

Matt glared at him. "You should've notified someone."

"If I'd called the police, I would've been there for hours while they interrogated me. Then I would've been forced to tell them about you, your tail, and Katie, and then you'd have had more than just the Marshals and the hitman on your case."

"He's right." Katie mumbled from the center of Matt's arms. "He only would've made matters worse by reporting what he found."

"Hagen deserves better than to be left lying dead on his floor."

Luke threw up his hands. "Hey, I called it in. Once I was halfway here, that is. I just don't have your obsessive need to follow the rules, Matt."

Katie straightened on Matt's lap and shot his brother an angry look. "It's your brother's obsession with rules that makes him a good cop and it's what makes people trust him. Like me."

So stunned by her defense of him, Matt didn't fight her when she pushed on his arms and rose from his lap. He watched her grab her coat. "Where are you going?"

"Just out on the porch. I need some air." She glared at his brother. "And for your information, your brother isn't nearly as hung up on following the rules as you think."

Luke watched her leave. "Wow, what did you do to her?"

Matt grabbed him by the collar and hauled him out of his chair. "I haven't touched her and neither will anyone else while I'm around. Got it, bozo?"

"Whoa, Matt. I didn't mean anything disrespectful." He lifted his hands in an innocent gesture. "I only meant how did you get her to change so much in two days?"

Releasing his grip on Luke, Matt took a few deep breaths. He'd never once in his life wanted to punch one of his brothers so much as he did now.

"The lady's been through a lot, Luke." He pushed his hands through his hair. "All I know is she's tough on the outside because she's had to be. But inside…well, I'm just getting to know her is all and doing so with a great deal of patience."

"Whatever you did, the lady seems willing to defend you."

A slow smile tilted the corners of Matt's lips. "She did, didn't she?"

———

After a dinner of fajitas and some nachos, the trio once more sat at the table going through the Family's pictures. Matt was sure that somewhere in them lay the clue to finding who Strict had sent as a hitman.

"So this is Billy Hagen and his brother Bobby," Luke asked Katie, holding two wallet-sized pictures.

She nodded. "I didn't really know Bobby much. Billy followed me everywhere."

"Did he have a crush on you?"

"Maybe. At the time I thought so. But now that I think back on it, I think he just wanted me to teach him my special skills."

Her words piqued Matt's curiosity. "What skills, sweetheart?"

She shrugged, staring down at the table. "My daddy, my real father, was a blasting expert for a coal mine. He kept blasting caps in the back shed. When I was a very little girl I used to follow my father out to his work shed. Daddy liked to make homemade fireworks as a hobby. Apparently, I'd inherited his skill and dexterity. Mama used to get mad when he let me help him design the display he built every summer for the Fourth of July. When I was sixteen, Strict discovered this. He immediately had me start building him bombs. Small ones at first.

"This newfound status eased my stepfather's demands on me in regards to training with the others. I became something special among all his people. No one else had the knowledge or ability that I did. He needed me." She paused for a moment.

Her eyes took on a faraway look. "When Mama married Strict, I was different. I didn't fit in. He treated me like a piece of dirt for so long. But then one day I found some powder and caps, like Daddy had. I took it to the woods and made a little rocket like he and I used to build. When it went off, the colors were so pretty."

"The Devil found out about it. I knew he'd be mad at me. I thought for sure he'd punish me. But he didn't. He asked me if I could do it again. I said sure and before I knew it, I had a little shack all to myself where I could sit and build my little bombs."

She paused, blinking several times. "Then one day Billy came into the shack. He begged me to teach him. I was proud someone asked something nice of me. When Strict found out, well, he seemed pleased, too."

She stared into the flames in the fireplace for a few moments.

"What happened to Billy, Katie?" Luke prodded.

"I found out the bomb was going to be used on a bus. Strict wanted to show the government he had the power to destroy things. I begged him not to use it. But he wouldn't listen. He made Billy get the bomb from the shed."

She looked at Matt, her eyes full of pain. "I watched Billy explode right there in the compound's center. Watching him die I realized that what I was doing wasn't special. My skill would kill people. Strict wanted me to build another one, but I said no. I wouldn't build him any more."

"What did Strict do?"

"He whipped me. Every day for a week, he whipped me."

"And you still refused."

She nodded, tears streaming down her face. "Then he turned the dogs on you."

She nodded more.

Luke cursed. Matt agreed.

"Is that when you gave in?" Matt asked.

She shook her head.

God, he didn't want to hear this. But he read in her face and her eyes the need to tell it. "When did you give in to his demands?"

"He grabbed one of the younger girls. She was all of ten years old. He said she'd take my punishment if I didn't do what he wanted."

"I told him I wouldn't build the bombs, but I'd teach the others how to do it. Only he had to let the girl, and her mother, leave the camp first."

"Did he keep his word?"

She nodded and lifted the picture of a young girl with dark bangs and pigtails. "The day after they left I started teaching the men how to build bombs. Then they used two of them to bomb the Federal Building in Philadelphia."

Matt took her hand in his and squeezed it tight. Katie stared at the table.

Silence filled the cabin.

Luke let out a deep breath. "So Bobby Hagen helped whoever this hitman is and now he's dead, too."

"Looks that way." Matt continued to hold Katie's hand, his thumb rubbing her knuckles. "So we're no closer to finding this guy than we were yesterday."

"Except we know he's cleaning his trail behind him." Luke

leaned his elbows on the table.

"True."

Katie lifted her eyes and studied them both. "So, now what do we do?"

"Now we go to plan B." Matt pulled out his cell phone.

"What's plan B?" she asked.

"We kidnap a Marshal."

"What?" Both Katie and Luke stared at him.

Matt shrugged. "Someone sold you out. We can't find the hitman, but we can find this Marshal…what was his name?"

"Castello," Katie replied. "Frank Castello. But you can't do that, Matt. You'll get into all kinds of trouble."

Luke nodded enthusiastically. "Kidnapping is a federal offense, especially kidnapping a U.S. Marshal, Matt."

"If it helps us find this killer and keeps Katie safe, then I don't see that we have any choice. We get him to meet with me early tomorrow morning. Somewhere public."

"This is crazy. You can't be serious." Luke stood and started to pace the cabin.

"We bring him back here and find out if he's the one who gave information to Strict or his man." Matt leaned back in his chair. "If he is, we turn him in. If he didn't, then we have one more person to help us find the guy."

"And if he presses charges?" Luke stopped and stared at him. "Then what?"

Matt shook his head. "He won't press charges. Either way we win. We catch the leak at the Marshals or we help him find out who it is."

"When do we do this?" Luke smiled, warming to the idea.

Matt looked at Katie "You call him and have him meet us in the morning. Then instead of you, Luke and I'll show up."

"I'll be the driver, you be the hard-ass. I like it." Luke gave him a high five.

"It won't work." Katie's quiet voice stopped their self-congratulations.

Matt rubbed her hand with his. "Sure it will."

"He'll be looking for me."

"Well, too bad. You won't be there." Suddenly, he didn't like where she was going with this.

"If I'm not there, he'll know something's wrong."

"No. No way are you going near this guy until we're sure he didn't set you up." Matt pushed himself from the table, his turn to pace.

"I have to go."

"No! I won't let you get hurt again."

"She's right, Matt. If she isn't there, he'll bolt."

Matt slammed his fist into the wall's exposed wood beam. "I promised to protect you, Katie!"

"And you will." She stepped between him and the wall, cupping his face in her small hands. "You and Luke will be right there with me. If you mean to do this, then we have to do it right. That means I have to meet with Castello. With you there, nothing is going to happen to me."

18

Castello lay on the couch in his office grabbing what little rest he could. Sleep was completely out of the question. Until he had Katie in protective custody he doubted he'd sleep again. Then there was the small matter of finding the department's mole.

After he'd interviewed the two police detectives that morning, he'd met with their captain. Once they were informed that their case involved a Witness Protection program member, all the police files had been turned over to Frank's task force.

From there, the case just got murkier.

The information told him only that Katie had been injured and taken to the hospital. After that, she and her patrolman disappeared without a trace.

Hell, even Edgars' captain had stonewalled him.

Castello thrust himself off the couch. He paced his office like a caged tiger. He wanted to put his fist through something. Since Strict's face wasn't an option, he might just have to redecorate a wall or two with holes.

"Frank?"

He stopped mid-stride to turn to the office door. "What is it, Crestview?"

"Well, sir, something strange has occurred with our investigation in the Strict file."

"What?"

"Do you know of any current case involving Strict that the FBI might be running?"

The muscles in Frank's jaw tensed. "Not that I'm aware of Bob, why? What have you walked into?"

Bob shrugged slightly. "Turns out a local FBI agent requested the visitor log for Strict."

"When?"

"Christmas day, sir." He handed Frank a faxed copy of the request. "He also obtained the picture file that our witness smuggled out of Strict's camp."

Castello studied the paper. "This request was signed?"

"Only by the division commander who was covering for Christmas. He's out of the country until after New Year's, so I haven't been able to ascertain who the agent was that filed the original papers."

Damn. Another dead end.

"Well, add it to our files. If we haven't found our killer or our missing witness by New Year's Day, we'll contact him when he returns."

A soft knock sounded on his door. Leslie stood there with his cell phone in her hand. He'd given it to her to monitor his calls while he uselessly tried to get some sleep.

"Who is it, Leslie?"

She hurried the phone over to him. "It's her."

He grabbed the phone. "Katie?" He mouthed the words *trace this line* to Crestview.

"Yes, it's me, Marshal. I'm safe."

"Where are you? I need to bring you in." He listened carefully, trying to hear any background noises that would pinpoint her whereabouts.

"I want to talk with you tomorrow. Alone. Can you meet me?"

"I can do it tonight, just tell me where."

She hesitated a moment. "No. Strict has someone in your department working for him. I don't want to come in just yet."

So she'd figured out there was a leak. *Smart girl.*

"Okay. Tell me where and when you want to meet. I'll be there." He grabbed a pen and paper.

"Tomorrow, on the corner of Third and State Streets, near the Capitol building. About nine in the morning." He heard her whispering something to someone, but couldn't make out exactly what they were saying. "You walk up State Street to Third, and then I'll find you. And Marshal?"

"Yes, Katie?"

"If you bring anyone, and I mean anyone, with you, I'll leave. You'll never hear from me again. Do you understand?"

The phone went dead before he could reply. He looked out his door at Crestview. Dave shook his head. She didn't stay on the line long enough to be traced.

As he closed the phone he wondered what Katie and Edgars were planning with this meeting.

Castello was no fool. He could smell a setup a mile away. This meeting reeked of it.

———

Just before dawn Katie, Matt and Luke loaded their gear into the SUV Luke rented the day before to lose the tail at the mall. They left Luke's sportscar at the cabin in case it had been identified when Matt picked up Katie. As they headed toward Columbus, Katie reviewed the plan in her head.

She was to stand in the doorway of the Ohio Theater, the historic landmark just across the street from the State Capitol building, until she saw Castello pass by on his way to the corner.

Matt would position himself on the opposite corner. When he saw her coming toward him, he would cross the street and approach Castello from behind. Luke would stay with the car in the parking garage. If all went well, they would get Castello into the garage, and subsequently into the car.

Katie slipped her right hand into her pocket, to feel the weight of her gun. For a decade she'd been able to forget how it felt to walk around armed, or to actually point her weapon at a human target. Now, in less than a week, she'd drawn it twice, and was about to do so a third time.

"We won't use them unless it's absolutely necessary, sweetheart." Matt's right hand covered her left one. "But we want him to know we mean business."

She nodded then focused her attention on the scenery passing outside the passenger window.

He couldn't possibly know how much having him with her, taking her welfare so much to heart, meant to her. It felt good to have someone on her side for once.

It also scared the hell out of her.

Her whole life she'd depended only on herself. She didn't want to trust him to always be there. There would come a time when he'd fail her. Everyone did. If she continued to let him get close, she doubted she'd survive when he left.

"Hey Matt, how'd you get these pictures?" Luke asked from the backseat where he sat flipping through the picture file.

"Jake got them for us."

Luke leaned in between the two front seats. "No, I mean, where did they originally come from?"

"I gave them to the FBI and the Marshals," Katie answered.

"You handed them over?" Matt asked and squeezed her hand.

"Yes. The night before I escaped the bunker, I saw Strict hide his keys to the filing cabinets in his office. The night after the bombing, there was a lot of drinking and celebrating going on over their success. No one really noticed me."

She took a deep breath. "I waited until everyone was passed out or asleep, then I snuck into Strict's office. In a strong box he kept locked in a file cabinet I found files on all the plans for the Federal Building bombing and several others. I took the pictures off of as many files as I could. I shoved what I needed to prove the case against Strict and the Family in the deaths of all those people into my backpack and hid the strong box with the rest of their plans."

"Wow. No wonder the feds had such a strong case against Strict and his conspirators." Luke sat back, nodding his head approvingly. "You're one tough lady."

"How did you manage to carry all those files and your belongings when you escaped?" Matt asked, concern on his face.

Flashes of that night filled her mind. The loud party noises. Guns fired into the air in celebration. Her hovering in the corner of her small room tears streaming down her cheeks for the people who'd died in the explosion. Tears for the three men who'd been killed, especially Gideon, who'd been so kind to her, tears for the strangers who'd died innocently.

Slowly the sounds had faded away. She peeked out her window into the dark night. Small campfires flickered throughout the compound as bodies staggered past. Family members lay sprawled on the ground where they'd collapsed in drunken abandon.

Her eyes adjusted to the shadows playing around the building's edges. When she was sure no one was left awake, she grabbed her backpack and crawled out her window.

Her heart raced. She would either succeed, and escape with enough information to convict Strict, or she'd die. Either way she'd finally be free of her nightmare existence.

"I couldn't carry all the files. The ones that pertained to future plans I hid." Shaking off the dark memories once more, Katie gave a brittle laugh. "I ran out with the clothes on my back, the backpack full of papers and pictures, and this." She patted the gun in her pocket.

"A trucker and his wife were passing by, and gave me a lift into Pittsburgh. It took me two more days to find the Marshals. Believe me, had I stopped in any small town between the bunker and Pittsburgh, I wouldn't have lived to testify."

THE COPPER SMELL OF FRESH BLOOD STUNG THE ANGEL'S SENSES, whetting his appetite for more. After losing track of the trooper yesterday, he'd summoned his source here.

Since the arrest and trial of The Prophet, the traitor's whereabouts was a highly guarded secret. Try as he might he'd never been able to get a lead on her. Then a few years back The Angel had suggested they try following the traitor's handlers, the two U.S. Marshals who'd guarded her through the trial. If anyone were to know where she was hidden or would contact her, it was those two men.

In preparation, they'd called upon a young woman from the Family whose father was still in prison because of the traitor's testimony. The Prophet had paid dearly to have her name changed, give her plastic surgery, and arrange extra training in hopes that somehow they could get her close to one or both of the agents. A few years ago a small window opened and they'd maneuvered their own spy into the government's system.

Unable to find the traitor's files, she had provided them with whatever information she could about the movements of the agents. Now, the Angel needed more.

When he'd first called for a meeting, she'd agreed, but he'd heard the hesitation in her voice. So he wasn't surprised when she'd arrived last night announcing she was done helping him and The Prophet. In fact, he'd anticipated just that reaction—relished it even.

She'd been very upset about the death of the older agent and wanted to end their relationship.

He'd already planned to sever ties, but first he needed more information, some clue to his true target's trail. She'd refused, said she couldn't help him kill anyone else, that her life was about saving people now.

Wiping the blood from his knuckles with a cold cloth he studied the woman tied to the metal chair in the center of the storage locker. The Prophet had accomplished one thing all those years ago. His training had made the girls in the Family tough. This one was almost as strong as Sarah—almost, but not quite. Both eyes swollen nearly shut, her head hanging down in defeat. Blood dripped slowly from her busted lip and broken nose, down her chin to pool on her breasts, spreading slowly over the white of her blouse.

Walking around her, he admired his work. Nothing like breaking the will of someone this determined to keep their secrets. There was so much more he could enjoy doing, but the sun was rising and time was running out.

With a smile he picked a stainless steel scalpel from the table of instruments near her chair. In the hands of a skilled surgeon its laser-sharp blade could be used to open a body with as little pain as possible. In the hands of someone as skilled as the Angel, it inflicted greater degrees of pain than any human could imagine.

"Please…no more…I can't…take any more."

"Shh, shh, my dear," he said as he smoothed the damp hair back from her face in a soothing fashion, his other hand holding the blade near her jugular, but not touching her. "You can end this now. The decision is yours. Are you ready to tell me where the traitor is, Leslie?"

19

Matt pulled his coat collar tighter around his neck. From his vantage point he could barely make out the navy blue of Katie's Peacoat peeking out from behind the brick wall, where she hid farther down State Street.

After leaving Luke and the SUV parked in the underground garage beneath the State Capitol building, he'd walked her to the Ohio Theater. He hated letting her wait by herself, tucked into the entranceway, but he needed to position himself farther away to provide the element of surprise if they hoped to take Castello off guard.

He stamped one foot then the other. The freezing morning air had seeped into his boots. His toes felt like ice.

He looked at his watch. Eight forty-five. If everything went well, he'd see Katie headed his way soon.

His stomach clenched.

At that point, she would be the most vulnerable. Completely out in the open, her only protection would be the multitude of people hurrying to work.

She'd insisted on coming, and his head told him she was right, but his heart wished she were in the garage with Luke, completely out of harm's way. She was so tiny, so feminine. No matter how tough an exterior she presented to the world, he knew she could be hurt. He knew how much that tough shell had cost her to earn.

He just prayed Castello hadn't sold them out to the hitman. Matt slipped his hand into his pocket, his fingers caressing the hard metal of his gun.

If anything happened to Katie, the Marshal was a dead man.

Katie peeked around the brick wall to her right. In the milling foot traffic and gray exhaust-clogged morning air of downtown Columbus, she glimpsed Matt's dark head in the building's doorway where he stood inside.

Her heart flipped.

She wasn't alone this time. Matt was less than a hundred yards away—her own personal knight protector.

Sucking in more of the frigid air, she stepped back farther into the vestibule's shadow. As comforting as it was to know she had someone out there who cared about her, it frightened her to know every moment he spent with her he endangered himself.

A month ago she hadn't even known he existed. Now, she worried as much for his safety as her own. For a woman without a future, she'd let her heart get involved.

She glanced at her watch. Eight-fifty.

Looking down the block to her left, she watched the opposite side of the street. Her heart pounded in her ears as she concentrated. She took her right glove off and shoved it into her left pocket. Then she slipped her right hand into her other pocket to grip her weapon.

Her eyes focused on the faces drifting past her vantage point. Most wore caps or scarves to protect them from the chaffing cold wind that swirled through the downtown streets. Heads lowered, men and women hurried to their jobs.

Then she saw him.

His head uncovered, Marshal Castello walked steadily against the flow of traffic, his dark hair visible above the crowd. His dark sunglasses screamed government agent.

Watching him pass by, she almost forgot to scan the sea of people behind him. She studied the flowing mass of humanity for a moment, trying to see anyone following Castello.

No one.

Good. He'd come alone.

Taking a deep breath, she slipped out of her hiding place, and followed the Marshal parallel along the street's opposite side. When she got to the corner, she saw Matt approach the light on the far corner.

Her heart double-timed a few beats. Funny how just his presence gave her more confidence. She could do this. Holding her head higher, her lips pursed with determination. For the first time in her life, she was calling the shots.

Crossing with the light, she zeroed in on her target. Then she stopped in front of Castello.

———

MATT SAW KATIE APPROACH THE CORNER. AS SHE WAITED FOR THE light to change, her head came up and she stood straighter. He recognized that determined look on her face. She might be scared, but she'd be damned if she'd let him or anyone else know.

As she crossed the street and headed toward the tall man with dark hair and black sunglasses, Matt dodged his way against the few cars that didn't make it through the light.

"Katie," the man said.

"Marshal Castello."

That was his cue.

Matt pushed his gun barrel into the Marshal's back.

Castello didn't even flinch. "And Patrolman Edgars. Nice to meet you."

"You knew he'd be with me?" Kate sounded surprised.

"He wouldn't be worthy of protecting you, if he wasn't with you, Katie."

The tenderness in Castello's voice irritated Matt. Did he have a thing for Katie? Well, too damn bad. She was *his* now. If she needed protecting, he'd be the one to do it.

"This is touching, but we're a little out in the open here." Ignoring the puzzled look Katie gave him, he pushed the gun a little tighter into the Marshal's back. "If the reunion is finished, let's take a walk."

"I'm thinking we should stay right here," Castello replied, not moving an inch when Matt pushed him. "At least until you tell me what you have planned."

"Since you or someone in your department sold her out to the Prophet, I guess your opinion doesn't really matter much." Matt stepped forward, forcing the Marshal to move a little.

Castello shot him an annoyed look. Matt lifted one eyebrow at him.

The crowd around them thinned out as the light changed again.

Castello focused on Katie once more. "I didn't sell you out. But I'm trying to figure out who did."

"I want to believe you Marshal Castello."

Matt ground his teeth as sadness and hope both crossed Katie's face. He glanced to his left, then to his right. No one seemed to be watching them.

"Katie, Edgars is right, we need to get out of this open space."

She nodded and led them toward the parking garage entrance. A sound from beside him stopped Matt in his tracks.

A white van slowly passed him and continued through the light to the corner, until the vehicle came to a complete stop.

Matt watched it move in slow motion, reading the Pennsylvania plates.

The driver's door opened. A tall, blond man jumped out, turned and lifted his rifle. It was a horror movie in time-lapse photography.

"Katie!" Matt pushed Castello to the side, and jumped into the path between the hitman's rifle and Katie's body.

Fire seared through his shoulder just before he landed on top of her, his arms breaking their fall—sort of.

Katie turned as Matt called her name.

In that split second she saw the blond man leaning over the white van, the morning light glinting off the long black gun barrel he aimed at her.

A moving blur of deep blue filled her vision.

A gasp escaped her when Matt's body careened into hers. His hands covered her head, just before they smacked into the concrete sidewalk. The wind was knocked out of her and she stared in a daze at the sky.

Women around them screamed. People scattered and crouched.

"Get down," Castello yelled to her left.

"Matt?" she finally whispered.

He lifted his head, his beautiful blue eyes searching hers. "You okay, sweetheart?"

She nodded. "I think so. You?"

"Yeah." He eased up just a little, looking to his left, but still covering her body with his.

Damn him. He's acting like a human shield.

Well, she wouldn't let him sacrifice himself for her.

She wiggled beneath him, pushing on his shoulders with her hands. "Let me up."

"Stop it, Katie." He pressed his body harder against hers. "Stay down."

"I won't let you die for me." She tried to grip his coat in her hands. Her right hand felt wetness beneath it. "Oh God, Matt, you've been hit."

"Shh, I know. Now hold still."

He laid his head into the crook of her neck. His breathing rasped in her ear. She stopped trying to get out from beneath him, and held him as tight as she could.

Tears stung her eyes, and her chest ached. "Don't die on me, Matt. Please don't die on me."

He kissed her ear. "I'm tougher than that, sweetheart."

Castello's face came into view. "He's gone. You two can get up now."

Slowly Matt pushed his body off of Katie's and struggled to his feet. He grabbed his shoulder, cursing at the same time.

"Let me look at it." Scrambling to stand beside him, she worked to open his coat.

"Wait, Katie. We have to get out of here." Matt grabbed her hand to still her efforts.

"I need to see the wound." She stared into his eyes, reading both pain and desire there.

"You can look at it, once we're safe somewhere." With a glance over his shoulder, he pulled her against him then jogged to the parking garage. "You coming, Castello?"

"Right behind you, Edgars."

Behind them, the sound of sirens blared. In front of them, the black SUV screeched toward them. Castello tried to jump in front of them, but Matt stopped him with a hand. "He's with us."

Luke stopped beside them. "Where we heading? And what the hell happened up there?" he asked as Katie opened the rear door, and helped Matt inside. Castello climbed in front.

"We'll tell you later. Go out the State Street entrance and drive slow." Matt leaned back against the seats.

"Do you three have a place close by?" Castello asked from the front seat.

"Nowhere safe," Matt replied.

"What about the cabin?" Luke asked as he pulled onto the street.

"It's too far away." Katie said, looking at Matt's wound.

"Then head into German Village. We'll go to a safe house I have there," Castello said.

"Pardon me, but I don't trust any safe house of the Marshals right now," Matt ground out as Katie probed his wound.

"This one isn't on the books. I use it for the rare time I want to hide a witness from danger. This qualifies." Castello gave directions to Luke, who'd maneuvered them away from the area that was beginning to fill with police vehicles and curious pedestrians.

Katie unfastened Matt's coat and gently shoved it off his left shoulder. She sucked in her breath. The front of his shirt was covered with blood.

"We've got to get you to a doctor." She dug through her backpack and pulled out a white t-shirt. Pressing the material against his shoulder, she worked to stem the flow of blood.

"No, doctors," he whispered between clenched teeth. "We don't want this reported."

His gaze met hers and she understood. If they went to a doctor, it would be reported and their faces would be all over the news. She'd have to fix him.

"You can do this, Katie."

His eyes told her he had complete trust in her. Heat filled her face and she lowered her gaze, focusing on applying pressure to the wound.

Leaning his head against the seat, he closed his eyes. For a moment her breath caught in her throat. Had he lost too much blood already? Then he lifted his hand and stroked her hair.

She trembled.

"I saw that gun, and I had to protect you." Gently, his fingers slid between the strands, and he pulled her closer, so her head rested on his uninjured shoulder. "Did I hurt you when I landed on you?"

"Nothing I couldn't handle."

"That's my girl. Tough to the end." A chuckle rumbled through his chest.

"You're injured. There's nothing funny about this," she scolded him, but smiled anyway. If he could tease her, he must be okay.

Luke, following Castello's directions, drove them through the downtown area into the renovated historic district of German Village. They stopped in front of one of the restored brick townhouses originally built around the turn of the century by German immigrants.

Katie stuffed the t-shirt into Matt's coat and closed it to hold the makeshift compress in place. Then she scrambled out of the car behind him. Luke already had one arm around Matt and Matt slung his good arm over his brother's shoulder.

Once they had Matt inside, she helped him out of his coat. He flopped onto a kitchen chair in the almost austere kitchen and started issuing orders. "Luke, park the truck in the alley. We don't know if anyone saw us and can identify it as ours."

Castello entered the room with a large plastic toolbox. He set it on the table by Katie. "This is a first aid kit."

"Thank you," she replied. Opening it, she found gauze, tape, disinfectant, even some sealed packets of sutures and steri-strips for sealing wounds.

Matt unbuttoned his shirt for her to see his injury. "This guy has been one step ahead of us all the way."

"What did you see before you were shot?" Castello pulled out a chair, turned it around and straddled it, leaning his arms on the back.

"I saw a white van with Pennsylvania plates." Matt hissed as Katie pulled the shirt away from his shoulder.

"Couldn't this wait until later?" she asked. "We need to get this wound closed."

"Katie," Matt's hand closed over hers, and he waited for her to lift her eyes to look at him. "The distraction will keep it from hurting too much."

"Fine." *Great. Wonderful.* If he didn't mind hurting while they talked, why should she try to be gentle? Still, she worked the shirt carefully away from his shoulder, then dabbed his wound with a clean gauze. It looked like a furrow in freshly tilled ground across the top of his shoulder. "The bullet just grazed your shoulder. I think you'll live."

He smiled at her.

A warm heat filled her cheeks. They both remembered him lying on top of her, and her plea for him not to die. Quickly, she broke the visual connection and concentrated on cleaning his wound.

"Geez." He hissed as she dabbed the astringent on the open wound. He sucked in air then panted a few breaths.

Mr. Big and Tough wasn't so big and tough.

Katie bit the inside of her mouth and retrieved the tube of antibiotic cream Matt's sister had sent her for her injuries, smearing it on the wound. The smoothness of his warm skin beneath her fingers sent shivers through her body. She wanted to caress even more of it.

"Why did the Pennsylvania plates tip you off?" Castello asked.

"I saw it the day before Katie's car exploded. The same day her tire was shot out."

"He was with you the day you called me to relocate you?" Castello asked, nodding at Matt.

She taped gauze on Matt's shoulder. "That's how I figured out my cover was blown. He came upon me standing by my car on the side of the road and offered to change my tire."

"So you figure this was the same hitman?" Castello asked Matt.

Matt nodded. "I saw him step out of the van and take aim at Katie. The rest you know."

"What did he look like?" Luke asked from the rear door as he entered.

"Tall. Blond. Older, maybe in his late fifties." Matt nodded at Castello. "Did you get a look at him after I hit the ground?"

An image flashed in Katie's brain. Just before Matt drove her to payment she'd seen *him*. Her breath froze in her chest. Her heartbeat pounded in her ears. She squatted on her heels.

Castello shook his head. "No. It was pandemonium."

"Damn. I was hoping you got a better description for Katie to ID him."

"I don't need it," she whispered.

All three men looked at her.

"Katie? What's wrong?" Matt gripped her by the shoulders and helped her into a chair.

"I know who it was."

"Who?" the men asked in unison.

She stared at Matt, barely seeing him through her own pain, her own sense of another betrayal. "But it can't be him. He died ten years ago."

20

"Katie, tell me who you think it was," Matt asked with quiet tenderness.

"Gideon. Strict's second in command, the one he called the Angel of Retribution."

"I thought you said Gideon died in the Federal Building blast?" Matt took her hands in his.

They felt like two blocks of ice. She stared at him with huge, unseeing eyes. The color had completely drained from her face. Fine tremors shook her body.

He glanced at Castello. "Do you have any whiskey here?"

"I think we do somewhere," the marshal replied already searching the cabinet. "It's been a while since we placed anyone in this house."

"Luke, find me a heavy blanket or quilt." Matt instructed his brother, as he unbuttoned Katie's coat and worked it off her body. He rubbed his hands over her arms and shoulders. Wincing with the effort he ignored the pain in his own shoulder and his rising panic. He needed to get her warm. He went to the kitchen and brought back a warm wet dishtowel. First he wiped her brow then cleaned his blood from her hands, rubbing briskly to get them warm.

Somehow he had to get the spirit back in her and pull her out of this. Right now, he'd be glad if she'd try to kick him or even point a gun at him again. Anything was better than seeing this quiet corpselike figure frozen in the chair.

"Katie, look at me. You can survive this. You've survived so much. Don't let the bastards win now."

Luke returned with a blanket and draped it around her stiff, quiet body. Worry etched his features as he looked to his brother for reassurance. Matt nodded that he was just as concerned.

"Here." Castello handed him a tumbler containing two fingers of whiskey.

Matt held the glass to her lips. "Drink this, sweetheart."

She took a sip then gasped as it burnt its way down her throat. "That's nasty," she whispered in a hoarse voice. She blinked a few times, finally raising focused eyes to Matt's.

He exhaled in relief.

Then she started shaking. Hard. Body-wracking. She nearly shook right off the chair.

Grasping her by the shoulders, he tried to steady her. "Easy, Katie. It's over now. You're safe again."

"He's evil." Anger and betrayal filled her beautiful eyes.

"Gideon?" he asked.

She shook her head. "Strict. He allowed Gideon to tend me after every beating." She gulped in air. "He hoped I'd give in, and he could control me if Gideon gave me some measure of compassion, some hope that I mattered."

Matt's gut twisted. He hated asking, but had to know. "Did you love him?"

"Gideon?" She covered his hand with hers. "No. I felt grateful to him, and I thought of him as a father figure, but I did trust him. When they told me he'd died, well, that was when I knew I had to get away from the bunker and the Family. Without Gideon there to restrain him, Strict would've killed me with the next beating."

"He beat you?" Luke asked.

Katie nodded.

Matt glanced at him. His brother looked incredulous. Matt's gaze shifted to Castello, who remained nonplussed by her revelation.

Understanding slammed into Matt. Castello knew about Katie's beatings, and he'd still forced her to face Strict in court, day after day.

"You bastard. You knew what that scum did to her. Still you used her, just like everyone else."

"She was our only witness." Castello's gaze didn't waver. "You know she had to testify as well as I did, no matter how badly Strict beat her."

Matt saw red. He wanted someone to blame for everything Katie had suffered. Right now he didn't really care who.

"Ease up, Matt." Luke crossed his arms and leaned against the wall. "He's no more responsible for what happened to Katie than you or I. If you quit thinking like a guy protecting his woman and more like a cop, you'll see he's right."

Matt eyed his brother. "He may not have been responsible for what Strict and his Family did to her years ago, but he's damn well been responsible for her safety since then."

"Please let it go. The Marshall isn't the leak." Katie laid her hand on his face. "I need you to focus on the problem at hand. If we're ever going to solve this mess, we're going to need Frank's help, too."

Matt stared at her, the rage in him subsiding with the plea in her voice.

"Please, for me?"

For a moment he hesitated, then nodded. He shoved himself away from the table, grabbed his shirt and headed out the back door. If he didn't get out of the house, he might explode.

"Matt?" Katie called, heading out after him.

"Let him go." Luke stepped between her and the door.

"It's freezing out there."

"And Matt's a big boy." Luke took her arm, steering her into the living room. "Besides, all he's going to do is slam his fists into the side of a tree or two."

Memories of Matt kick-boxing the other night warmed Katie more than the whiskey and blanket combined. "Does he do that often?" she asked, curling into the sofa's corner.

"Hit things?" Luke flopped onto an oversized chair across from her. "Not since he was fifteen. Before that he was pretty much a loose cannon, headed straight for the bad side—disobeying rules, getting into fights."

That didn't sound much like the man she knew. "What happened to change him?"

"You mean what stopped his wild ways and gave him his stubborn insistence about following the rules?"

Katie nodded.

"When his friend Chris died, Matt changed overnight. He's never talked about what happened that night to any of us. He just shut himself in this emotional box and stayed there." Luke shot her a grin. "Until you popped into his life. You've sure changed him."

Katie shook her head. She and her problems had endangered Matt twice now. They'd also made him go against his personal beliefs. "I'm sorry I caused him so much trouble."

Luke held up his hands. "Hey, don't be sorry. I'm glad to see him taking chances. You're just what he needs. Keep pushing his buttons, and maybe he'll be human like the rest of us again."

Katie pulled the blanket tighter about her. Staring at the crystal vase on the coffee table, she mulled over everything Matt's brother had told her. What happened all those years ago to make him change a hundred-and-eighty degrees? Had he caused his friend's death in some way?

Castello, who'd been talking on his cell phone in the other room, entered with it pressed against the side of his face. "Yes, sir. I intend to match notes with the parties here. As soon as you've got each task force member in the building, I'll be in to conduct the interviews myself."

He closed the phone and sat on another chair, next to Luke's. He closed his eyes for a moment, rubbing the bridge of his nose.

"What task force were you just talking about?" Katie asked.

"When you went missing after the car bomb, I came to the same conclusion that you did." Castello met her eyes with a steady, unwavering gaze. "That someone in my department had given your identity to Strict or one of his people."

"Did you find out who it was?" she asked. A sound from the kitchen caught her attention. Her heart flipped a little in her chest. Matt was back, safe and more in control of his emotions.

His dark hair fell to one side from the wind's force. His cheeks were flushed pink, whether from exertion or the cold she couldn't tell.

It didn't matter. He'd come back. The consequences of how that thrilled her were something she'd have to think about later.

"You'd better join us, Edgars. I'm sure you'll want the details of what I've learned so far," Castello said.

"Damn right I do." Matt joined Katie on the sofa. She automatically shifted to give him room.

He wrapped an arm around her, and she shared the blanket to warm him.

"Katie, ever since the death threat Strict issued for you on the day of his sentencing, my partner Pete Halloran and I have kept your file, including your new identity, under lock and key." Castello began his story. "When I realized there had been a leak, I knew it could only have come from one of two people. Me or Pete. Pete retired a few years ago, so I went to see him."

"Did he admit to selling out Katie?" Matt asked, pulling her closer. His body radiated tension.

"Not exactly."

"What do you mean, not exactly?" Katie's stomach twisted in a knot.

"Katie, the information came from Pete." Castello paused for a moment and he seemed to age five years. "It was tortured out of him, before he died."

Suddenly, the room closed in around Katie, and her lungs hurt to breathe again.

The marshal sitting across from her, and his partner who'd died trying to protect her new identity, had provided a concrete ground of support when she'd needed it most. If Strict and Gideon could kill one of them, what chance did she stand against them?

She forced herself to take a slow deep breath. For years she'd known she'd have to face Strict. She'd known it would be ugly, maybe even bloody when she did. Never in all that time had she thought someone else's blood would be spilled instead of hers.

"You okay?" Matt's deep voice rumbled against her ear.

She nodded. "The news just took me by surprise, is all. Mr. Halloran was always nice to me."

"You sure you want to hear more? We could do this later." Concern laced his words.

She shook her head. No matter how much she wanted to take refuge in his protectiveness, she had to depend on her own strength to get through this.

"I don't know how much time we have. Ever since this started, I've felt like I'm racing against a ticking clock." She eased herself away from him. Only a fraction of an inch, but enough that they both knew she was strong enough to handle whatever else she'd learn. "Marshal, when did Mr. Halloran die?"

"The M.E. puts it at a little more than a week ago."

Matt withdrew his arm from her shoulder and leaned forward. "He couldn't have given Gideon the time and place for our meeting this morning."

Castello nodded. "You're right. When we realized Katie's disappearance and Pete's death were connected, my boss and I formed a task force to investigate both." He stood and paced to the fireplace. "When you called me yesterday, all four members were present for the call."

Matt let out a string of expletives questioning the mental fitness of the Marshal's co-workers.

Luke voiced his agreement.

With growing irritation, Katie fought the urge to scream at all three testosterone-based beings in the room. "So, you're calling them all in to interview them?" she asked instead.

"Not exactly," Castello leaned against the mantel. "As we're speaking, all four are being placed under guard until we can determine who leaked the information."

"About damn time you started taking her safety seriously."

"Matt." Katie laid a restraining hand on his arm. "He's not responsible for what someone else has done."

He shook off her hand and strode over to stand nose-to-nose with Castello. "His department's leakier than a storm drain. You've nearly been killed three times, not including the staged accident with the rifle shot." He pushed Castello back a step. "I, for one, hold him very responsible for all of that."

Castello pushed his chest into Matt's. "Look, Edgars, if you want to try and take a piece of my hide, I'll be happy to step outside and oblige you."

"In a heartbeat, Castello. You deserve a beating for putting her in danger." Matt shoved him.

Castello shoved back. "Maybe if you'd convinced her to come in, like you should've the first night, she would've been better protected."

"And if I had, she'd be dead now."

Glass shattered behind them. Both lawmen jumped apart.

Waterford crystal lay shattered on the hardwood floor where Katie had thrown the vase at their feet.

If she wasn't so pissed off, the looks on their faces would've been laughable.

"*She* is right here in the room, gentlemen." Katie ground out each word, her hands clenched in fists at her sides. "*She* doesn't like being ignored or discussed in third person. S*he* doesn't need protection. *She* doesn't need stupid macho one-upmanship out of you two, either." She sucked in a deep breath, looking from them to Luke, who sat grinning uselessly from his chair. "What *she* needs is a hot bath, a warm meal and a plan—in that order."

Before any of the men could respond, which frankly was the only reason they still breathed, she turned on her heel and stepped over the crystal shards. With her back ramrod stiff and only slight control of her own temper, she headed up the stairs in search of the first item on her list.

Gideon tightened the strap of his duffel bag on his shoulder and sauntered away from the South-side dump. The van was a liability now. He needed an alternative means of transportation and quickly. That patrolman the girl hooked up with was smart. Somehow he'd recognized the van then prevented the shot from getting its target. He wouldn't waste any time getting an all-points bulletin out on the vehicle.

After stashing the van, Gideon had changed from his dark blue coveralls and into a pair of camouflage pants and khaki shirt. With his appearance changed somewhat, he'd hitch a ride into downtown and find a car in a used lot.

Gideon smiled. No one would be looking for a hitman traveling on foot.

Of course if the girl had recognized him, she'd give the police a good description for the APB. Sarah knew him too well to forget any feature, including the thin scar across his jaw.

Absently, he caressed the scar as he made his way to the highway for a ride.

Strict had given it to him the day after he'd interfered with Sarah's punishment. "Never fail me again."

He'd never failed Strict before, not since they'd served in the Vietnam War together. The Prophet had dragged him out of a firefight swarming with Vietcong just before the last big battle of the war, Operation Linebacker. With shrapnel in his back and three bullets in his leg, if Strict hadn't hefted him on his shoulder and carried him five miles through the jungle, Gideon knew he would've died an agonizing and torturous death at the enemy's hands.

From that moment on, his life belonged to the Prophet. He'd follow Strict straight into the bowels of Hell if he asked. There was one last task he promised to complete. He needed the damn girl.

He muttered a curse as he flagged down a semi.

"Need a lift?" The grizzled old trucker asked after he'd slowed to the side of Route 23 just south of the city. A thermos of coffee and a bag of donuts sat in the passenger seat.

"Just into town, if you don't mind." Gideon flashed him a smile. Everyone was always a sucker for his smile. "My old truck died yesterday, and I'm looking for a new one."

"Sure thing." The trucker eyed Gideon's duffle with the nylon gun case attached. "Going hunting?"

"Yep. Looking for big game." Gideon moved the man's food over on the seat and slid into it. The trucker pulled the rig onto the highway, heading toward the center of town. This was the older man's lucky day. The semi was too cumbersome to be of use to Gideon. The man would keep his truck and his life today. Gideon had his priorities.

First and foremost, he needed to find the girl. Leslie had served her purpose, and he'd disposed of her. Now his conduit to the whereabouts of his prey was gone.

Standing out in the open this morning guaranteed that Sarah would recognize him. That had always been the plan. Then she'd quickly figure out why Strict had ordered her death. In that case, Gideon knew where she'd head next. Which meant he had to get there before she did. His next attempt had to succeed. He needed to get the information from her and silence her before the execution on New Year's Eve.

There were less than two days left.

21

Half an hour after Katie had regally departed the living room, Matt went in search of her. She'd locked herself in the bathroom and hadn't emerged yet. If anyone deserved to stay locked behind a door, Katie did.

As much as he wanted to let her hide from reality, they needed her description of Gideon for an APB. The sooner it hit the streets, the more likely they'd be able to apprehend the hitman.

At the bathroom door, Matt inhaled deeply then exhaled slowly. Every time she faced another piece of her past his heart tore at her anguish. He really hated being another person who wanted something from her.

"Katie?" He knocked lightly on the door. Silence came from the door's other side.

His heart beat faster. Was she okay? Had she used taking a bath as a ruse and fled while no one was looking? Didn't she know how dangerous it was for her to be on her own now?

Fighting his own rising panic, he knocked a little harder. "Katie, open the door."

No immediate response occurred. He took a step back, ready to shove his shoulder into the door.

Then it opened. She stood there, wrapped in a fuzzy white robe, rubbing her wet dark hair with a white towel. She looked so tiny and vulnerable. *Innocent.* No one looking at her would know she'd lived such a hard life.

Relief flooded him.

"What's wrong?" Lifting her arms, she wrapped the towel over her hair. The movement pulled the robe's top apart, revealing her creamy skin and the soft swells of her breasts.

He swallowed hard. "I need you."

"You need me?" Confusion etched her features, but a slow heat lit her eyes. Oh yeah, he needed her.

Closing the gap between them, he stepped forward until only a millimeter separated them. He leaned in close, forcing her to tilt her head back to look at him.

She licked her lips.

What little resolve he had left flew right out the window.

Lowering his head, he held her still as his mouth devoured hers in a kiss. He ground his lips against hers, his tongue sliding in to taste the soft, warm, velvety feel of her mouth.

A groan escaped him.

God, she tasted so good.

His mouth never broke contact with hers as he wrapped his hands around her shoulders and dragged her closer. The robe parted further as his hands massaged her soft skin beneath.

He forced his mouth to leave hers then slowly trailed a path down her neck to the juncture of her shoulder. Lightly he nibbled there. The fragrance of gardenias filled his senses.

"Oh God, Katie." He dipped his head farther, tracing his lips back across her throat and down between the swells of her breasts. Trying to rein in his desire, he slowly lifted his head and eased her body a fraction of an inch away from his. "You tempt me in ways I never dreamed possible."

"I can't take another rejection," she muttered between panted breaths, her eyes fixed on the third button of his shirt.

"Katie, I'm not rejecting you." Once again, he took her face between his hands, gently forcing her gaze to meet his. He pressed his hips into hers, trapping her between the doorframe and his raging hard-on. "Does this feel like rejection to you? Believe me, sweetheart, I want nothing more than to slip you out of that robe and between the sheets of that bed over there."

"Then why...why are you stopping?"

Her breath felt like jets of sultry heat across his skin. "Because I won't be like every other man in your life. I won't just use you for my needs."

"But I want it too, Matt. Truly, I do."

With determination he released her shoulders and gently secured the belt of the robe back in place. "I know you do. But now isn't the time or place for us to be together. When it is, I promise neither one of us will take advantage of the other."

"Hey, Matt. We need Katie down here to talk to the sketch artist on the phone," Luke called from the first floor.

Confusion of a different kind crossed her face. "Sketch artist?"

"I only got a glimpse of Gideon. No one else saw him at all. Castello couldn't see through the pandemonium that broke out." Matt brushed his thumb across her jaw. "You lived with Gideon for years and know what he looks like. We need you to give them a description, and any distinguishing marks you can remember."

"Hey, you two coming, or do I need to bring the phone up there?" Luke sounded closer. A soft groan of frustration escaped her.

"You'd better go ahead. I'll join you in a few minutes." Matt released her and stepped away from the door, giving her room to slip into the hall. "I need a moment to calm things down."

Katie took a few steps, then stopped and turned, a mischievous smile on her lips. "You're wrong, you know."

"I'm wrong? About what?"

"When you decide the time is right for us to be together," she pulled the top of the robe closed, and took a step backward, "I intend to take full advantage of you."

―――

"Height?" Fifteen minutes later, dressed in the jeans and sweater Sami had sent with Luke for her, Katie leaned against the kitchen counter and stared into space, trying to determine Gideon's height. Since she stood just an inch above five feet, almost everyone seemed taller to her.

Matt walked through the door, and she motioned him closer. Holding the phone away from her, she asked, "How tall are you?"

"Six feet, three inches."

He reached past her to pull a glass from the cupboard. She inhaled the spicy scent of his aftershave again. His body heat brushed past hers, sending tingling awareness across her skin.

When the woman on the phone's other end said her name, she couldn't remember what they'd been talking about. "Excuse me?"

"Do you know the suspect's height, ma'am?"

"Oh, yes. He's over six feet tall. Maybe one or two inches." Heat filled her cheeks. Katie turned away from Matt, forcing herself to concentrate on Gideon's description as the woman continued to ask her questions. "Blue eyes, very crystal clear blue eyes. Hair color? Blond, but I'm not sure. He might've changed the color."

"The man I saw had white hair, and he wears a short military cut," Matt said, then drank long and slow from his glass of water.

Katie swallowed hard as his neck muscles worked then she repeated what he'd said into the phone. "Distinguishing marks? He has a scar from his right ear to the corner of his mouth. No, ma'am, the scar is a very old one."

When she couldn't provide any further information, the artist promised to send a copy to Marshal Castello later that evening.

After hanging up the phone, Katie joined the trio of men who were digging into the box of fried chicken and biscuits on the table.

"Who cooked?" She sank her teeth into the tender chicken. Still warm. That took care of number two on her list. Now all they needed was a plan.

"Luke went out for it while you were in the tub." Matt offered her some french fries. "He's always good for food, if nothing else."

Luke grinned at her between bites of chicken. She glanced at Castello who was listening to someone on his cellular phone as he ate. For the first time since they'd left the cabin that morning, she relaxed.

"So, Katie, why does Strict want you dead?" Luke sat back in his chair, his plate completely clean. "I mean besides the whole you-got-him-convicted thing. Why now?"

Katie almost laughed at the comical way the younger brother ignored the glare Matt shot across the table. "You mean why now, when he's had ten years to find me and do it?"

Luke nodded.

She considered his question a moment or two, logically. This time she didn't feel any of the panicky need to run and hide like she had the past few days.

Why now? Good question.

Katie wiped her mouth with a paper napkin. "I guess because Strict has this need to control everything. His ego is so dependent on always succeeding, always being a step ahead of everyone else. If he can't keep the government from killing him on New Year's Eve, then he'll settle for making sure the girl who betrayed his cause doesn't outlive him. The fact that I'm female makes it an even bigger slap to his pride." She took a long drink of her iced tea. "Women are lower than dogs on his hierarchy of evolution, you know."

"Okay, that explains why you feel your death is on a time limit," Matt said, focusing his attention solely on her. "But now that we know who the hitman is, I think there's another puzzle piece we need to establish."

"What?" Curiosity and apprehension filled her. Where was Matt going with this? She wasn't sure she wanted to hear the answer.

"If Gideon was Strict's right-hand man, why did Strict hide the fact that Gideon survived the Federal Building blast from his own people? Why has Strict kept Gideon hidden from everyone and everything for the past decade?"

"Because he wanted to use him to hunt for Katie?" Luke answered.

Matt shook his head and laid a hand on Katie's. "Didn't Strict announce to the clan that all three men died in the blast before you left and turned them in?"

Katie nodded, her appetite suddenly replaced by nausea. "He labeled all three as martyrs for his great cause. That was when I decided I had to leave."

"And Strict strikes me as a man who never does anything without a reason behind it, right?" Matt asked.

Again, she nodded.

"So, maybe, Strict had other uses for Gideon. Some other plan he intended him to carry out?" Luke asked, following his brother's line of thought.

"It could be you're on to something, Edgars." Castello closed his phone. Anger, hard and tense, etched lines around his mouth. "Gideon is apparently leaving no witnesses behind."

The nausea in Katie's stomach turned to cold fear. "Why?"

"We're pretty sure who the informant in our division was."

"Was?" Luke asked, all humor gone.

"They found my personal secretary dead in a storage locker." Castello swallowed several times before continuing. "She'd been tortured, just like Pete."

"You're sure she's the leak?" Matt asked.

"She sent a text message to my captain, tendering her resignation and that she was responsible for Pete's death. They traced her cell phone GPS to the storage locker where they found her."

"Why would she leak information to Gideon? She didn't even know me."

"Money?" Luke asked.

Castello shook his head. "Leslie didn't live extravagantly. Seemed a sweet kid with a boring life outside of work when she came to work for us a few years back. Hell, she didn't have any access to any information about you, Sar..er..Katie."

Katie smiled softly at his stumble over her name. "Then how did she know about me or where I was?"

"She didn't." Matt said.

"Then how did she blow my cover?"

"She didn't blow your cover. She blew mine and Pete's." Frank locked gazes with Matt.

"My guess is she was a plant. Once they figured out they couldn't get any information about Katie's whereabouts, they started following the movements made by you and your partner."

"Shit. And we eventually led them straight to Katie."

"I take it this lady was on the task force?"

"Stupid rookie mistake. I assumed the leak had to come from someone with clearance to access files." Castello rubbed the back of his neck, his gaze meeting Matt's. "Leslie's and Hagen's deaths means our man's making sure no one can identify him."

Matt slid his arm around Katie.

"What's this guy up to, besides filling the local funeral homes?" Luke asked.

"Preparing." Katie's one word pronouncement caught all their attention.

"For what, sweetheart?"

"This has all the earmarks of some big plan of my stepfather's. I would almost bet that my death is not Gideon's only assignment."

"Do you know what they might have planned?" Castello asked.

She shook her head. "No, but it'll be big, I guarantee it. The Prophet always said he would be immortal. What better way to make people believe it, than to strike from beyond the grave."

"Damn, I wish we knew what he was planning." Castello stood and paced the room. Katie felt Matt studying her.

"You're sure you don't know what Strict might be planning?" Matt asked.

"No." She swallowed hard. The answer was so obvious and so frightening. "But I bet I know where to find the answers."

"Where?" Castello and Luke asked simultaneously.

"No." Matt shook his head. "I'm not letting you go there."

"We have no choice, Matt." She laid her palm on his cheek. Suddenly, there was no one else in the world but the man seated next to her. His pain at knowing what she had to do touched her very core. He alone understood what this would cost her. "The answer has to be buried there."

"We'll send someone else to get it. I don't want you going back to that nightmare."

"No one else can find it. I have to go."

"What are you two talking about?" Castello asked.

Luke stood and started cleaning the table. "Papers Katie stole from Strict and hid ten years ago."

"Where do you have to go to get them?" Castello asked.

Matt shook his head again trying to convince her to put the idea out of her mind.

Katie stared at Matt and slowly nodded her head, willing him to understand one more time. Not taking his eyes off her, he slowly bit out the words.

"She has to go to Strict's compound, the Bunker, in Pennsylvania. Back to her nightmares."

22

Four hours later Matt drove the SUV on I-70 across the Ohio-Pennsylvania border. He and Katie were headed to Strict's Bunker in the farmland of Western Pennsylvania to retrieve the papers she'd hidden on the compound years earlier.

"This plan sucks," he muttered for the hundredth time.

Katie quit answering him at least an hour ago, which only increased his agitation. She wanted to dig around the compound immediately, get the papers and get out. The only flaw in her agenda was the fact that they would reach the compound after dark.

No matter what she said, he wouldn't allow her to search through her nightmares in the cold and dark. He also wouldn't let her spend the night out there.

Anger and something close to fear settled in the pit of his stomach.

Every time she delved into her memories of her time with the Family, it tore her apart just a little more. He didn't know how much more he could witness or how much of the woman he'd come to love would survive the process.

He glanced at her still, quiet figure in the passenger seat. With every mile they closed in on the Bunker, she withdrew further. Tension radiated from her. She looked so frail and fragile, like spun glass hanging by a thread. If he touched her, he feared she'd shatter into a million pieces.

"When you get to the I-76 junction, take State Route 119 north." Tension laced her voice. She didn't consult a map. *You never forget your way into hell*, she'd said.

"How much farther?" He focused on the highway. Fat snowflakes fell before the car's headlights. Semi-trailers and the occasional pick-up truck were their only traveling companions on the highway.

"I'm not sure. I lost track of time when I left the Bunker behind me." She glanced at him and he knew she already remembered the fear she'd felt that night. "It seemed like forever at the time."

"You're safe with me, Katie." He laid his hand over her entwined fingers in her lap. "Strict can't come after you tonight."

"But Gideon can."

He squeezed her hands tighter, trying to infuse some confidence in her. "As far as we know, he's still in Columbus somewhere. If Castello is right, with the secretary dead, Gideon will have no way of knowing where we're headed or why."

"I wish I could believe that." Her gaze met his. Nothing but despair filled her face.

"Last time you were in Strict's compound, no one was there to help you or fight for you. This time, you have me. I intend to stick to you like white on rice."

A quick, hesitant lift to her lips let him know she appreciated his effort to lighten her mood. It disappeared as quickly as it came.

"Do you think the secretary was the leak in the Marshal's task force?"

"Probably. The question remains, was she the only leak?" He released her hands to grip the steering wheel with both of his.

"The way your hitman is leaving dead bodies behind him, unless Castello finds another member of his task force dead, it's more than likely she was Gideon's main source of information."

Katie shook her head. "I never met her. I did meet Pete's first secretary a few times."

"You did?" His hands tightened on the wheel.

"She was very nice. The morning the FBI agents brought me to the Marshals as a witness for them to protect, she served me hot tea at her desk." Katie's voice caught, like she was trying not to cry. "I kept thinking my mom would've liked her."

The same mother who put her in the hands of a monster? He glanced at her. A tear ran down her cheek.

"Who are you crying for? That woman? Or your mother? Please don't say your mother. She put your life in danger."

"Castello told me when his secretary died in that car accident three years ago. Do you think it was an accident?"

"You can't possibly think her death was your fault." He took his foot off the accelerator as he came to the turnoff to Route 119.

With a soft grunt, she closed her eyes and rubbed her forehead. "I know I didn't kill her, if that's what you mean. But if the Devil wanted someone to take her place, then her death could be because of me."

Matt tried to rein in his anger. He wasn't going to let her take the blame for this. "If, and I'm not saying he did orchestrate her death, the first woman's accident was intentional, you are not to blame. Strict and this Gideon are.

"While we're on the subject, you don't get to take the blame for these two other deaths, either. They chose to help Strict's hitman. You get in bed with the devil, you best be willing to pay the price. They were dead the moment they agreed to help him find you. No way are you responsible for any of this."

"I disagree." Katie closed her eyes a moment against the intense anger rolling off Matt. Finally she opened her eyes to look into his blue ones. "Can we talk about something other than Strict or my past?"

He nodded. "Sure. What do you want to talk about?"

"Let's talk about your past for once. I mean, you know my secrets, it's only fair you tell me one of yours."

Obviously she had something in mind. "Ask away."

"How about your friend Chris?"

Whoa, he hadn't seen that coming.

"Who told you about Chris? Oh, wait a minute. Luke." He swore under his breath that Luke wouldn't survive to see his fortieth birthday. "One of these days my little brother's gonna learn to keep his nose out of other people's business."

"Don't blame him. I asked him what made you such a by-the-rules cop." She laid a hand on his arm, squeezed it, then returned her hand to her lap. "He told me you didn't use to be this…intense."

"What else did the family clown tell you?" He clenched the steering wheel tighter.

"That when your friend died you changed drastically. He didn't know the details, but implied that you were with your friend when he died."

A movement to his right told him she'd turned her head to watch him. "Luke said you never talked about it with anyone."

Sweat beaded on his forehead, and the truck's close confines crowded in around him. In a desperate attempt to stave off his panic, he turned off the heater and opened his window.

God, I don't want to do this.

Prepared to refuse her request he inhaled the cooler air deeply. Then memories of holding her while she bared her scars, both literally and figuratively flashed through him. Could he have less courage than she did?

"Chris and I lived next door from to each other. From the moment we met we were inseparable. Climbing trees, playing football, fighting my brothers in games of cops and robbers, Chris and I were always together."

"He must've been a good friend."

Matt snorted. The sound rang harsh even in his own ears. "Luke really didn't tell you much, did he?"

"No. What did he leave out?"

"Chris is short for Christina. She was the biggest and toughest tomboy in Columbus."

"Oh."

"Of course, she had to be. She had four older brothers. The whole family was tall and redheaded, each one meaner than the one before. Chris learned early on to defend herself. No one ever tried to coddle her and when she came up with an idea, there was no talking her out of it." He swallowed the lump that suddenly filled his throat.

Why hadn't he learned to refuse Chris? If he'd treated her more like a girl to be protected and less like a buddy would she be alive today?

"What happened?"

"When we were fifteen, a heavy metal band was playing a concert in Cleveland. Chris got it into her head we needed to go. The only problem was our parents wouldn't take us." He released one hand from the steering wheel and wiped his sweaty palm on his jeans, then repeated the process with the other one.

"So Chris waited for her parents to go out that Friday night, like they always did, then she and I took their family's extra car. I knew it was wrong, but she said she'd go with or without me. I couldn't let her go by herself."

"No, you couldn't."

"But I should have told someone, anyone. I should have tried to talk her out of it."

Katie's hand settled on his arm once more. "You said no one could convince her an idea was bad."

"But I knew the rules. Taking a car without permission and driving without a license were both illegal."

"Then what happened?"

"We were about an hour north of Columbus. The radio blaring. Chris driving. It was dark. Chris was looking at me, laughing when it happened." He saw the scene in his mind like it was yesterday. "The headlights ahead came out of nowhere. They swerved into our lane. I yelled at her to watch out. She looked back out the driver's window and screamed."

Inhaling, he blinked a few times to clear his vision then exhaled slowly—his pulse slowing some.

"The next thing I knew, the car was lying on its side in the field beside the road. The front was crinkled up like an accordion against this massive oak tree. The smell of smoke and blood filled the air. I thought I'd throw up. Then I realized I couldn't move, and Chris lay on top of me."

The words wouldn't stop, even if he'd wanted them to. His mind needed to purge the story, to tell Katie everything. "I tried to move her, but she simply moaned. My hands touched something wet and sticky. She was bleeding. I was pinned in between the dashboard and my seat. Later I found out I'd broken my left leg and my right arm. Chris had fractured her ribs and pelvis."

He swallowed again. "There was no one around to help her. The drunk left the scene and never reported it. No one came for hours. She might've lived if someone, *anyone* would've stopped."

Suddenly, unable to see through his unshed tears, Matt pulled the car onto the shoulder of the highway. He turned to Katie, who was wiping away her own tears. "She slowly bled to death in my arms."

Without hesitating, Katie unfastened her seatbelt then scooted over, wrapping her arms around him in a fierce hug. He gripped the back of her coat in his hands, crushing her to him, his face buried against her neck.

For the first time since that night, he wept for Christina.

Time passed. Katie moved back and forth, and he realized she was rocking him for comfort.

Whether hers or his, he wasn't sure.

Finally in control of his emotions once more, Matt eased his hold on Katie. "I'm sorry to lose it like this."

"It's okay. You've never told that to anyone before, have you?"

He shook his head, pulling away from her a little more.

"Thank you for sharing with me." She kissed him softly then scooted back to her seat, fastening her belt once more. "But you have to let it go. You aren't responsible for what happened to your girlfriend."

Forcing the memories of Chris' death out of his mind, Matt pulled the SUV back onto the highway. "I know I wasn't responsible, but I made two promises to myself that night. I would always protect people weaker than me, especially women. Secondly, I would never again put someone's life in danger by breaking rules."

"I'm sorry you've had to go against the rule book for my sake, but I've got news for you, Matt. I'm not some weak little woman that needs protecting." Anger laced her words.

He studied her. Her lips were pressed together in a thin line and her cheeks were flushed. "Believe me, I know you aren't weak, even though you're little. But I intend to watch your back as much as I can."

Silence ruled in the car for the next ten miles as they both fought their personal demons. They passed a group of fast food restaurants and motels then traveled deeper into the countryside.

"You want to take the Farm Road 544 turnoff ahead," Katie's voice broke the quiet. "And head west."

He glanced at her. Her face resembled a harlequin mask, flat, pale, motionless. Her left hand lay in her lap, limp. But her right hand held onto the armrest of the passenger door in a death grip, the knuckles tight and white.

If he had his way, he'd turn the car east, and head straight into the Poconos. He'd find a cabin so isolated, no one would ever find them. Then he'd make love to her until neither of them could walk.

"We don't have to do this," he said as he pulled off the main highway onto the farm road. "We could go anywhere you want, lay low until after Strict's execution, and let the feds worry about Gideon."

She shook her head, her gaze fixed on the road ahead. "I turned a blind eye once before and fifty people died. I'd never forgive myself if something in those papers will prevent one more innocent life from ending, and I did nothing about it."

Matt nodded. He understood. In order to live with herself, she had to at least attempt to prevent another disaster. His job was to see she survived the ordeal.

Signs for a bed and breakfast appeared on the road's right side. The sun slid farther behind the bare maple and oak branches. The gray mist of dusk deepened by the minute.

He had to make a decision.

When the second sign for the B&B appeared, he turned the car off the highway and into the drive.

"Where are you going? This isn't the way to the Bunker." The sudden change in plans snapped the semi-trance Katie had been drifting deeper into.

Good.

"It's too dark for us to search around the compound for papers that may or may not still be there."

"Oh, they're there, alright."

"You're sure you can find them?" He pulled up outside a three story Victorian, parked the car then turned to study her.

"In a heartbeat." A spark sounded in her voice.

"That compound had to have been covered from top to bottom by the FBI when they cleaned out the Family. You don't think they would've found those papers years ago?" Maybe he could goad her completely out of her fears.

"I hid them in a safe place. Believe me, no one, not even Strict would've looked where I hid them." She crossed her arms over her chest. "So why are we stopping here? We need to go to the Bunker and get them."

"We'll spend the night here, and get an early start in the morning." He held up his hand when she started to protest. "Relax, Katie. If those papers are so well hidden no one's found them in the past ten years, they'll keep for one more night."

She opened her mouth again then shut it, her lips compressed into a thin tight line. She shook her head as she climbed from the car, muttering something about testosterone.

Matt hid his grin as he opened his door, watching her jerk her backpacks from the SUV's backseat.

Every time the past reared its ugly head to haunt her, he thought she'd go down for the count, only to find she'd bounce back, tough and sassy as ever.

23

Thomas Pike pulled at his shirt collar and loosened his tie, the stricture making it hard to breathe as he sat in the Federal Penitentiary's visiting room. Sweat covered the palms of his hands.

He hated these interviews with Strict. If things were going his client's way, Strict would pace the interview room like a rooster in the henhouse. But when he didn't get the results he wanted, like today, the Prophet sat still as a statue. Only the muscle twitching in his left cheek suggested he wasn't made of granite.

"Our friend said his date didn't work out the other morning." They spoke in code to keep the guards from eavesdropping. This did little to ease Thomas' conscience. If he got caught acting as the conduit between Strict and a hitman, he'd be disbarred. If he didn't do as Strict asked, there was every possibility he'd end up dead.

"What happened?" Ice dripped from Strict's deep voice. Oh yeah, he was upset.

Thomas pulled on his collar once more. "Apparently another man got in the way of their rendezvous."

"Any word on his next planned encounter?" Strict lifted both eyebrows in question, staring straight into Thomas' soul.

The sweet spiced aftershave Strict always wore wafted around Thomas. His stomach roiled in protest as nausea hit him. Despite the cold weather outside and the draft inside the visitation cell, Thomas' palms grew wetter.

"He said they'd meet where they last saw each other."

A slow smile transformed Strict's face into pure evil. "He is sure she'll meet him there?"

A shiver of dread slithered up Thomas' spine. "He seemed to think she'd go there of her own volition."

Suddenly, Strict pushed away from the table. He paced the room in several quick strides. "This is good. This is very good."

"You think he'll succeed this time?" Thomas whispered.

"Without a doubt, Thomas." He chuckled at his own play on words. "Gideon has never failed me. He'll meet his date, take care of his assignment, and retrieve my property at the same time."

"Will it be in time, though?" Some of Thomas' tension eased. His master was pleased. "The execution is scheduled in two nights."

"Once he has completed his first assignment, the other will take place without question." He stopped pacing and stood below the prison interview room's high windows. A few stars twinkled in the sky above, despite the searchlights flashing through the window.

Thomas' pulse pounded in his ears as quiet spread throughout the room.

Strict turned, his intense crystal-blue gaze on Thomas. Thomas nearly jumped out of his chair when Strict finally spoke.

"With the stroke of midnight, this false government will cease my physical existence. But my immortality will be etched in the history of the world forever and that little bitch won't be able to stop me."

An older gentleman, quite tall and as lean as a fence post, with snow-white hair and wrinkled, leathery skin, answered Katie's quick knock on the Bed and Breakfast's door. "May I help you?"

Before she could answer, Matt stepped onto the porch behind her. "My fiancée and I were wondering if you had any available rooms for the night?"

Katie forced her gaze to remain fixed on the proprietor's face. *What possessed Matt to call her his fiancée?*

"Well, we weren't expecting any more customers this late in the year, young fella."

"The name's Matt Edgars, sir." He held out one hand to the other man, while slipping his free arm around Katie's waist. "This is Katie Myers. We were on our way to see her family, but it will be long after dark before we get there. We hoped you might rent us two rooms."

"Who is it, Charlie?" a squeaky voice called from behind the older gentleman.

"Two travelers wanting rooms for the night, Penelope," he called over his shoulder.

A tiny woman, half the height of her husband, suddenly appeared at his elbow.

For the first time in her life, Katie came in contact with an elf. Her white hair was pulled back in a bun on top of her head, with wisps of white curls framing her face. Her eyes tilted at the corners when she smiled. Katie swore they twinkled.

But the most wonderful thing about this elf was her smell. Cinnamon, nutmeg and orange spices filled the very air around her.

"Goodness gracious, Charlie Watts, let the poor souls inside. It's nigh on to freezing out there." She elbowed her husband away from the door. Taking Katie by the hand, she led her into the old Victorian farmhouse's front room.

Matt followed them inside and finally Charlie closed the door while grumbling about calling ahead and reservations.

"We really hate to impose," Kate tried to ease the older man's complaints.

"Dearie, never mind Charlie. If he didn't have something to complain about, he wouldn't talk for days." Penelope led them through the house to the kitchen. She directed them to the large country table decorated with Christmas linens and plates. "Pull off your coats and have a seat. I'll fix us some supper. It's always so lovely to have unexpected guests."

Katie looked at Matt. He simply shrugged and started removing his coat.

"Charlie asked me why I was baking pies and starting bread for the morning. I just knew we'd be having company tonight. The other guests have all just left. Charlie thought we'd have a few days to clean the rooms before the next reservations arrive. Luckily we still have one room clean and available."

The tiny pixie bustled around the room, chattering almost without taking a breath as she spooned vegetable soup into bowls. The flavors smelled so hearty, Katie could taste them from across the room.

Penelope set heaping bowlfuls before Katie and Matt. "Now you just warm your outsides in front of the fire here, and let the soup warm the insides."

Meanwhile Charlie, took his seat at the end of the table, packed his pipe with tobacco, and lit the bowl. Sweet tangy smell of oranges wafted from around him.

Katie looked at Matt. He winked at her, and she fought the urge to laugh. It was all a little surreal for her.

Anyone observing this domestic scene would have no idea she and Matt had a mission of such vital importance. And yet, for the first time since they left Columbus on their trek, the ache of tension between her shoulder blades loosened.

"So, Mr. Watts, you said you have one available room for the night?" Matt asked between bites.

Charlie puffed on his pipe a few times before answering. "Sure do."

"Oh, Charlie, quit being so obstinate," his wife said from the across the kitchen. "It's the honeymoon suite and he doesn't want to tell you because we usually only rent that to married couples. But since you're engaged, that's almost the same thing, now isn't it? And a very lucky thing too, given how late it is and how cold it's turning outside."

Katie blinked hard at the sudden rush of words, then realized Mrs. Watts spoke to her. The lie they'd told the couple stuck in her throat. She focused her attention on her bowl and tried to swallow the food in her mouth that had turned to paste.

"It is fortunate for us, Mrs. Watts." Matt took over the conversation. "We've been traveling for hours, and still have a nightmarish trip ahead of us. It's great to enjoy your hospitality for tonight."

He intended to perpetuate the falsehood to these nice people. Katie didn't know whether to hug him or kill him.

"Have you been engaged long?" Penelope smiled at Matt, but Katie saw her glance at her left hand first. Heat filled her face. Their story shone for the lie it was.

Matt laughed. "You'll have to excuse Katie. The change in our relationship is still new to her."

New to her and everyone in the free world.

He leaned forward as if telling their hostess a secret. "We just became engaged on this trip. I haven't had time to buy her a ring, yet."

"Well, don't spend too much on one, son. You'd do better to invest in a house." Charlie puffed on his pipe a few more times.

Katie glanced at Matt. He straightened in his chair, any hint of humor gone, he watched her with such intense desire it set every fiber of her being on high alert.

What was he thinking?

"You know, Mr. Watts, I might do that." He reached out and took Katie's hand in his. "I imagine a home of her own is just what Katie needs."

———

SEVERAL HOURS LATER, KATIE CLIMBED OUT OF THE COOLING BATH in the honeymoon suite's bathroom.

She wiped the fog from the mirror and studied the woman reflected there.

The young features and clear open gaze didn't fit the ancient way she felt inside. Was she really only twenty-seven? She felt sixty. Lord knows she'd lived a life hard enough to fill that many years.

She pushed her wet dark hair off her temples. And yet there were so many things she hadn't done in her life. She'd never gone to a high school football game, a prom, fallen in love, gotten married, or had children. For that matter she hadn't ever made love. Of course, until a week and a half ago, there hadn't been a man she trusted enough to fall in love with or make love to.

Visions of Matt filled her mind. The tall patrolman stopping and insisting she take a Breathalyzer test. Oh, he'd irritated her with that, yet softened it by insisting she drink hot chocolate.

The way he came to her rescue, insisted on helping her, despite her attempts to keep him at arm's length, showed his unwavering courage. He even put his own life at risk to protect her and taught her to trust him.

The memory of his fingers caressing her scars and his lips kissing each one as if he could take the decades-old pain away from her, made her heart ache with longing.

Each scalding kiss they'd shared played in her mind again.

Her fingers still remembered the feel of his skin beneath them. Her body ached to press against his solid frame once more.

Again she studied the woman in the mirror.

This time a smile played around the corners of her lips, her pupils dilated, her cheeks grew flushed with excitement.

Never had a man treated her with such respect, such protectiveness or made her want the normal things every other woman dreamed of in this world.

And oh, did she want him. The ache low in her stomach spread throughout her body. Her entire body craved more of his kisses, his touch, him.

"You may be dead tomorrow," the young woman in the mirror said to her. "Be greedy. Make love to the man in the other room. Feel alive."

"I have no future to offer him."

"He hasn't asked for one. But you have here and now. He's won your heart. Let him know it. If fate decrees you'll survive Strict's plans, then you can worry about futures."

"If he rejects me again, I don't think I'll survive it."

The look on his face at dinner when he'd held her hand and promised her a home flashed before her. That wasn't the look of an indifferent man.

"Katie?" Matt's voice sounded from the door's other side. "You okay in there?"

She blinked and her heart jumped a few beats. "Yes. I'll be out in a minute."

"Don't be a coward," the woman in the mirror said. "For once in your life, take what you want."

Her decision made, Katie slipped on her nightshirt.

Not exactly a sexy negligée for seducing the man of my dreams. But she couldn't walk out naked. That was too daring for her, no matter how much she'd come to trust him.

Taking a deep breath, she opened the bathroom door and stepped into the honeymoon suite's bedroom.

Her breath caught in her throat.

Soft candlelight cast the room in a romantic glow. A low fire crackled in the fireplace. The scent of pine filled the room. The covers on the bed had been turned back in anticipation and Matt leaned against the window frame across the room, watching her.

She couldn't meet his eyes—not yet. Her gaze started at his bare feet on the hardwood floors. Slowly she let it travel upward. His jeans stretched against his firm thighs and hips, hugging his waist. His shirt was off. No signs of love handles existed at his waist. He didn't have the washboard abs so many infomercials said men needed, but his flat stomach came close.

She licked her parched lips. Heat flooded her from her head to her toes, settling deep between her thighs.

Oh, she wanted this man.

The only flaw she saw on his body was the white bandage she'd taped to his shoulder earlier in the day. Beneath it lay the wound he'd gotten protecting her.

"Katie?" He held out his hand.

Without hesitation, she cleared the distance between them. She place her hand in his, letting the other rest lightly over his bandage. "I'm so sorry you got hurt because of me."

"It wasn't your fault, sweetheart." He kissed her knuckles.

A shiver ran through her. "You could've been killed today."

"So could you. We were lucky." He wrapped one arm around her and drew her closer. He gave her a boyish grin. "Besides, you saved my life once, seemed only fair I return the favor."

The heat of his body warmed her, despite the slight draft from the window. She stared into his deep hazel eyes. "Is that why you knocked me away from the bullet? To return a favor?"

His face lost all humor. "As long as I'm able, I won't let anything happen to you. You have to trust me on that."

She laid her free hand on the side of his face. Her thumb stroked the taut muscle along his jaw. "I do trust you, Matt. More than anyone in my whole life, I trust you.'

"I'D NEVER HURT YOU." HE LOWERED HIS LIPS TO HERS, OFFERING her a soft, gentle kiss. The scent of gardenias clung to her. He tightened his arm about her waist, pressing her closer. She felt so right in his arms. He deepened the kiss. The need to possess her raged through him.

A soft whimper escaped her.

It was like ice water to the raging fire inside him. Slowly he eased her away from him, their lips lingering for an extra second before they parted.

He'd just promised not to hurt her. He wanted this night to be special to her. He wanted no memory of her past to infringe on this night. If she'd lived the life other women trapped in the male dominant society of Strict's Family had, then Matt doubted she'd escaped being raped. Tonight had to be all about Katie. She had to want his lovemaking.

If she couldn't, no matter how much it would kill him, he'd simply spend the night holding her. "Penelope insisted on making the room romantic, sweetheart. I didn't know how to stop her."

He stared into Katie's deep violet eyes. His hand splayed against the small of her back. "If it's too much for you, we'll blow out the candles and just get some sleep. Nothing else has to happen tonight."

"I think it's all lovely." She leaned in and kissed him, her lips barely touching his. "I've read about this kind of romance in books. It's every normal woman's dream. Matt, I've never had normal. Not since I was six years old. For once in my life I want something good."

"I don't want you to feel pressured about this. I was worried about taking you to the compound tonight. I only brought you here so you could rest."

She placed a finger on his lips, stopping any more words.

"Please don't give me a reason to act the coward now, Matt. I've never made love to anyone before."

His heart pounded in his chest. The implication was huge. He'd be the first man she'd ever given herself to, not just another man using her for his needs. Could he do it?

For a moment he held her in his arms, then he lowered his head to hers, stopping a hair's breadth from her lips. "If you're sure this is what you want."

"What I want, Matt, is you."

24

"I've never felt like this about anyone in my life, Matt." Katie cupped his face. His five o'clock shadow tickled her palms. She wanted him to understand what she was asking. "You're the first man I've ever trusted to make love to me. Please make this special."

His Adam's apple moved as he swallowed. Understanding lit his face, and something deeper.

Need. The intensity of it thrilled her. In all her life, no man had looked at her like she was a five-course meal to be devoured.

Suddenly, she felt feminine, sexy and in control.

She pressed her body against the length of his solid frame. With her hands still holding his face, she stood on her tiptoes, pulled his head toward hers, and kissed him with all the need she held inside.

His arms tightened around her. A growl ripped through him, and he crushed her to him, bringing her slightly off the ground. Katie wrapped a leg around his, clinging to him as her body pulsed with desire. His hands slid down to cup her bottom and lift her higher.

"Yes," she murmured against his lips. "Teach me. Show me what it's like to be a woman."

He broke the kiss and studied her face once more. She thought he meant to set her aside.

Instead, he cradled her in his arms and carried her to the bed. He laid her down, stretching out beside her. With one hand he smoothed her hair off her face. The intensity in his eyes once again thrilled her.

Without shifting his gaze from her face, he reached for the hem of her nightshirt. He pulled it to the base of her rib cage, splaying his hand across her soft abdomen. She sucked in her breath.

He pushed her nightshirt over her breasts, then off her body. It was his turn to suck in his breath. "God, you're beautiful, Katie."

This man knew all her secrets. He'd seen all her scars. Touched them, kissed them. And still he saw her as beautiful.

No man had ever seen her naked. A shiver coursed throughout her body. Embarrassed to be so exposed to him, she reached for him, but he captured her hands in one of his.

"It's okay, sweetheart," he whispered, raising her arms above her head. "We're going to go slow with this. If we go too fast, I'll hurt you, and I mean to show you how it is to be loved. Trust me, Katie," he said, pushing her fingers against the headboard's spindles.

Didn't he know how much she trusted him? Tomorrow held every possibility that she'd die. This might be the only time in her short life she'd feel loved. If he wanted to take the entire night, she'd follow his lead. Her fingers curled around the headboard's spindles, and she gave him a tentative nod. Words were beyond her now.

He stretched his body along the length of hers. "I've been thinking of having you, like this, for days." He leaned in and kissed her slow and deep. With his hand he made a light trail along the far side of her body, slowly moving from hip to ribs, his fingers caressing the tips of the scars that crisscrossed her back. Finally he brought his hand to rest with his palm covering her breast.

"Then why did you wait so long?" she managed to whisper. Her taut nipple tingled beneath the heat of his hand. Then he began to knead the flesh and pluck at the peak. Fire and ice spread through her body.

"Because you weren't ready."

Oh God, she was ready now.

He dipped his head and kissed the side of her neck, moving slowly along the column of her throat. He blazed another trail of electricity along her skin with his lips. Every nerve in her body jumped to hyper mode.

Then he shifted his body lower beside her. The friction of skin against skin sent shivers dancing throughout her.

She moaned softly.

He paused, his head suspended a millimeter above her breast. The warmth of his breath caressing her nipple thrilled her. She wanted more. Her fingers gripped the spindles tighter. She closed her eyes, waiting for his lips to claim her.

Instead, his tongue, soft and wet, drew a lazy circle around her nipple. Then his lips suckled softly on it.

She arched her back off the bed. "Oh, Matt."

"More, sweetheart?" he murmured against her breast.

"Yes, please."

He shifted again, his body covering the lower half of hers. He repeated the process on her other breast until she quivered beneath him.

Then he moved lower. Gently, he pushed her thighs open, settling his body between them. His lips never left her flesh. He tasted every inch of her stomach, then across the junction of one leg at her groin.

His fingers opened the folds of her sex. "You're so wet for me already. You're so beautiful, Katie."

She opened her eyes to see him staring at her, his face cradled between her thighs. Desire burned in his eyes. Then he dipped his face.

Surely he didn't mean to kiss her there?

Oh yes he did.

Fire shot through her. Her body lurched off the bed as his tongue slid between her tender folds. Her eyes closed and her world centered on the sensations he caused. She whimpered with need.

"Shh, sweetheart," he murmured against her most sensitive flesh. "Try to relax and let it happen."

Relax? How could she relax with him playing Ravel's *Boléro* on her body?

Then he began his assault once more. Gently licking, sucking, teasing her into a new frenzy.

Her body wiggled and thrust to the ballet's sensual movements he directed.

He coaxed every bit of control from her, until she reached the crescendoed peak he wanted. Finally her body, taut with desire, fell into the abyss. Spasms wracked her, and her grip on the headboard slowly eased.

The bed shifted as he moved away from her body. She whimpered. "Don't go."

"Believe me, I'm not going anywhere." His voice was a deep rumble from the bedside.

Katie opened her eyes. His back to the bed, she watched him strip out of his jeans and boxers—his legs firm, hips lean, each muscle delineated in the candlelight. Then he turned. She inhaled deeply at the sight of his erection. Warmth spread through her. She'd done that. She'd aroused him to the point that he wanted her as much as she wanted him.

"Are you sure, Katie?" he asked.

After the orgasm she'd just had he still asked her for permission. She knew if she said no, he'd stop. She'd learned to trust him enough to believe that. But she didn't want him to stop. She wanted him, all of him.

"Please make love to me, Matt." She held her arms open to him.

He took a moment to protect her with a condom then moved between her thighs once more, this time kneeling with his erection pressed against the swollen, moist folds of her. His hands on either side of her torso, he leaned in and kissed her, slow and deep. She tasted her own desire on his lips.

"Tell me, Katie," he murmured. "Tell me what you want."

She bent her knees, and rubbed her wet sex along the firm, hot length of him.

Tell him? Couldn't he feel what she wanted?

He kissed her again. Slipping his tongue into her mouth, teasing, thrusting against hers. "Tell me, Katie."

"Inside me," she whispered. "I want you inside me, now, Matt."

Pulling back, he shifted his weight onto his arms then slipped his tip between her folds. She inhaled as he stretched her open then wrapped her legs around him.

"Oh, God, Katie," he moaned in response, and with one thrust, he buried himself deep inside her.

Something tore and a sliver of pain shocked her. She gasped.

———

HE FROZE.

"Dammit, Katie, I didn't know." He started to move away.

She tightened her legs on his, and grabbed at his back, holding him to her. "No. Please don't stop."

Her actions pulled him in deeper.

"Katie...don't move...sweetheart," he managed between

breaths. If she moved again, he'd hurt her more, despite his promise. "I need…one…second."

Her eyes opened. Unshed tears filled them. "You won't stop, will you? I don't want you to stop."

The desperation in her voice touched his soul. "I won't stop." He smoothed her hair from her face, and trailed kisses against her eyes, then her nose, and her chin. He felt her hold on him relax a little.

"Is it better, yet?" He kissed her gently, fighting with all his might to control his own raging need to thrust into her tender flesh.

She nodded. "I think so."

He leaned all his weight onto his elbows, then slid back a fraction of an inch, letting her adjust to the feel of him moving inside her. He thrust forward again.

"Oh, yes," she murmured against his lips, dragging his head down to hers. And he was lost.

All thought fled his mind, and the need to join with this woman, to bring them both to fulfillment grasped him in its reins.

Her fingers dug into his back, her heels into his thighs as he increased the rhythm. With each thrust another of her little moans of pleasure filled the room. The feel of her around him, squeezing him, pulling him drove him to fill her faster until they both hovered at the brink.

"Love me, love me, love me," she whispered into his ear.

He smothered her moans with a searing kiss. When the first of her shudders coursed through her, he let his own orgasm rip through him.

The firelight cast a soft glow in the hearth across the darkened room opposite the bed. Matt had extinguished all the candles and crawled back into bed with Katie. He lay on his back, one arm above his head, the other holding her pressed against his body.

"Why didn't you tell me you were a virgin?" Smoothing her dark hair from her face he kissed her forehead.

"I told you I'd never made love to anyone before." She whispered beside him. "I guess I should have said I'd never had sex before, but I thought you understood."

"I thought you meant something else."

"What else could I have meant?" She leaned on her elbow to study him.

He swallowed hard. "You lived with Strict's family. I knew women in that type of environment were sometimes, um, used... um, as sex objects—"

"You thought I was a camp whore?" She pulled away from him, climbed out of bed, and searched the floor for her nightshirt.

"I never said I thought you were a whore." He jumped out of bed, going after her. "Katie, come back here."

"Back off." She raised one hand to ward him off.

He stopped, panic mixing with his own anger. "Come back to bed, sweetheart. It's freezing cold tonight."

She scrambled into her nightshirt, then pulled a quilt off the chair near the fire and curled up in it. "I'll sleep here."

"Dammit, Katie." He knelt in front of her. God, he wanted to take her in his arms and carry her back to bed. But she had to come to him willingly. So many had forced her to do what they wanted. He wouldn't be one more. "Sweetheart, I never believed you'd do anything willingly."

"What did you think?" she asked, her eyes filled with hurt and unshed tears. He reached for her hand.

She drew it away. "Don't touch me."

Patience. He needed to make her understand, but he'd have to tread carefully.

"Katie, you've been through so much at the hands of that madman. Abused, both physically and mentally. When I saw the lash scars on your back, I assumed you'd..." He swallowed.

"You assumed I'd given in to whatever he wanted, even if it meant giving my body to him and his men?"

Matt shook his head. "No, sweetheart. You're too strong to just give in. Each of those scars attests to that."

This time she reached for him, the smooth skin of her palm settling against his face. His heart ached with her tenderness.

"What did you think, Matt?"

His shoulders sagged under the weight of how his assumption had hurt her. He lowered his eyes, his head bowed. "I'd thought you'd been raped."

Except for the logs crackling on the fire, silence filled the room.

She laid her hand on his head, bringing his face to rest on her knee. He slid his hands around her thighs, watching the fire dance around the logs' edges.

It took a few minutes, but eventually she spoke.

Matt rubbed her thighs with his hands. Whatever she was telling him needed to come out. His heart ached with each word, but he wouldn't stop her.

"That day after Billy died and I refused to build Strict anymore bombs was also the day my public whippings started. No one refused the Prophet. For a week he lashed me to the flagpole, and whipped me with that horse whip. Each day I refused him. Even setting his dogs on me wouldn't break my resolve.

"After a week, he threatened to have me raped by every man in the group. I told him to go ahead, I wasn't going to let one more person be harmed because of me." She snorted heavily. "I'd forgotten what a sick man he was. He used my own words against me. That day he grabbed the ten-year old girl from the crowd, I watched him stroke her hair in a sick, perverted fashion. He said I would teach his men to build his bombs or she'd take my new punishment."

Nausea gripped Matt. He couldn't listen to any more. "Oh

baby, I didn't know, really." He scooped her into his arms, kissing her frantically.

"I wouldn't let them use me, but I couldn't let them use her either." She gulped in air. "There was no other choice. I caved in to his demands. He killed fifty people because of me. In the end, I was too weak to stop him."

Matt sat in the chair with her cradled in his lap. He framed her face with his hands, forcing her to look at him. "You're wrong, you know. I've never met anyone stronger in my whole life."

She tried to shake her head, but he held her.

"You survived a life of such persecution that would've killed most people. You managed to save your virtue in a sea of perverted animals. You fought to save people, and managed to save one small girl." He kissed her slow and deep then lifted his head to stare at her. "And in the end you were the one person who defied Strict. You put him in that prison cell. You alone are the reason he's getting the punishment he deserves."

"If I can't find those papers, and stop whatever plan he has in place, he'll win again." She leaned in against Matt's body. "You're right, though."

"About what?" Rubbing his hands over her back beneath the quilt, he enjoyed the feel of her cuddled in his lap.

"It's freezing cold tonight," she murmured against his neck. He pushed the quilt off her shoulder and kissed her collarbone.

Shivers rippled through her, even as she tilted her neck to offer him more creamy skin to taste. He obliged her with a nibble of her neck. "And what would you like me to do about it, sweetheart?"

"I think you should take me to bed and warm me." Tracing a finger across his chest, she made a soft purring sound. "From the inside out."

With a growl, he lifted her in his arms and carried her back to bed. "Anything you want, sweetheart."

Castello knocked on the door of the three-story colonial nestled in the historic district of Harrisburg. It was near midnight, and his head and shoulders ached. The red-eye to Philadelphia had been long and miserable.

He glanced at the man beside him. Luke Edgars had stuck to him like gum on the sidewalk. Even though he'd had no business at the crime scene of Leslie's murder, Luke had insisted on coming along.

Frank gave the guy credit though. Unlike most rookies Luke hadn't lost his lunch during the crime scene walk-through.

Remembering Leslie's tortured body tied to that metal chair in the storage locker nauseated Frank. An ache to smash his fist into something ripped through him.

"And why is it we're here visiting Strict's lawyer instead of on our way to find my brother?" Luke asked, stepping back to look around the well-to-do neighborhood.

"I'm here because with Leslie's death, we have no idea where Gideon is going, or what he has planned next. One way or another, I'm getting information out of Strict's lawyer." Castello rapped on the door once more. Harder. "You're here to keep an eye on me for your brother, get in my way, and generally piss me off."

Luke gave him a lopsided grin. "Okay, just so we know what our roles are."

"You should've stayed in Columbus."

"Like I told you before. If anything we find will help my brother, I'm gonna call him."

Castello ground his teeth as lights in the house turned on. "And like I told you, I'll call him myself. I want Katie safe as much as you two do."

Luke just grinned that good-buddy grin at him once more. "Frankly, your track record sucks with Matt and me."

Before Frank could punch half of Luke's teeth down his throat, the front door opened.

"Who the hell are you, and why are you pounding on my door at this hour of night?" The fiftyish, heavy-set bald man asked, as he squinted at them with a scowl on his face.

Oh yeah, he was going to like making this guy sweat.

"Frank Castello, U.S. Marshals, Mr. Pike." Frank shoved his ID in the man's face.

Strict's lawyer instantly paled. "You could've made an appointment with my secretary in the morning," he blustered, trying to cover his first reaction.

"This matter couldn't wait." Frank stepped forward. "You don't mind if we talk inside, do you, Mr. Pike?"

"Might as well come in and get this over with." Pike held the door for them then led them to a wood-paneled library. "But I can assure you, I'll be speaking with your superiors, Marshals."

"Oh, I'm not a Marshal, Mr. Pike," Luke announced from the library's doorway. "You'll have to contact my boss separately."

Frank wanted to hit him.

"And who are your superiors?" Pike seated himself in a leather chair, and motioned them to take a seat.

Luke gave the man a movie-star smile and handed the lawyer his ID case. "The Treasury Department. IRS investigator Edgars at your service and I'll be looking into all your finances from this moment, back to the very first dollar you ever made. Unless of course you'd like to cooperate with my friend the Marshal here."

If possible, the lawyer paled further.

Castello reconsidered decking Luke. Instead, he went to the side bar, located the whiskey and poured Pike a tumblerful. "Here. You're going to need this."

The lawyer took the glass in his shaky hands. Drinking the whiskey a little too fast, he coughed and sputtered a few times, then set the glass aside. "What is it you want from me, gentlemen?"

"You're Jacob Strict's lawyer, correct?" Frank asked, flipping open a pocket notepad.

"You know I am, or you wouldn't be here." Pike seemed to relax. "And you also know that anything said to me by him is privileged information. So you have wasted your time coming here, and cost me valuable sleep."

Frank leaned forward. "And you also know that as an officer of the court you're obliged to divulge to the authorities any information Strict may have given you of future crimes he's planning."

Still holding onto his bravado, Pike gave a shaky laugh. "In twenty-four hours the man will be dead. Where is he going to commit these future crimes from? The grave?"

"That's actually what we believe he has planned." Frank flipped a few pages in his notebook. "In fact, we believe he has already sent a hitman after his stepdaughter, Sarah Strict, in the hopes of silencing her before he dies. Is this true?"

"I have no knowledge of this rumor."

"How is Strict financing the hit on his stepdaughter?" Luke asked from where he lounged on the corner of the leather sofa. "Are you dispersing the funds for him?"

Pike took another sip of whiskey, his hands shaking slightly. "It would be illegal for me to pay out funds to finance a felony, gentlemen."

Frank flipped another page in his notebook. "We also have information that Strict is planning an act of terrorism against the United States Government, scheduled for some time after his execution tomorrow night. Is this true?"

The lawyer blinked. His calm facade cracked slightly.

Frank smiled. "You didn't know we knew that, did you?"

"Again, I have no knowledge of this alleged plan."

"If you did, you'd be honor-bound to report it, wouldn't you, Mr. Pike?"

"Of course. I am an officer of the court and know my duty."

Castello fought the urge to gesture he'd just scored a touchdown. Instead, he pulled out his pocket tape recorder.

"What's that?" Pike gripped the tumbler of liquor tighter.

"Just a little something we picked up on our way to see you." Castello set it on the table. "Are you sure you don't want to change your statement?"

Then he hit play.

Jacob Strict's voice filled the room.

"With the stroke of midnight, this false government will cease my physical existence. But my immortality will be etched in the history of the world forever..."

THE MISTY GRAY LIGHT FILTERED THROUGH THE BEDROOM curtains as dawn inched its way onto the horizon. Katie stood across the room, dressed in her jeans and hiking boots, watching Matt sleep beneath the quilts on the honeymoon suite bed.

Already she missed his warm body pressed against hers, the subtle spices of his cologne and the feel of his lips. Her body and soul screamed for her to climb into bed with him and never come out.

But her heart and mind knew she couldn't come to him as half a person. Until she dealt with her past demons, they'd haunt her future forever. Matt taught her that. He'd helped her learn not to hide from her painful memories. His great patience was one of the things she loved about him.

The idea surprised her, then warmed her.

She did love him. She loved him with all her heart.

How had she come to love this man in such a short time? From the moment he'd offered her that steaming cup of hot chocolate on the roadside almost two weeks ago, he'd laid siege to the concrete walls surrounding her heart. Like a knight of old, he'd stormed the citadel and finally found the maiden trapped in the ice tower.

God, now I sound like some medieval troubadour.

Katie shook her head then slid her hand in Matt's coat pocket. Without jangling them, she eased his car keys out, along with his cell phone.

With a last glance back at the bed, she wished one more time her life could be different. She really hated doing this. He'd probably never forgive her. But she wouldn't let him put himself in danger for her. If anything happened to him, she'd never survive it. He'd come to mean that much to her.

An hour earlier she'd written him a letter explaining where she was going and why. Now she set the envelope on top of his boots. Then grabbing her backpacks, she slipped out the door and away from the one man in her life who'd stood by her.

25

Outside in the cold, Katie eased the SUV into gear and headed back onto the road. Matt had been right. It was much easier to face your nightmares during the light of a new day instead of in the dark of night.

She smiled and felt her cheeks heat remembering all he'd shown her the night before. In the intimate confines of their suite he'd replaced all her fears of the dark with images of love and sharing.

Five miles down the road, she flipped open his cell phone and punched the call list. Finding the number she wanted, she hit speed dial.

"Luke? This is Katie." She turned the SUV around a series of curves. A few more miles and she'd be at the right turn.

"Katie? Man, I'm glad to hear from you. You two okay?"

"Yes. We're both fine."

"Did you make it to Strict's compound okay? Have you got the stuff?"

Through the static on the phone, he sounded a little worried. God, she hated cell phones. "No, we didn't make it there last night. But I'm getting the papers today." She watched the road up ahead. The road to the compound should be after the next bend. "I need you to do something for me. Pick up something, actually."

"Sure, whatever you need kid. Put my brother on first. I need to talk to him a sec."

"Um, that's what I need you to do for me."

"What, Katie? I can't hear you through this connection. What do you need me to do?"

"Pick up your brother. He's at a bed and breakfast on Farm Road 544 heading west from the state route. If you leave Columbus now, you should get there in about four hours."

"Katie…not in…trouble." Luke's voice faded in and out as she headed under power lines.

"No, Matt's not in trouble. Just go get him for me." She slowed for the turn onto the snow-covered, gravel road. "This connection is breaking up, Luke. Tell your brother…tell him I'm sorry."

She tucked Matt's phone in the seat next to her amid the wires she'd stolen from the truck at the bed and breakfast. Lord knows she had plenty to apologize for this morning.

Shifting into a lower gear, she turned onto the unplowed road that led her back to the hell of her youth. The passing years since she'd hiked her way along this path, through the dark night, fearing each second that someone would find her and force her to return, had taken their toll on the landscape. The oaks and maples, now devoid of their leaves for the winter, towered higher than four stories. The evergreens spread like giants among the bushes and underbrush.

Would she be able to find the place? People depended on her memories, the memories of a frightened teenager, to find the missing piece to the crazed mind of a maniac.

She maneuvered the SUV along the deepening forest's winding curves. Then an electric security gate appeared out of nowhere. Startled, she slammed on the brakes. The front wheels skidded on the ice and snow. The car fishtailed. Without thinking, she spun the wheel the opposite direction, eased her foot off the brake, downshifted, and prayed. The vehicle straightened, and she pumped the brakes. The SUV stopped, sideways, right next to the gate.

Panting, she slumped in the seat, her arm and head resting on the steering wheel.

"Well, that's one lesson Strict taught me that came in handy." She inhaled and exhaled deeply to help calm herself.

Silence. She shook her head. In all the years she'd lived in the Family's noisy confines, she'd learned to fear the silence in these woods. It always meant trouble.

"This is an army, and you are all soldiers. You'll spend the next forty-eight hours in this forest, learning to survive. You will hunt your own food, make your own fire, and conceal yourself at all times from the enemy." Strict's voice rang in her ears.

The ten other teens he'd ordered into the forest that freezing morning thought they were preparing for some revolution against the government. They believed Strict's claim that the government was their enemy.

But she'd known the truth.

The enemy was Strict. If she failed at one step of the exercise she would've been disciplined in front of everyone. Humiliation had been his favorite weapon.

But this time you won't win, you bastard.

She shrugged off her memories and pulled her weapon from her pocket. Checking the magazine by rote, she slipped the gun back into her pocket. *Never hurts to be prepared.*

Standing in front of the padlocked gate, she shivered in the cold. For years she'd dreamed of leaving these gates. Never in the past decade had she dreamed she'd need to scale her way back into this place.

Now she had to go through this hellish place one more time. On the other side lay the woods she'd trekked through and the cliff she'd climbed down in order to hide Strict's precious papers. If she couldn't stop him, no one could.

Better get on with it. An unpleasant task is best done quickly. Wow, she hadn't remembered her father telling her that in years.

Katie glanced back at the car where his picture remained safely nestled in her backpack, then smiled. If Dad was talking to her after all these years, then maybe he was watching over her again. Or maybe he always had been, and Matt helped her open her heart enough to listen.

Years before, the gate in front of her had sizzled with electricity when locked each night. Strict told them it was necessary to keep out the enemy. But she knew it was to keep them inside as prisoners. Every inch of remaining fence was topped with barbed wire.

Again she heard her Dad's words. *"Always check for danger before crossing the street."*

Bending, she gathered a handful of snow and packed the material into a tight snowball. She took a step back and hurled the white ball at the gate. The cold missile hit a bar then fell to the ground in pieces, without a single spark or crack of sizzling electricity.

"Good. At least I won't end up like fried chicken."

She grasped the bars to begin scaling. The rusted padlock caught her eye. Perhaps the metal had rusted through in the past ten years. It couldn't be that easy to get into the place, could it?

Oh hell, why not?

Bracing herself in front of the padlock, she grabbed the bars on either side, and pulled hard. The lock hinge snapped, and the gate opened in front of her. She stumbled back a few steps and laughed. "Well, that worked. Strict was right about one thing. The government hasn't paid much attention to maintaining the security here."

Taking a deep breath, she opened the gate and took a step inside the grounds. Slowly, she exhaled, willing her heart to slow to a normal pace.

Nothing happened. What had she expected? To be transported back in time, like some time-warp thing? She headed along the path to where the main buildings were. On her right stood the vacant dog kennels. Out of habit, she moved to the path's far left side.

"What's a matter, girl? Scared of some dogs? Never met a bigger coward than you."

Katie shook her head once more to clear her mind of Strict's voice. Was he going to haunt her every footstep in here?

She stepped into the compound's main circle known as the common. Some would've compared it to an old town square. The main meeting hall sat in the center. Strict's office had been inside. Surrounding it were the mess hall, the barracks for the single men on one side, and the single women and teens on the other. In the rear sat the munitions hall. Her bomb-building shack lay nearly fifty yards to the left and rear.

Slowly, she moved around the circle to her left. It was like walking in one of those Western ghost towns. Everywhere she looked, she expected to see someone from the past step out and walk across the common. The eerie feeling left her sweating in the cold.

Once she passed in front of the main meeting hall she froze. There it was. The object of many of her nightmares.

To the casual observer it was simply an abandoned flag pole. But if you looked closely, you could see the fine lines where the whip had curled around her body and dug into the pole's wood.

She began to shake again, fine tremors that gradually increased until she couldn't stand. She fell to her knees, her arms wrapped protectively around her body. She keened, rocking back and forth, a low moan filling the air around her.

Then she curled into a ball, lying on her side in fetal position. The pain was so great. Pain she hadn't allowed herself to feel all those years ago. It swept over her like a tsunami.

Darkness closed in on her as her wails bounced off the

compound's silent walls surrounding her, echoing into a giant symphony of despair.

———

Feeling better than he ever remembered, Matt stretched in the bed, his hand reaching for the warm body on the other side. He met only the cold linens and pillow.

"Katie?" He sat up in bed, and scanned the room in the dim early morning light. It was empty.

Her bags were gone. She'd taken everything. She'd gone on without him.

Fighting his rising panic, he swung his feet over the bedside, and pulled on his jeans. "Damn the woman. She knows how much danger waits for her there. Why did she go alone?"

He reached for his boots. An envelope lay on top, addressed to him.

> Matt,
> *Please don't be mad that I've gone to the compound by myself to get the papers. You can't protect me from this. I have to stop Gideon from killing more people for Strict. No matter what I have to do. Thank you so much for last night. It was the most beautiful night of my life. I will treasure it as long as I live. All my love,*
> Katie

"She loves me." Matt stared at the last line of the letter. "She tells me she loves me then leaves me?"

A sinking feeling in the pit of his stomach joined the panic in his heart. She didn't expect to come out of that compound alive. Dammit, didn't she know she'd become his life?

He thrust his feet into his boots, grabbed his coat and

searched for his keys. No keys. No cell phone. She'd left him stranded. Only his gun and wallet remained in his pockets.

Man, he wanted to shove his fist into something. Instead he thrust both hands through his hair. He glanced at the bed. The sacrifice of the virgin. Had that been all last night had meant to her?

He read the letter again. No, it had to have meant more to her. She gave him "all her love".

Katie had never used that word about anything.

Think. Did she leave any clues where this place really was?

"I can't let another innocent person be hurt because of me." Her words echoed in his head. "No. She knew I'd come after her. She planned this. She's willing to be the martyr if it stops Strict."

And she still didn't trust him enough to let him help her. That's what hurt the most. All the conversations, the kisses, making love, none of it had gotten through to the core of her, to her heart. She might think she loved him, but if she couldn't trust him to be there for her, then she truly hadn't learned to love him.

He paced to the window. In the fresh layer of snow he could make out tire tracks on the drive.

They headed west on the road.

To his left, in the periphery of his vision, the garage caught his attention. Thrusting one arm into his jacket he ran out of the room. He had the other arm in the jacket when he found Mr. and Mrs. Watts in the kitchen enjoying their morning coffee.

"Mr. Watts, do you have a car I can borrow?"

"No. Don't have a car."

Matt looked out the window and cursed. He needed transportation and fast.

Charlie took a big gulp of his coffee. "But if you're wantin' to go after that little woman o' yours, I'd be happy to loan you my truck."

When the older man handed him the keys, Matt could've kissed him. He ran out the door toward the garage, only to stop a few feet from the door. Small footsteps in the snow led from the front of the house to the garage.

Oh she wouldn't. She didn't.

Inside the garage he lifted the truck's hood. His heart fell to his feet. *Shit.*

She'd taken the distributor cap and some wires.

After slamming the garage door in frustration, Matt stomped back through the snow to the bed and breakfast. She'd left him little choice but to contact the sheriff. He hated the idea of involving the local police, especially complete strangers, because he'd promised her he wouldn't, but he needed to get to her before Gideon did.

As he rounded the corner, a black SUV pulled into the drive. Matt stopped in his tracks, his hand sliding into his jacket pocket to curl around his weapon. Out of the corner of his eye he saw Charlie step out the porch as the vehicle neared.

"Friends o'yours?" Charlie asked, puffing out a ring of smoke from his pipe.

"I was just about to ask you the same thing," Matt replied, his attention fixed on the car.

A moment later the car stopped. The front passenger door opened. Luke climbed out and held the door.

"You gonna go with us to rescue your damsel in distress, or stand there like an icicle?"

Relief flooded Matt. For the second time in his life, both in the past hour, he felt like kissing a member of his own gender.

"Just a second, I have a bill to pay." He pulled out the cost of one night's stay and an extra five twenties, handing all the money to Charlie.

"This is too much, young fella," the older man said, trying to hand him back some of the money.

Slinging his duffle over one shoulder, Matt dodged his hand and jumped off the porch and ran to the car. "No, sir. You're gonna need a mechanic to fix your truck," he yelled before climbing into the back of the SUV.

He sat in the middle of the bench, leaning in between the two front seats, tapping the leather upholstery in a nervous rhythm with his hands. "She's headed west. I don't know exactly where the compound is, but that's where she's gone."

"I know where the Bunker is," Castello said, pulling the car out of the drive and back onto the road.

"Tell me you've been there." Matt needed a break.

"Twice. Both times about ten years ago."

"Think you can find your way back?" Hope grew inside Matt.

Castello nodded. "This area hasn't changed much in all that time. If the government didn't do too much to the compound itself, I think I can find it."

His answer satisfied Matt. He sat back in the seat. "Just hurry, okay?"

"It's snow on top of ice, Edgars. I'll get us there as fast as the damn road lets me."

Matt nodded, tapping his foot in frustration. His heart and mind both raced. What if they didn't find her in time? How could she just leave him after last night? That still stung.

She thought she was protecting me.

The idea shook him. She wanted to safeguard the person she loved. Hadn't that been what he'd been trying to do for days? Protect her?

In order to shield him, she'd made sure he couldn't follow her. If Luke and Castello hadn't arrived, he'd still be sitting in that house, waiting.

"How did you find me?"

"Katie called and told us where she left you," Luke answered.

What the hell? "She left me stranded, even disabled that old guy's truck, then called you to come get me? What kind of game is she playing?"

"I don't think she's playing any kind of game, Matt." Luke

turned in his seat and looked at him, all teasing gone. "The lady believed we were four hours away, back in Columbus. I think she has every intention of dying to keep you and anyone else safe from these crazy bastards, but especially you."

His brother's words sank in. The idea angered and overwhelmed Matt. She valued her life so little she planned to throw it away to stop this madman. Yet, she'd cared enough about him to try and keep him safe.

Something Luke said seeped past Matt's emotions. "Luke, where were you when Katie called?"

His younger brother flashed him a grin. "About an hour east of here, headed to find you."

"What were you doing east of here?" That feeling of dread tap danced across Matt's spine.

"Funny you should ask. The Marshal here and I had a long talk with a lawyer."

He paused, and Matt knew he'd have to drag it out of him. "Luke, cut to the chase. I'm not in the mood for twenty questions. What lawyer and why?"

"Strict's lawyer in Harrisburg," Castello added, apparently as irritated with Luke as Matt. "The slimeball knew about the plot to kill Katie and never reported it."

Matt surged forward in his seat. He wanted blood—anyone's. The lawyer's would do.

"Tell me you beat the confession out of him."

"For a minute or two I thought I'd have to. Believe me, I would've liked nothing better." Castello gave him a knowing look in the rearview mirror then concentrated on driving. "Then Junior there," he pointed to the passenger seat, "gave him a reason to sweat all on his own."

Luke laughed. "You're just pissed a Treasury agent had him squealing like a baby more than the big bad Marshal."

"Would've been nice to know I had an IRS investigator with me, not just someone's kid brother," Castello muttered.

Matt stared at his brother. "You threatened him with an audit?"

"You'd be amazed at my powers, big brother." Luke suddenly grew serious. "What we found out was worth the effort. It seems Strict doesn't want Gideon to kill Katie, yet."

"What the hell do you mean by yet? He's firebombed her car, shot out her tires, tried to kill us both with that shotgun, and even took a shot at her downtown."

Suddenly, Matt slapped the front seat's leather. Now the whole picture made sense.

"It's an ambush. The bastards wanted her to go back to the bunker to find their papers she hid. It's a trap." His chest hurt with the knowledge. "And she's walking right into it."

Luke and Castello both nodded.

"Did the lawyer say what they needed the papers for? What their plans were?"

Castello shook his head, his eyes meeting Matt's in the rearview mirror. "He claims no knowledge about that. Only that they wanted to force her to return to the compound and find the papers for them. He also said it's important they be found before Strict's execution tonight. After he gets the papers, Gideon is to kill Katie."

―――

The cold eventually penetrated the pain surrounding Katie. The sun wasn't too high in the sky, but she didn't know how long she'd lay there, reliving every beating she'd taken in this place.

After all these years, her body had decided it couldn't function until her mind purged itself of the pain and anguish she'd buried so deep inside.

Great, what a wonderful time for repressed memories to rear their ugly heads.

Slowly, she uncurled her body. She needed to get a grip on her nerves. Nothing but ghosts lived here. Nothing in this place could hurt her anymore.

"Suck it up, Katie," she ordered. "A job needs doing, and you don't have time to wallow in self-pity."

Forcing all the memories back to the past, she shoved herself off the cold ground and rubbed her hands together to warm them. Despite the urge to stare at the whipping pole longer, she skirted the meeting hall and headed for the munitions shack. The government probably carted off all the weapons and explosives, but she hoped they'd left behind the one thing she needed today.

Rope—hundred-foot rappelling rope to be exact.

The doors creaked open, and musty air from a decade of disuse wafted out to greet her. In the gray, dust-mite filtered light she studied the building's interior. Every time she came into this place, the metallic taste of blood filled her mouth. She'd received her first bloody lip from Strict here, quickly learning the penalty for failure.

She shook off the eerie feeling that Strict lurked in the corner ready to jump out at her any moment. It wasn't doing her any good to remember any of this. She headed to the back cabinets.

Nylon ropes hung like long colorful loops of spaghetti inside. She pushed on the cabinet's rear wall. It sprung open. Strict's paranoia led him to build hidden compartments for weapons storage.

Luckily, the government hadn't found this one. Still hidden from unknowing eyes hung several knives. She took one out of its scabbard. Man, she hadn't held one of these in years. The weight still felt balanced lying in her palm. Another lesson she'd learned at this hellhole. It had taken her a few months of practice, but eventually she'd been able to hit a target the size of a fifty-cent piece from more than fifty yards away.

The feds must've been so busy taking out the big weapons—

the explosives, assault rifles and semi-automatics—that they missed finding this stash of small knives.

Might as well take this with her. Who knew what she'd encounter the rest of the way to the papers.

She slipped off her coat, put her arms through the scabbard's leather straps and felt the knife's weight settle between her shoulder blades as she pulled her coat back on. "Just like old times."

At the cabinet's base lay drawers containing miscellaneous items, including flashlights and batteries. With practiced movements, she put the batteries into the flashlight then switched it on.

"Let there be light," she said as a thin beam cut through the room's murky darkness. She snapped the flashlight off and shoved it into her other coat pocket, opposite the one holding her Glock. Then she took two lengths of rope, slung them over her head and thrust her arm through the loops.

Fully rigged for what she needed to do, she hurried out of the shack, and headed for the back fence. If luck was with her, no one had filled in the ditch beneath the fence where she'd crawled through the night of her escape.

The thin layer of ice underneath the snow crunched beneath her feet as she trekked through the pristine woods. She paused at the fence to listen for anyone following her. Not a sound. The eerie quiet surrounded her. She'd give anything to see Matt coming through the snow toward her. Even angry, he'd be a welcome relief to the quiet solitude.

No use in wishing for something that wasn't going to happen. He was back at the bed and breakfast, probably so pissed off he never wanted to see her again. She couldn't blame him. What she'd done was unforgivable, but she'd do it all again if it kept him safe.

At the fence, she edged her way along to the farthest corner, near the tree line. Kneeling, she pulled on the fence, yanking the edge up from the snow.

Great. At least she wouldn't have to waste time going back for wire cutters. Removing the ropes she shoved them under the fence, then lying on her back, she wiggled beneath the chain-link. A metal snag caught on her injured hip, tearing at the material and bandage beneath.

"Oh, damn," she said with a growl as pain shot through her. She'd gained weight in her hips and thighs since leaving here.

Once through the fence, she leaned against it, panting. She pressed her gloved hand against her thigh. Small spots of blood appeared on her palm when she lifted her hand. Probably tore a stitch or two, nothing major.

Good thing. If Matt were here, he'd fuss at her about injuring herself again. Funny how in such a short time she'd gotten used to someone worrying about her.

She slipped the ropes back on her shoulders again and headed into the woods.

———

Gideon watched the girl wiggle under the fence through his field glasses. A smile split his lips. No wonder he or the feds hadn't found the papers in the compound. They weren't here. The girl had hidden them in the woods.

For years he'd told the Prophet his stepdaughter was smart. Strict never believed him. Even now she still had a few tricks up her sleeve.

Gideon grabbed his rifle and slipped the strap over his shoulder, then headed down the stairs from the meeting hall's roof. All night he'd camped there in the cold, waiting for his prey to come to him. Now he'd track her.

At the fence he saw drops of blood.

"Sarah, you know better than to leave a trail."

He scaled the fence, pausing at the top to snip the barbed wire with his wire cutters. Landing on the other side, he paused to listen. Faint sounds of snow and branches crunching in the woods ahead. Nothing behind.

Since she took rappelling gear with her, he already knew where she was headed. Years ago she'd struggled with the rappelling cliff behind the compound. Compared to places in the Rockies, it wasn't a high cliff.

But Strict had been relentless with Sarah. He'd drilled his stepdaughter repeatedly on the ropes, humiliating her every time she froze. Gideon couldn't count the number of times she'd hung suspended in air while the other trainees went home for dinner. Finally, she'd made it down the cliff in one attempt.

"Leave it to Sarah to hide the plans to Strict's ultimate revenge in the one place Strict assumed she'd avoid."

Every time she'd been given an obstacle, she'd overcome it. Gideon had always admired that in her. Such a shame to have to snuff out her light. But he had a higher calling. He had the Prophet's bidding to fulfill. Not even a sweet, smart thing like Sarah could get in the way.

———

KATIE STOOD ON THE CLIFF'S EDGE, THE ROPE WRAPPED AROUND her body and secured to a thick oak some twenty feet away. The other rope dangled over the edge beside her. She'd need both ropes to get herself and the strong box she'd lugged down the cliff a decade ago back to the top.

To calm her nerves, she took a deep breath.

"You can do this, Katie. You did it once before in the dead of night, cold, scared and desperate. This is no big deal."

She took a step backwards out into space, and let the rope take her weight.

Oh God, she hated this feeling. Her body hung suspended in

the air for a second then her feet made contact with the mountain wall.

"You only have thirty feet to go. You can do this."

Slowly, she worked her way down the mountainside—sweat beading on her brow with each push off. Her arms ached with the force of inching down the rope and supporting her weight. Her breath fogged out around her each time she exhaled.

Finally, she hung suspended in front of a small cave. For years, this was the place where she'd frozen while Strict hurled insults and obscenities at her from above. The night she'd escaped, she knew he'd never look for her or his stolen papers here. Now she prayed they'd stayed safe from the world in this little divot in the mountainside.

Taking a deep breath, she pushed with her legs until she swung out, then back in, landing on the dirt and moss-covered cave's floor. She untied her rope and pulled the flashlight out of her pocket. Swinging the beam to the cave's farthest corner, the light flashed on the flat rectangular box's dull metal exactly where she'd left it a decade ago.

She knelt beside it and pulled the knife from the scabbard to pry open the latches, which had rusted shut through the years. She slipped the knife back in place, sat in front of the box and lifted the lid. "Now what does Strict have hidden inside you, that he needs so badly?"

Katie lifted out a pile of papers.

"Lists of names and money donations. Ooo, a senator and a couple of congressmen. Bet they don't want this to see the light of day. But I'll also bet this isn't what he's looking for."

Plans for buying more land and building training camps nationwide, lay in the layer beneath. "Great, just what we need—more compounds to abuse and brainwash people. One wasn't enough?"

She rifled through order forms for weapons, computers, even

satellite-television installation. "Probably wanted to watch his face on all the international news stations."

In the bottom lay an envelope sealed in plastic. "What's this? And how did I miss it before?"

Well, that was easy to explain. The night she'd escaped, she only wanted to find enough evidence to put the man on death row. Strict's future catastrophic plans weren't high on her priority list that night.

Carefully, she opened the plastic and pulled out the envelope. She peeled back the sealed flap and laid the contents on the box's metal lid. Holding the flashlight she read them.

The first page contained lines of sixteen digit numbers. The second, an army memo stating that a shipment of surface-to-air missiles was missing from a nuclear munitions cache on the eastern seaboard. It was dated five days before the Federal Building bombing had taken place.

"Holy shit!"

No wonder Strict was desperate for this. Gideon could take out any target he wanted if he had the right codes. Strict could use it to leave a parting mark on the United States and the devastation would continue for years afterwards.

She needed to destroy the numbers before Gideon found her. It was only a matter of time before he figured out she'd come back to the compound to find the papers. Too bad she didn't have any matches. Best to keep them on her person until the job was done. She slipped them into the back waistband of her jeans for safekeeping.

She tied the extra rope to the strong box. For a moment she studied the cave. It had served its purpose. Hopefully, she'd never see the inside of it again.

She secured the rope around her, and swung free from the cave, hanging a moment, before beginning her slow ascent up the cliffside.

Once she reached the top, she turned and tugged on the other rope. The strong box's weight pulled on her already aching muscles, but she knew from experience the pain would be worse if she stopped and started again.

Finally, she had the box beside her on the edge of the cliff. She untied the rope then hefted the metal container into her arms. Turning, she froze.

Gideon stood between her and the forest. He had a cigarette in one hand and a .357 Magnum in the other, pointed right at her.

"Hello, Sarah."

26

Matt jumped out of the SUV as soon as they stopped beside the car where Katie left it. He knelt and studied the ground. Luke squatted beside him, a long-distance sniper rifle he and Castello'd picked up along the way slung over his shoulder.

"No other vehicles have been in this area." Matt pointed to the untouched snow all around them. "And the only tracks leading into the compound are Katie's."

Luke nodded. "If Gideon's here, he didn't come in this way."

"You check the perimeter and see if he's here." Matt said, pulling his weapon from his pocket.

At least Katie left him his gun. "I'll take the Marshal and search the compound."

"You're sending the kid to fix the perimeter?" Castello asked, taking out his own weapon. "I know he's your brother, but this guy's dangerous and millions of lives may be at stake."

"Right now I'm worried about only one life—Katie's. You ever been deer hunting?"

"No. What's that got to do with finding Katie or stopping Gideon?"

Matt stalked up the path with the Marshal close on his heels. "When we were kids, our dad and uncles took us deer hunting. Luke was going through this Indian scout phase, and developed a great love for tracking. If Gideon came in here, my brother will find where."

"Hell, even I could track him in this snow," Castello muttered, following Matt.

Matt traced Katie's tracks to the path's far side, away from the abandoned dog kennels. Her old instincts of self-preservation had taken over again. Even though no dogs were in the cages, she was avoiding them. "True, but Luke can find him if he came in before last night's snowfall."

Castello nodded and walked to the path's other side.

They didn't exchange another word as they entered the compound's center. The place reminded Matt of a cross between an army barracks and one of those pictures of the abandoned concentration camps in Europe just after World War II. The cold starkness of it drilled home just how desolate Katie's life must've been here.

Her resiliently strong spirit amazed him more every minute. No wonder he loved her. He paused, staring down at her tracks. What if he never got a chance to tell her? The idea scared the hell out of him.

"Find something?" Castello whispered from the opening's other side.

Matt shook his head, and motioned for him to move around the right side of the compound and he'd go to the left. Watching every building as he approached for any kind of movement, he followed Katie's tracks around the periphery of a central building.

Directly opposite the building's main entrance the tracks grew jumbled He studied them and the large circle on the ground. Why had Katie stopped here? And why did it look like she had fallen or lay down in the snow? Had she been injured? Which of her nightmares had come to haunt her here?

Then he saw the flag pole directly across from where she'd stopped. Anger and disgust swamped him. That was where her whippings took place. That was why she stopped here. God, he wanted to raze this fucking place to the ground.

He forced his mind to concentrate on finding Katie. Her footprints picked up again going around behind the main building. As he started to follow them a movement to his left caught his attention.

He raised his gun and waited.

Luke appeared from between two buildings, both hands raised in surrender. "Whoa, big brother. Don't shoot. Just your friendly scout here."

"I ought to put a hole in you just for sneaking up on me like that," Matt whispered, lowering his weapon.

"You're the one that sent me looking for another entrance and any sign of the hitman. Which I found, by the way. Besides, you can't shoot me. Mom wouldn't like it."

"What'd you find there?"

"A second gate sort of hidden in the woods, tracks from last night with fresh snow in them, and a late model, four-door Ford sedan."

"So he's here."

Luke nodded. "We'd better find Katie before he does."

"I think he already has. See the tracks coming out of that center building?" Matt pointed to the path. "He must've been in there watching for her to arrive. Then followed her."

They continued tracing her path until they met Castello coming out the munitions shack's open door.

"She came in here, and must've gotten rope. A cabinet is open and it's stocked with tons of the stuff."

Luke pointed around behind the building. "She headed down there."

When they reached the spot where Katie had crawled beneath the fence, Matt's heart sank more. "She's re-injured her thigh. See the blood trail she left?"

"Our man saw it, too." Luke pointed to the second set of tracks in the snow on the fence's other side. "Where's she headed that she needs rope?"

Matt knew exactly where and what she was doing. His sense of urgency doubled. He'd seen her frozen in the air, hanging out a window, unable to move up or down. If she'd gone over the side of a mountain, and Gideon caught her in the middle of a memory, she'd be easy prey.

He scaled the fence, catching his jacket sleeve on the barbed wire. He pulled the material loose and dropped to the other side, heading for the woods at a dead run.

Suddenly, something hit him from behind, and he landed in the snow with Luke on top of him.

He pushed him off, coming up with both fists swinging. "Get out of my way, Luke."

Luke ducked his punch and head butted him. They landed in the snow again. "Think for a second, man. If we go storming in there without knowing where he is or what she's doing, we could get her killed."

"He's going to kill her anyway. I can't let that happen." Matt shoved him off again, scrambling to his feet but reining in his urge to run.

"Your brother's right." Castello stood between them. "Gideon thinks she's alone out there, Edgars. He's focused on her and getting those papers. Until the cavalry gets here, we're her element of surprise and the only hope she's got."

"Cavalry?"

"The Marshal made some calls while we were en route to you," Luke said, picking up his sniper rifle from the snow. "Help is on its way."

"How many?" Matt asked, looking at Castello.

"Could be two or could be twenty. But they're at least an hour behind us."

"Let's get moving then, but we'll make it quiet." Matt hated admitting it, but they were right. If they didn't get Gideon this time, he'd keep coming after Katie. He wanted her safe and in his arms right now. But more importantly, when he had her there, he didn't ever want to lose her again.

―――

"Whatever's in this box won't do the Prophet any good anymore, Gideon. He's going to die at midnight tonight. There's no way that will be stopped." Katie took a step toward him, and away from the cliff's edge. "Can't you let his crazy dreams die with him?"

"Stop right there, Sarah." He shifted his weight.

She froze again. "My name isn't Sarah anymore. Sarah ceased to exist the day I escaped this place. Call me Katie."

"Of course, *Katie*." A smile split his lips.

She'd forgotten how handsome he could be when he smiled. It was one of the things that made people trust him so easily, especially a young, frightened teen. But she'd seen him shoot at her yesterday, knew he'd ruthlessly killed three people to get to her, and he held a gun on her now.

That smile didn't fool her one bit. At this moment she knew she stared into her own angel of death's face.

"Now set the box down, Katie. I've always admired your brains. Don't make a fool out of us both by trying anything heroic."

"If I set this down, Gideon, you'll kill me."

He tilted his head to one side, almost innocently. "My dear girl, I'm afraid I'm going to kill you anyway."

"Why? Why are you following his orders without question and without hope of any reward?" If she could keep him talking, maybe she could think of a way out of here. She wished Matt was nearby.

He's not here. You stranded him ten miles down the road. Where he'd be safe.

"My life belongs to the Prophet." Gideon's voice sounded so natural, as if they were discussing the weather, not her death.

"I never understood your loyalty to the Devil. You aren't one of those mindless people who believed the crap he dished out any more than I did. What made you so loyal to him?"

"I really do owe him my life. He dragged me out of a Viet Cong trap in the middle of a South Vietnam jungle when everyone else would've left me to be tortured to death." Gideon took a long drag off his cigarette. "No one had ever cared if I lived or died, but he did. If he wants me to wipe out half the East Coast I intend to do so."

"Is that what he wants you to do? Kill all the people on the East Coast?" Maybe she could get him to tell her about Strict's big plans. Anything to keep him talking and not shooting.

"It's a brilliant plan, little girl. Only we aren't going to kill a few people. This is a gift that keeps on giving. You might say the power we have will be nuclear in devastation." He put out his cigarette. "Now put down the box."

"What you want isn't in this box." Even to her own ears she sounded desperate, but he didn't know she spoke the truth.

"Katie, Katie. There's no use trying to fool me. You wouldn't have hidden that box all these years then scaled the side of a mountain again to retrieve it if what I wanted wasn't inside. The sooner we get this over with, the better it'll be for both of us. Let's not make this harder than necessary."

He sounded like he was planning to pull out a splinter, not shoot her. His quiet, calm voice didn't ease her nerves one bit. The instant the box hit the ground he'd take her out. As long as she held on to the container, he couldn't shoot. The bullet's impact might send her and the box into the ravine and river below.

She also knew he'd take the chance if he had to. His patience would only last so long. If she didn't think of something quick, she was a dead woman.

Matt listened to the conversation in the clearing ahead as he inched his way closer. She was stalling.

Attagirl, Katie, keep him talking. They just needed a few more minutes to get into position.

He'd taken point, heading down the center, while Luke circled to the left and Castello to the right.

At the tree line's edge, Matt hunkered down behind a tree trunk, his gun aimed right at Gideon's head. Matt dragged in a slow deep breath. Katie stood twenty feet in front of the man, a few steps from the edge of a cliff, a metal strongbox in her hands and a rope around her body.

In his whole life he'd never been as glad or as scared to see someone. A movement to his right told him Castello was in position.

"Just put the box on the ground, Katie," Gideon ordered.

Where the hell was Luke? They needed to make their move.

Light flashed to his left. Luke lay on the ground. The only thing visible was the scope of his rifle. Gideon was not leaving this clearing alive.

Now, how to get Katie out of the line of fire?

For a moment he studied her beautiful face, listening to her ask Gideon why he was so loyal to Strict. God, she was magnificent. So calm, so strong, even though he knew how frightened she must be. Then his gaze traveled lower, to the rope harness she'd made for the trek down the cliff. Then he followed the rope to the tree she'd secured it on.

"Katie," he called to her.

Startled, she looked toward the woods. "Matt?"

Gideon never took his eyes off her. "Nice of you to join us, Patrolman. You're just a little late."

"Katie, do as he says, take a leap of faith, sweetheart." He hoped she understood what he wanted her to do.

Without hesitation or questioning, she dropped the box and dove over the side of the cliff.

27

Gunfire erupted from every area of the clearing. Gideon managed a second shot before bullets ripped into his body. Matt fired twice, both shots finding their target. The hitman's body lifted off the ground then slammed back down, limp and still.

An eerie silence fell as the three lawmen ceased firing. The air around them smelled of gunpowder and blood.

Then Matt scrambled to his feet and ran through the snow to the spot where Katie had disappeared. "Katie?"

Please let her be on the other end of that rope.

"Matt?"

Yes! "I'm here, sweetheart."

He stretched out on the clifftop and peered over the edge. About twenty feet below she'd pressed herself against the mountainside, her hands clinging to the rock crevices, the rope taut as it secured her from falling farther.

"Is it finished?" She let go and grabbed the rope with both hands, her beautiful face looking at him.

"It will be when you get up here." He grinned at her, willing his heart to slow.

Grabbing the rope, he pulled her up as she scaled the wall one more time. When she reached the top edge, he released the rope and latched onto her hands, dragging her onto the top.

Once she was beside him, he pulled her away from the precipice and into his arms.

"Oh God, Katie. You scared the hell out of me." He kissed her hard, as much to reassure himself that she truly was safe in his arms, as to let her know how he felt.

She clung to him, matching his kiss with as much fervor. "I couldn't believe it when I heard your voice," she said when he lifted his head to stare at her. "Then you asked me to take a leap of faith. For a second I didn't know what you meant."

"But you did what I asked. You trusted me." He smoothed her hair off her face, and rubbed his thumb across a smudge of dirt on her cheek. "You trusted me."

"With all my heart."

"Katie, is this all there was in the box?" Castello asked from his position by the box as he rifled through the papers. "I don't see anything they could've used in here."

"I wasn't taking any chances." She reached behind her and pulled out a packet of folded papers from inside her jeans and handed them to the Marshal. "These are codes for surface-to-air missiles that went missing right before the bombing took place."

"Damn." Luke said, securing Gideon's weapon before coming to read over Castello's shoulder.

"Is he really dead?" Her voice broke over the question.

Matt moved between Katie and the gruesome sight. She didn't need to see that. She had enough fodder for her nightmares already. "He and Strict can't hurt you anymore, sweetheart."

"Can we leave now?" Tears glistened in her eyes. She probably had a thread's width of emotional control left after nearly dying.

"We'll go anywhere you want."

"Anywhere?" She dashed her hands over her eyes, wiping

away the tears. Her jaw tightened, and that distant, wary expression filled her face once more.

Matt's heart sank. He knew where she wanted to go. He didn't think he could stand to watch her go there.

But he loved her, and he wouldn't stand in her way. "Just name it."

"I need to go to the Lewisburg Penitentiary." She headed into the woods again, determination in her stride as she retraced her path. "I'm going to an execution."

———

KATIE SAT IN THE SUV WAITING FOR MATT. AS SOON AS THEY'D gotten back to the compound's main gate, several government vehicles had pulled up behind them, surrounding the cars.

They'd been searched, interviewed and their weapons confiscated for ballistics testing. She'd watched from a window in the meeting house as Gideon's lifeless body, wrapped in a gray government issue blanket, was carted off on a stretcher to a waiting van. Now that the threat was completely gone, it was hard to believe Gideon had been the one trying to kill her.

Then federal agents had questioned her about the box's contents, where she'd hidden it, and any other details she could remember about Strict's plans that might help the FBI find them.

"All Gideon said to me was if Strict wanted him to take out half the East Coast, he'd do it," she'd told them. "And that whatever they had planned would be nuclear in its devastation."

That news started a flurry of phone calls and activity. She didn't know if they'd ever find the missiles, but she'd done her part by finding and handing over the codes to them.

Forgotten, now that all her information had been passed on, she'd come out to the SUV to wait and stay out of the way. She had one more thing to do before she could put this place behind her forever. One last monster from her past to confront.

Matt broke away from the group of men clad in blue jackets. His lips were pressed into a thin hard line. The muscle in his jaw flexed and relaxed as he stalked toward the car.

"Can we leave now?" she asked when he was in the driver's seat.

"They're done questioning us. Castello took the heat on this," he answered without looking at her.

Oh yeah, Matt was pissed.

Too bad. She'd done what she believed necessary to protect him. Given the choice, she'd do it again, a thousand times if necessary.

They drove in silence until they reached the interstate. When he headed east, she turned to study him. "Are you ever going to speak to me again?"

The silence stretched for another ten miles. Finally, she couldn't stand it. "I'm not going to apologize for leaving you."

"If Castello and Luke hadn't come along, you'd be dead now, and it would be your body instead of Gideon's they just took to the county morgue, sweetheart." He rolled his head from side to side, exhaling hard. "I've seen one too many women I cared for end like that."

"I'm not your girlfriend Christina, Matt. I can take care of myself."

"Believe me, I don't have you confused with Chris. She was an impulsive teenager who simply borrowed a car for a joyride, then had the misfortune of getting in the path of a drunk driver." He glared at her then focused on the highway once more. "No, you decide to step in front of a hitman determined to kill you. Take care of yourself? I don't think so. You don't think before you act. You just do."

"I'm sorry your male ego is bent out of shape. I wanted to protect you as best I could from dying because of something in my past." She stared out the window, nibbling on her lower lip. "I'd do it again, if I thought you'd be safe."

Suddenly, he pulled the car off the road and onto the shoulder. He shoved it into park. Katie grabbed onto the door handle. "What're you doing?"

He turned to her, cupping her face in his hands. Anguish and pain filled his eyes. "When I woke up and you were gone, I panicked. I knew you'd gone after the papers alone. You'd left me no way to follow you, and no directions if I had a vehicle. All I could think was, you would die and never know how much I love you."

"You love me?" She shook her head. She couldn't be hearing him correctly.

"Sweetheart, believe me I do. I love the way you fight your fears, no matter how real they are. When you learned to trust the Boxers back at Craig's house, I knew you could learn to trust me. When you threw yourself in front of that shotgun ambush, I knew you'd never let someone take a punishment meant for you." He leaned in and slowly kissed her, deep and slow. "But when you let me see your scars, your pain, your nightmares, I knew just how strong a woman you are and I've fallen for you hard, Katie Myers."

"But you can't love me," she whispered behind her tears.

"Why do you say that, baby? Can't you feel how much I love you?" He lay one hand against her heart. "Here? Inside? Can't you feel it for yourself?"

The tears ran unchecked down her cheeks. "No one's ever loved me, Matt. No one since my dad died."

A soft smile spread over his face and he pulled her into his arms. Cradling her head against his shoulder, he whispered in her ear. "I love you so much I'm doing something I hate."

"What's that?"

"I'm taking you to visit the monster in your nightmares."

Once again Matt looked at his watch as he paced outside the back gate to the prison. Almost midnight. Was Katie okay? Was she scared? Even though she made him promise not to follow, he knew he never should've let her go in there by herself.

He'd wanted to go with her. She'd refused.

"I need to do this alone, Matt," she'd said, kissing him for the hundredth time on their trip east. "Did you ever believe in the boogeyman when you were a little kid?"

He nodded.

"This is my own personal boogeyman. Until I prove to him and myself I can stand up to him, unafraid, then I can never have a future free of him."

"Does that future include me? Because I want it to." He tried to make her understand what he wanted.

She kissed him then climbed from the car. "I hope so, Matt. I hope so."

For the past week he'd watched her face one nightmare after another. Every time she put one behind her, she came out stronger.

This was different.

This was the demon that'd tortured her and humiliated her. Seeing him face to face, after reliving all her other memories, might be the one test of mental strength she couldn't win. What if she went into that mental cave and never came out?

How long would it take to end Strict's life?

In the cold, crisp air the anti-death-penalty protestors' voices sang Silent Night on the penitentiary wall's other side. If Strict could hear them, he'd scoff at their choice of words. If he'd succeeded, pandemonium and wails would've filled this night, not silence and peace.

They protested for a life that wasn't worth the oxygen used to say the words. If Strict had his way, the very freedom they used to gather and speak their minds would've been forfeit.

Matt wished Katie had never gone inside. How long would

she have to stay? How long until she was back in his arms once more?

He glanced at his watch for the millionth time. Just a few more minutes.

Katie stood inside the warden's office, as he talked on the phone to the President of the United States. Castello had pulled out all the stops to get her on the witness panel for Strict's execution.

"Yes, Mr. President. She's right here. No sir. The media is outside the main gate. No one will know she's here, except those in the witness room. Yes sir, I understand. We all owe her a debt of gratitude. I will, sir."

The warden hung up the phone and held out his hand to Katie. "The President wanted us to extend his thanks to you for stopping a disaster today. The FBI found three missiles programmed with coordinates for nuclear power plants along the Eastern seaboard."

Several gasps came from the guards and other witnesses in the room as they heard for the first time what Strict had planned for his final act of terror.

"He also said we were to sneak you out the back gate that you came in to help protect your identity from the media. Everyone on the panel will sign a privacy agreement to keep your presence here confidential. It's the least we can do to thank you for what you did."

Katie blushed under all the praise. She'd only done what was necessary to stop the nightmares. "Thank you for including me on the panel at such short notice."

A knock sounded on the door. A guard entered and spoke into the warden's ear.

"Ladies and gentlemen, it's time." The warden led them down

the hall from his office and into the witness room. Wooden seats lined the room in three rows. All of them faced the glass window where a black curtain was closed.

Katie took a seat on the end of the first row. She laced her fingers together tightly in her lap.

Her heart raced. She pulled her upper lip between her teeth.

She didn't want to be here. She wanted to run back to the car and curl up in Matt's arms forever.

But she'd promised herself she'd see this through to the end. She wouldn't go to Matt half a person. She wasn't hiding from her nightmares anymore.

The curtain opened, and they could see Strict lying serenely on the table, a smile on his lips. Leather straps across his chest, arms, abdomen, thighs and calves held him down. IV tubes in his arm connected him to the machine on the room's back wall that would end his life.

"It's not fair that he die so painlessly," a woman cried softly. "My husband died in pain from third-degree burns, ten hours after the bombing."

"He looks happy," a man murmured behind Katie.

Katie knew why Strict looked so peaceful. He believed his final plan was still in effect—that millions would die when he did.

"Someone should wipe the smile off his face," another man said angrily.

There was only one person in this room that could do that. Slowly, Katie walked to the glass wall's other end, and stood facing Strict. She whispered something to the warden.

The warden picked up the phone and called into the death chamber. A guard leaned down and whispered to Strict.

His face snapped to the left.

Katie stepped closer to the window.

Strict's eyes grew wide as he recognized her. Then he began struggling against his bonds, screaming obscenities that the witnesses could only lip-read in their soundproofed room.

The clock's second hand passed the eleven-fifty-nine and thirty-second mark. Two men at the machine pushed buttons and the chemicals started to flow down the IV lines.

"What happened?" someone asked. "What did she do?"

Katie turned away and stepped out the door. She didn't need to see any more. She'd finally confronted her own personal monster, and won.

FIVE MINUTES AFTER MIDNIGHT THE BACK GATE OPENED AND Matt held his breath, watching as Katie stepped out into the night. She walked straight toward him, a smile lighting up her face. With each step her pace increased until she was running.

He shoved himself off the car's hood and caught her up against him, wrapping his arms around her in a fierce hug.

"Thank God you're okay," he whispered against her hair. He drew back just enough to press his lips to hers, all his fear and need infused in the demanding kiss.

Minutes later, when he could release her without fear she'd vanish into some midnight mirage, he stared into her eyes. "Is he dead?"

"I suppose so."

That surprised him. "What do you mean, you suppose so?"

"I didn't stay to watch." She laughed. "Let's get in the car, it's freezing out here."

Once inside with the heat running, Matt turned to her. "What was the purpose in coming here if you didn't stay for the execution?"

She leaned in and kissed him. "I wanted him to know I'd survived. If I was alive, he'd know his plans were going to be as dead as him."

"What happened then?"

"He went crazy. He'll scream in torment every moment in hell, knowing I beat him."

Matt laughed. "That's my girl, sassy to the end."

"I couldn't have done any of this without you." She touched his cheek when he started to protest. "You helped me face my past, my nightmares. You were my strength through the whole thing. I love you, Matt."

He pulled her to him once more, letting his kiss tell her how much he loved her.

"Now I have something to ask you," she said when they finally broke apart.

"Oh? What?" He pulled out of the parking lot and away from the prison.

"Can we find someplace to talk about that future you wanted to share with me?"

EPILOGUE

Katie slowed the car and pulled in behind Matt's truck at the address he'd given her. He'd asked her to meet him here after her therapy session.

From the day after she'd walked out of that prison, they'd both been in counseling. They went twice a month as a couple, and she went twice a month by herself. Today was one of her private meetings. She felt stronger every day now.

Matt stepped out of the house as she approached the door, a paper in his hand and a smile on his face.

"What're you up to?" she asked as he hugged and kissed her.

"Now what makes you think I've got devious plans?"

"Besides the grin on your face? The fact that I'm standing in front of some stranger's home? Or maybe it's that paper you keep hiding from me."

He laughed. "Two months ago you promised to love and honor me, now you're impugning my reputation for honesty?"

"I didn't promise to become stupid." She smiled, remembering the boisterous Edgars' clan's acceptance of her and the beautiful wedding she'd shared with this man. In all her life, she'd never believed she'd be this happy.

He led her into the house, which was decorated like it came right out of a magazine.

"Who lives here?" she asked, trying to take in everything at once.

"No one. It's a model home." He handed her the paper in his hand. It was a pamphlet for a new subdivision she'd passed on her way here. "I wanted your opinion on the house. If you like the style and design, we can build one of our own."

"Build one of our own?" She stared at the pamphlet.

He tipped her chin so she'd look at him. "You can build and decorate our home any way you want."

Tears sprang to her eyes. "I don't know anything about decorating. I lived out of two backpacks for years."

He laughed. "We'll hire a decorator if you want, or my mother and sister can help. Just take a look at the floor plans and pick the one you want. Maybe we'll even get a puppy or two."

As she giggled over the idea of puppies, he drew her into the safety of his arms.

He brushed his hand softly over her hair. "Charlie Watts advised me that night at the bed and breakfast to save my money and build you a home. I knew that moment he was right. Sweetheart, if anyone ever needed to put down roots, it's you. You deserve a safe home to call your own."

"I already have that, Matt." She smiled up at him through her tears. "I have you. Right here in your arms is my home."

NEWSLETTER SIGN-UP

Thank you for reading
HUNTED
Want to know more about my books and new releases?
Please consider joining my **newsletter** mailing list.
I promise not to SPAM you.
Your email will NOT be sold to other sites
and is only to be used for the purpose of sending
out my newsletter.

ALSO BY SUZANNE FERRELL

WESTEN SERIES

Close To Home, book 1

Close To The Edge, book 2

Close To The Fire, book 3

Close To Danger, book 4

Christmas Comes To Westen (book bundle):

Close To Santa's Heart

Close To The Mistletoe

Close To Christmas

EDGARS FAMILY NOVELS

Kidnapped

Hunted

Seized

Vanished

Capitol Danger

Exposed

HISTORICALS

Cantrell's Bride

Turner's Vision

ABOUT THE AUTHOR

***USA Today bestselling author*, Suzanne Ferrell** discovered romance novels in her aunt's hidden stash one summer as a teenager. From that moment on she knew two things: she loved romance stories and someday she'd be writing her own. Her love for romances has only grown over the years. It took her a number of years and a secondary career as a nurse to finally start writing her own stories.

The author of 16 novels and an Amazon best-seller for both her series, the Edgars Family Novels and the Westen series, Suzanne's books have been finalists in the National Reader's Choice Awards--SEIZED (2013) and VANISHED (2014). Suzanne was also a double finalist in the Romance Writers of America's 2006 Golden Heart with her manuscripts,

KIDNAPPED (Long Contemporary Category) and HUNTED (Romantic Suspense).

Currently working on more books for her Edgars Family series (KIDNAPPED, HUNTED, SEIZED, VANISHED, EXPOSED and Capitol Danger) and the Westen Series (Close To Home, Close To The Edge, Close To The Fire, Close To Christmas, Close To The Mistletoe, Close To Santa's Heart and Close To Danger), Suzanne hopes to bring readers more passionate and suspenseful books to fill your reading moments.

Suzanne's sexy stories, whether they are her on the edge of your seat romantic suspense or the heartwarming small town stories, will keep you thinking about her characters long after their Happy Ever After is achieved.

You can Find Suz at:

Website: http://suzanneferrell.com/

Made in the USA
Middletown, DE
19 May 2020